The
Honeysuckle Dream

(The Butterfly Storm Book Three)

by

KATE FROST

LEMON TREE PRESS

Paperback Edition 2019

ISBN 978-0-9954780-9-1

Cover design by Jessica Bell.

The
Honeysuckle Dream

by

KATE FROST

LEMON
TREE
PRESS

The Butterfly Storm Series

For Mum and Dad

who encouraged me to read

Norfolk, 2006

Stepping out of the car on to the weed-filled gravel drive of Salt Cottage, I push my sunglasses into my hair, put my hands on my hips and mutter, 'Fuck.'

The cottage is as I remember it; peeling white-painted windows and the Norfolk flint cladding its walls, but the garden's wilder and encroaches on the cottage more than before. Even the sunshine doesn't make it look more appealing. I sigh. What did I expect? It's been left empty for nearly a year.

A wave of nausea washes over me at the realisation of what I've done. There's no going back now. From city girl to bloody country bumpkin. Otherwise known as a new start. Admittedly I've had plenty of time to reflect during the five-hour journey from Bristol, but it's only now seeing the place in all its faded, dirty glory that reality has hit.

I have a couple of hours before the removal lorry arrives. At least I can start thinking about where everything's going to go. I've got the essentials in the car: a suitcase of clothes, wash bag, cleaning products, and a box of supplies for the kitchen, tea, coffee, a kettle and a toaster. I grab the box and crunch across the gravel to the paved path. Bushes and weeds attack my legs where they've outgrown the border. There are pockets of colour hidden amongst the green wilderness, flowers struggling to reach sunshine.

Balancing the box on my hip, I slide the key out of my pocket and slot it into the lock, battling with it until the door groans open. I'm greeted by a gloomy hallway and a waft of staleness. I wrinkle my nose.

'Fuck.'

I step inside and switch on the light. A bare bulb flickers to life. I pad across the hallway, the carpet sticky beneath my trainers, and push open the door to the kitchen. It's as bad as I remember. I place the box on the warped lino floor, hardly daring to look at the 1970s beige units, filthy worktops and cigarette-stained walls. Instead, I unlock the back door, push it open and breathe in the fresh, clean air, soaking up the lush green trees, grass, fields and hills. However bad it is inside, at least I have this to escape to.

I start by writing a list of jobs. I've decided to focus on just three rooms to begin with: my bedroom, the bathroom and the kitchen. I plan on getting them at least liveable, then tackle the living room before deciding on what to do with the remaining rooms. I practically fill a notebook with jobs. I've given myself two months to spend doing up the cottage before I have to focus on work, but at least financially the pressure is off for the time being with redundancy pay to keep me going and two wedding planner jobs lined up.

It's odd being here on my own, 240 miles away from my friends in Bristol, although actually I'm slightly closer to Sophie in Greece. Except that doesn't change anything, there's still a massive wedge in our relationship which is a bigger issue than a few thousand miles and a four-hour flight. I'm used to knocking about in a house on my own though. Since I stopped having lodgers, and once Sophie moved out, it's been just me. I don't even have a bloody cat, although I feel like I should do. A single, middle-aged woman, it's the done thing, isn't it?

The carpets are old and threadbare, so they're easy to pull up by hand. I start in the hallway, ripping out the brown flowery carpet, taking it outside and dumping it on the edge of the driveway. I add 'book a skip' to my ever-growing list. I need a wee but I can't bear to go without cleaning the bathroom first. There's no shower, just an olive-green bath, sink and toilet. Olive makes it sound too tasteful. In reality it's the colour a four-year-old would describe as snot green. The bottom of the bath is thick with dirt and a daddy longlegs has made its home by the plughole. I pull on gloves and squeeze copious amounts of cleaning fluid over the sink and scrub. I don't want to use the loo even after I've cleaned it.

After an hour of scrubbing, the bathroom is just about usable. I celebrate by putting the kettle on. The lorry should be here soon with what little furniture I decided to bring with me from Bristol. Seeing my sofa in the living room and my bed upstairs might make this place feel a little more like home.

I take my tea outside and sit on the step. I can't wait to start tackling the garden but I know my priorities have to be inside the cottage to begin with. The wind makes the tree branches sigh. There's a snort from beyond the weathered fence at the bottom of the garden. I leave my cup on the step, trudge through the long grass and peer between the bushes. A black horse with a white stripe down its nose raises its head and looks at me with big brown eyes. Sophie would love it here. I reach my hand towards the horse but there are too many brambles in the way.

The sound of a lorry coming along the main road disturbs the peace of fluttering birds and whispering branches, followed by loud beeping as a large vehicle begins to reverse down the lane. So much for my peaceful cup of tea. By the time I get out of the house and to the driveway, the removal lorry has backed all the way down the lane. I hope to God the farmer doesn't need to get a tractor down to the farm anytime soon. That'll be one way to introduce myself to the neighbours; blocking the shared lane. Never had that problem in Hazel Road with street parking. I got pretty nifty at parallel parking on a narrow road into a tiny space. Here, space is not an issue.

I smooth my hot palms down the front of my jeans, and sweep my messy hair out of my eyes. The afternoon sun beats down but there's a fresh breeze and it's good to be outside after breathing in cleaning products and staleness for the last couple of hours.

The lorry's engine shudders to a halt, and silence returns apart from the wind rustling the leaves. One of the delivery men jumps down from the cab.

'Good journey?' I ask, walking over and scraping open the gate.

'Would have been here a bit earlier but we followed a slow-going tractor for miles.'

'Ah, the joys of the countryside.' I place my hands on my hips. 'Think it's going to take some getting used to.'

'Rather you than me, love.' He yanks open the back of the lorry and I glimpse my furniture and boxes. 'Right, let's get this lot in then.'

'The kettle's just boiled. What do you fancy? Tea? Coffee?'

I make them coffee and direct boxes and furniture into different rooms. I got rid of a lot of stuff when I sold the house in Hazel Road. I thought it was a good opportunity to have a clear out. I was starting afresh; it felt right to get rid of the clutter at the same time. I kept big items of furniture like my bed, the sofa, the American-style fridge but got rid of a lot of other things. I've got boxes of Sophie's old stuff too that she didn't want to take with her to Greece. They were in the attic at Hazel Road and will go in the attic here too, for her to retrieve. I haven't given up hope that one day she'll visit.

'You've taken on quite a project, love.' One of the removal men says as he passes me, holding one end of my sofa, the last thing to be taken inside.

'Yep, I don't do things by halves.'

'Just you on your own, is it?' he calls back as they squeeze through the front door.

'Uh huh.' I nod. Just me. Has been for a while now.

The third removal man shuts the back of the lorry and waits for the others to return. I realise this is it; I'm in my new home, what little I brought of my old life with me.

'You need a hand with anything before we leave?'

He's young and good-looking, the type I normally go for and exactly the type I'm wanting to escape from. I'd love him to give me a hand, but really I want the day to be over, the removal lorry gone, and a bit of time to myself to get used to my new home.

'I'll be fine, thanks though.'

He winks, then saunters out of the driveway and climbs up into the cab with his workmates. They drive up the lane and I watch them until they turn on to the main road and disappear.

Silence.

I close the gate, dragging it across the gravel. I look towards the cottage. The sun is beginning to set, sending purples, pinks and orange across the sky. A flock of ducks fly over in formation, black against the softening light. A hoot of an owl, a whoosh as a car goes past on the main road at the top of the lane. It's fresher and cooler here than it was in Bristol and I shiver in my jeans and T-shirt.

I can't be bothered to connect the TV tonight. All I want is food and my bed. I'd thought ahead about tea, coffee, milk and biscuits, but I'd totally forgotten about something to eat for dinner and I'm starving. I drive five miles to the nearest Chinese takeaway in Holt. Five miles along dark winding roads. Our closest takeaway in Bristol was at the bottom of our road. The smell of rogan josh after getting off the bus after a night out used to be intoxicating.

I eat chicken chow mien on the sofa with my legs tucked beneath me, away from the disgusting carpet I have yet to remove, before heading upstairs.

I lie in bed, eyes wide open, unable to drift off despite the insanely long and tiring day. It's painfully quiet. I'm used to the stomp of footsteps going up the stairs next door and my neighbours Ella and Ken screaming at each other in the middle of the night. The darkness is going to take some getting used to as well. No street lights casting an orange-glow through the blinds like in Hazel Road. Here, blackness envelops everything, like an all-consuming hug. Only moon and stars decorate the velvety black.

Everything about this place is so far removed from my life back home. *My old life*, back in Bristol. It's no longer home. This ramshackle, stinking, dirty cottage is now home. It's a chance to change my life, change my attitude… to everything. Kiss goodbye to bad habits and my terrible choice in men. In fact, kiss goodbye to men completely for a while. Here it's going to be just about me, with no one to mess with my head.

I wake to birdsong and sunlight streaming through the curtain-less window. I'd managed to find a sheet, pillow and my duvet, but everything else remains in the unopened boxes surrounding the bed. The window's open and a cool breeze curls in. It's cold, but I prefer that to the stale stink of lingering smoke and damp. I can't wait to strip everything back and scrub away the dirt to reveal the cottage's hidden charms.

I swing my legs out of bed and slip them straight into my trainers, not wanting to put my bare feet on the grubby carpet. I should have ripped this one up first. Last night I'd managed to find soap, toothpaste and a towel, and when I go downstairs into the kitchen there's the kettle, mugs and coffee.

I switch the kettle on and unlock the back door, pushing it open to an early morning mist floating across the fields. The air is fresh though, and sweet compared to inside. The lawn, although overgrown, is lush and green and speckled with daisies and dandelions. I breathe deeply, acknowledging the start of panic building in the pit of my stomach, but realising a stronger sense of peace is taking over. My shoulders relax as I shiver in the cool morning air and look out on my wilderness. Without really understanding why, I know I've made the right decision.

Sheffield, 1979

The conversation stops the moment I walk into the living room. Three pairs of eyes look at me.

Mum, Dad and Elliot.

The tension in the room is palpable. 'What's going on?' I ask, but I know exactly what's happening.

Dad stands, picks up the newspaper from the coffee table and walks past me and out of the room. His reaction couldn't have hurt more if he'd slapped me in the face.

I know then that they know the truth.

'Elliot?'

He stands and smooths his hands down his trousers. It feels like there's an enormous distance between us emotionally and physically, his usual warmth has gone. He won't even meet my eyes.

'I'm sorry, Leila. It needed to stop. Particularly now.' He glances at my stomach. I fold my arms, as if to protect myself from the man I thought I knew, who I love and who I believed loves me. 'I've told your parents everything. We've come to an agreement and I'll support you as best I can through them.'

It takes a moment for his words to register. I feel like a child being told off by an older relative, rather than the man who until a few weeks ago was quite happy to put aside his marriage while he happily shagged me.

Mum gets up from the armchair. Elliot clasps her arm, his wedding band a glaring reminder of how married he is. How stupid I've been to think we'd get away with this. That I'd get away with it.

'I'll see you soon,' he says to Mum, like he's popped over for a brew and an innocent chat about golf. 'I'll see myself out.'

He walks past me, yet keeps his distance, pausing just long enough to say under his breath, 'It's over, I'm sorry.'

He's taken control, told my parents the truth about our affair before I've had the chance to put my side forward. He's taken the upper hand and left me to deal with the wrath of my parents while he waltzes back to his family.

The front door slams closed.

I have no idea what to say. Mum can't even look at me. My heart thumps, the knot of tension in my stomach building.

'Mum.'

'It's shameful.' Her voice cuts through the room. She's unable to disguise her disgust.

I know all she's thinking about is how horrified everyone else will be if they find out. *Her* friends. The rest of our family. *His* wife.

It's 1979, not bloody 1950.

Yes, I've done something wrong, it should never have happened, but I didn't choose who I fell in love with. Love chose me. Mum would think that's shameful too. Falling in love with a married man. I'm pretty certain she wouldn't see it as love. Lust, yes. Love, no.

But I do love him, so much it hurts.

'You had an affair. Are you out of your mind? And now this…' She gestures in the direction of my stomach, unable to say out loud that I'm pregnant.

I place my hands on my flat stomach. If it wasn't for this, then maybe we could have carried on with no one needing to know. Maybe one day he would have realised that he loved me more…

He's distanced himself from me over the past couple of weeks ever since I told him I was pregnant and *he* told me to not tell anyone. I expected support at the very least, but all I got from him was fear. Now I know why; he was trying to figure out a way to protect himself.

And now it's over. He made sure of that.

'You've been unbelievably stupid and reckless. How could you? He's your father's best friend. For God's sake, he's married to my maid of honour, my good friend. He has children. My goodness, Leila. I've disapproved of some of the choices you've made, but this… I don't have the words to describe how disappointed I am in you.'

I frown, not quite understanding. I know she's upset, but it seems she's only upset with me. What the hell did Elliot say?

'You're still friends with him?'

'Of course we're still friends. It's over. Done with. You don't ever see him again. We'll all move on as best we can.'

I laugh, because the situation is so unbelievable that's the only way I can control the churning emotions in the pit of my stomach. I feel like I'm going to be sick.

'How are you okay with this?'

'Okay?' Mum practically spits at me. 'I'm as far from okay as I can possibly be.'

'He was the one who made the first move…'

Mum shakes her head. 'Oh please, Leila, don't go giving me that. The past couple of years and your behaviour; I have no doubt you seduced him.'

I reel back. I'm open-mouthed yet unable to form coherent words. She's looking at me with pure hatred. Dad's retreated outside, probably locked himself away in his beloved shed, washed his hands of the whole situation. He's never been one for conflict and this is as serious as it gets.

'He should never have succumbed to your advances…'

'My advances? Are you kidding?'

'But,' Mum says firmly, cutting me off. 'He stepped up in the end and was honest and open with us.'

I shake my head, unable to fully comprehend her words. 'It wasn't just down to me.'

'You should have known better.'

'I should have known better!' My fists clench as my voice rises. 'Don't you think he's the one who should have known better?'

Her cheeks flush. 'Men can't control their desire.'

'Oh my God, Mum. Can you actually hear yourself? Are you seriously suggesting that he was unable to control himself because he's a man and that actually makes it okay? Because he thinks with his dick instead of his head.'

'Leila, enough!'

Her shout stuns me into silence.

'You're going to go and stay with Aunt Pearl until you've had the baby.'

'I'm not.'

'Oh you are, Leila. You've brought enough shame on us without parading it in front of everyone. Once you've had it, and given it up, then you can come home.'

'Wait, what? Given it up?'

She fixes her steely-blue eyes on me. 'You're hardly going to be able to raise a child on your own.'

'Why can't I?'

'You're living in a dream world, that's your trouble. You're not raising a baby in this house. That's the end of this discussion. You have no other choice.'

I storm upstairs and shut myself in my room. I yank up the sash window and breathe in cool fresh air to try and calm the tightness creeping up my chest. I didn't want this; despite knowing what the consequences could be, I didn't want to get pregnant, but I can't be cold-hearted like Mum. I can't disengage myself from reality like she can. I may be young and I may have made some unwise choices over the past few months, but I can't go through with this pregnancy and give birth to just give up my baby. I'm not someone who easily gives up on things. Mum's attitude and Elliot's cowardice has just made me feel even more determined to go my own way.

It's cold by the open window but I need the fresh air to clear the fog in my head. I grab the blanket from my bed, throw it round my shoulders and sit on the window seat. The sky is darkening, reds, oranges and gold merging with black and grey. This has been my home all my life and yet the past couple of years I've felt less and less like I belong here, through spending more time with friends going out and realising I want more from life than to be someone's wife. Mum's never been career-minded; Dad's the breadwinner, always has been, always will be. And although Mum has a creative flair, she's thrown that side of herself into gardening, cooking and looking after our home.

I stare down at the garden with its perfectly cut lawn, no weeds or daisies poking through. The borders are neat and regimented, filled with shrubs and bushes, carefully planted and maintained by Mum. The apple tree at the bottom of the garden always has an abundance of fruit and Mum spends hours in the kitchen making chutney and apple crumble. She's the perfect wife and mother, much like Elliot's wife…

Maybe this has been my way of battling against my parents' expectations to follow in Mum's footsteps. I want a career, not marriage, yet I've never been sure what job I want to do. And here I am, just turned nineteen, pregnant and facing a situation I never anticipated. I'm bloody sure I'm going to find my own way through life. I'm not going to follow my parents' wishes because they're ashamed of me.

It's just as well I've had loose morals over the past couple of years – at least that's what Mum believes. I've actually only had two boyfriends, the first when I was sixteen, but the one Mum had a problem with was the twenty-year-old boyfriend I had when I was seventeen. I know she thinks he led me astray, smoking, drinking, sex… But friends got me into drinking and smoking. I had fun with Duncan and Mum didn't approve, and yet here she is protecting a man who should have known better and placing all the blame on me.

Elliot screwed his best friend's daughter, yet I'm the one in the wrong.

I grip the window ledge until my fingers hurt. I breathe deeply, attempting to calm my pounding heart and still the panic in my chest. An idea begins to form. The only reason Duncan and I split up was because he moved down to Bristol for work. I don't want a relationship with him and I'm sure as hell certain he won't want to get involved with me now I'm pregnant. But we're still friends and he's a nice guy, someone I think would help me if I ever needed it. And boy do I need help now.

Dad and his silence can fuck off.

Mum and her high and mighty sticking up for Elliot over her daughter pig-headedness can fuck off.

Aunt Pearl can fuck right off too.

I open my desk drawer, pull out my address book and find Duncan's new number scribbled in the front. If he agrees to my crazy idea, this might work. I write his number on a piece of paper and put it in the pocket of my cords.

I creep downstairs. Dad's not inside yet and Mum's pottering about in the kitchen. I take my denim jacket off the hook in the hallway and slip out of the front door, closing it quietly behind me. It's nearly dark already. I power-walk down our road, shivering in the chilly March evening, the only sound my flares catching against each other. I sense net curtains twitching, neighbours watching and wondering where a young lady like me could be going after dark.

Fuck them all.

Mum's desperate to keep up appearances, unable to think about anything other than protecting herself, petrified that everyone will find out that her teenage daughter screwed her best friend's husband.

It's only a short walk to the pay phone a couple of streets away but it's enough to clear my head. The distance from home makes me feel like I can do this. I've been battling against my parents for as long as I can remember. I've always felt suffocated by them, probably made worse by being an only child. I've fought against their expectations, wanting a different life, to be challenged, to not be so narrow-minded. But they're set in their ways, and their reactions after Elliot spoke to them have simply confirmed what I already knew. One way or another I need to escape.

By the time I reach the pay phone, I'm defiant and determined about my plan however challenging it will be.

I pick up the receiver and slot coins in. The receiver is cold against my ear and cool air blows in beneath the bottom of the door. It starts to ring and I hold my breath, willing Duncan to pick up.

A female voice answers. My heart sinks.

'Is Duncan there?' I ask.

'Yeah, I'll go get him.'

Footsteps fade away and it feels like eternity before there's scrabbling on the line and Duncan says, 'Hello?'

'Hello, Duncan, it's Leila. I hope you don't mind, but I need to ask a big favour.'

Norfolk, 2006

'Knock, knock,' a deep voice says while knocking on the open front door.

I look up from the box that I'm rifling through. The man standing in the doorway is handsome. Tall, broad shoulders, clean shaven. What my friend Kim would describe as a 'silver fox', but not my type. Too old.

'Hi.' I wipe my dusty hands down my dungarees and walk over.

'I'm Robert.' He shakes my hand. 'I live in the village; own the pub by the village green. I just thought I'd pop by and see how you're settling in. And I brought you these.'

He hands me a bottle of wine and a box of biscuits, those fancy ones you get from M&S.

'Thank you, that's so kind.' I take them. 'I'm Leila. Do you want to come in and have a coffee?'

'Oh, I didn't mean to disturb you.'

I wave my hand. 'You're not. I could do with a break.'

'That will be lovely then, thank you.'

He shuts the door behind him and follows me through to the kitchen. I'm conscious it still smells damp despite every window and door being left open since I arrived two days ago.

'You'll have to excuse the state of the place; it's not exactly been well looked after...' I place the bottle and biscuits on the wooden table I brought from Bristol. It's the only thing clean in the kitchen, everything else, particularly the work surfaces, cooker and splash back are coated with a thick film of grease.

'Don't worry, I'm not really surprised. June was a bit of a recluse, wouldn't accept help from any of us in the village and wasn't on the best of terms with her sons. They rarely visited.'

'Well, they seemed to want a quick sale and were happy to take my cheeky offer. They obviously wanted to pocket the money.'

'I'm just glad this place didn't go to a developer; there are enough second homes around here as it is.'

'I got in quick.' I flick the switch on the kettle. 'Tea? Coffee? I have both. Got my priorities right.'

'Coffee, please.' He goes to lean against the work surface but thinks better of it. It looks sticky even from the other side of the kitchen.

'Have a seat.' I gesture to the two chairs on either side of the table. 'They didn't come with the house, so they're not a health hazard, I promise.'

His booming laugh fills the kitchen, making me glad of the company despite thinking my escape to the country was because I want to be on my own. He sits at the table and folds his hands together. The backs of his fingers are hairy and he has a gold band on his wedding ring finger.

'You've been the gossip of the village,' he says, smiling at me.

'I have?'

'Well, not you exactly but whoever was moving in here. There was great excitement when the For Sale sign went up. I think most people thought a family would move in.'

'Well, you've got just me.'

'No husband or children?'

It's quite a forward question for someone I've only just met, but I like that directness. I guess he's a bit like me in that respect. 'Definitely no husband.' I spoon coffee into two mugs and grab the milk, the only thing in the fridge. 'But I have a daughter.'

'Oh?' He glances around as if expecting to see her hiding like a little kid would.

I smile as I pour in boiling water and carry the mugs over to the table. 'She's grown-up, living in Greece.'

'You don't look old enough to have a grown-up daughter.'

'I had her young.' I reach across the table and open the box of biscuits. 'Help yourself. So, how about you?'

'I have grown-up children too. And grandchildren. My son Ben lives in London with his wife and their two children. My daughter Vicky recently got married and lives near Norwich.'

'Well, you don't look old enough to be a grandfather either.'

He laughs. 'I certainly feel old enough!'

I pick up my mug and the biscuits. 'Let's sit outside; it's a beautiful day and it's pretty much a hell-hole in here.'

We escape into the fresh air and sit on the back door step like I did the day I moved in. Once I've sorted out the worst of the inside, I'm going to get patio chairs and a table, maybe build another patio with a barbecue area further down the garden beneath the trees. I have so many plans. It's an exciting prospect cleaning the place up and putting my own stamp on it.

'It was this view that sold the house,' I say.

'It's pretty special. It has a perfect and enviable position on the edge of the village.' He reaches for a biscuit. 'Where have you moved from?'

'Bristol.'

'Really? You don't sound like you're a southerner.'

'I'm not. I grew up, up north.'

'How did you find this place?'

'Fate really. I'm starting my own wedding planning business – I did some bits in Bristol and then a friend of a friend wanted me to plan her daughter's wedding in Norwich next year. The idea of moving grew from there. I desperately needed a change. Countryside and being close to the sea appealed so I started looking for houses around this way and stumbled across this cottage.'

'So, you moved for a wedding?'

'Yep, I really did, despite being well and truly single.'

'You've never been married?'

I shake my head. 'Nope. Not the marrying type. But you obviously are.'

He rubs his fingers across his wedding ring. 'I was, to my wonderful Jenny, but she passed away years ago.'

'I'm so sorry.'

He waves his hand. 'Please, don't be. We've got our skeletons out of the closet early.' His booming laugh returns along with a smile that lights up his face. He's not my type but he is good looking. I have plenty of skeletons in my closet that I'd quite like to leave for the time being. I particularly don't want to share them with someone I've only just met.

He drains his coffee and stands up. 'I'd better let you get on. If you need a hand with anything then please do shout. You can always find me knocking about at the pub.'

'Thank you, that's kind.'

'Will you be getting some help to do the place up?'

I lead the way back inside. 'Maybe some of the bigger jobs. I think this kitchen pretty much needs gutting and starting again, but I plan to do most things myself. I've got a friend from Bristol coming up to help next week and I'm pretty nifty with a hammer and a drill.'

He's easy to talk to and down to earth – a good first person to meet in the village. I hope everyone else is as welcoming of a city girl.

We reach the front door and he pauses. 'I tell you what, come down to the pub this evening and have a meal. It's on me, as a welcome to our village,' he says when he sees I'm about to protest.

'If you're sure.'

'I'm positive. A good opportunity to introduce you to

some of the other locals too.'

'Well thank you, that sounds great.'

I wave him off along the path and across the driveway. I close the front door behind me and lean on it. I hope to God his invite for a meal at his pub is nothing more than him being neighbourly. I wonder if he'd be as generous if I was pig-ugly, old or a bloke. I'll give him the benefit of the doubt; he's friendly and welcoming and I appreciate the gesture. Plus, a bit of company and a proper meal somewhere other than my dirt-encrusted kitchen sounds like a bloody good idea.

Derbyshire, 1978

Elliot and Margaret's house is only thirty minutes away from us but it feels like another world. I've left behind suburban Sheffield for the wild beauty of the Peak District. Driving in this direction reminds me of family days out, going for a walk or a pub lunch together, on the rare occasions when Dad wasn't working at the weekend or when he actually fancied doing something together as a family.

I sit quietly in the back of the car and watch the landscape pass by, a blur of greens and browns with snatches of blue sky. Dad driving; Mum listening to Radio 3. School's finished forever, the summer's nearly over and I have a part-time job that gets me out of the house, but there must be more to life than this. At least there seemed to be some sort of purpose going to school and I got to see people other than my parents. Fine, there are new people where I work, but they're all loads older and seem so far removed from me.

We pull up outside Elliot and Margaret's house, park behind another car on the grass verge and get out. Dad takes some beers from the boot and Mum grabs the Tupperware with the potato salad, and hands me the burgers. I follow them around the side of the house. Smoke drifts into the sky and the barbecue smell gets stronger as we reach the back gate and let ourselves in.

We're greeted with hugs from Margaret, and eldest

daughter Amy shouts hello as she runs past, chased by her younger brother and sister. I sigh. Even though I no longer have a boyfriend since Duncan moved down south last month, I'm living for the weekends, being able to go out with my friends, smoke, drink, talk, stay up late, enjoy life. During the week, even though I'm no longer at school, the focus is on work and bettering myself. Dad scoffed when I mentioned the possibility of university. Even though I'm eighteen, they're still treating me like I'm twelve, trying to contain me, when all I want is to burst out of their suffocating constraints.

Elliot's by the barbecue and while Mum heads into the kitchen with Margaret, I follow Dad across the perfectly cut lawn. I wish I'd insisted they'd left me behind. A few hours to myself, away from my parents would have been fucking fantastic.

'Henry!' Elliot's standing behind the barbecue, a beer in one hand, tongs in the other turning sausages and burgers on the grill. 'So glad you could make it.'

Dad places the cans on the table to the side of the barbecue and slaps Elliot on the shoulder. 'How many people have you invited? You've enough food to feed an army.'

'We've brought burgers.' I hold out the Tupperware. 'Mum made them.'

'Great. Put them over here.' He motions with the tongs to a small table behind him filled with plates of raw meat. I set the container down and retreat from the smoke.

'You can never have too much meat.' He raises his glass to Dad and laughs.

I'm about to wander off to find Amy when Elliot turns to me. 'We've not seen you for a while, Leila. What are you up to these days?'

'I've started a secretarial job.'

I adore how he doesn't ignore me like other grown-ups. He's always interested in what I'm doing, or at least is polite enough to ask.

'It's only part-time though so I'd like to find something

else, something a little more challenging.'

'There's nothing wrong with the job you have.' Dad opens his can of beer and points it at me. 'It's a perfectly good job for a woman.'

'Well, I may not want to do that job just because I'm "a woman".'

'You could do some work experience in my office if you'd like?' Elliot says, flipping the burgers. 'It would need to be unpaid unfortunately and it wouldn't exactly be glamorous, you know, making coffee, getting paperwork copied, filing, that kind of thing, but it might help you understand the architecture business if that's something you'd be interested in?'

'Oh my God, yes, that would be incredible, thank you.'

'That's awfully nice of you, Elliot,' Dad says, patting him on the back, 'but unnecessary. I hardly think Leila has the qualifications or temperament to become an architect.'

'That's not what I meant, Henry, but an understanding of the business and gaining some extra skills to go alongside her secretarial ones would do no harm, now would it?'

I love Elliot for sticking up for me. Dad's hardly going to argue with his best friend.

'Well, as long as you're sure,' Dad says.

'Of course, it'll be my pleasure.' He smiles at me.

'Any trouble, send her back.'

I know full well the repercussions if I show Dad up in front of Elliot. I can't wait to leave home, to be earning enough to live somewhere else, away from a father who restricts me and a mother who won't stand up for herself. Maybe I should work my arse off this year, save up and apply to university in the next couple of years. 1980 seems like a good year to put a finger up to Dad and prove I can do anything I want if I put my mind to it. It's the end of the fucking seventies, not the fifties. Elliot has seemingly embraced changing attitudes, yet Dad is stuck firmly in the past.

I walk away to let them talk about golf or whatever other crap they find interesting. Mum's back outside chatting with Margaret and a few of their friends. I recognise some of them from other summer parties. All the children here are younger than me, and I feel stuck, no longer a kid, but equally I'm not regarded as a proper adult either.

Since Duncan moved away, I haven't had the chance to go out and meet anyone else. Friends are either working, a couple have already got engaged, and only one has gone off to university. Mum and Dad have never encouraged me to aim high or dream big. I think they expect me to settle down early like they did, and yet at the same time I know Mum's not happy. I wonder what she could have become if she hadn't met Dad and been tied down by his old-fashioned ways.

Amy, James and Susan are playing in the sandpit at the end of the garden. Amy's closest in age to me, and even she's eight years younger. There's a massive difference between being ten and eighteen. I scuff the perfect lawn with my foot and wander away from the house, my hands rammed in the pockets of my flares. I gaze past the trees screening the edge of the garden to the hillside dropping then stretching to the horizon and the rolling green hills studded with heather. I stand there for a moment, the smell of grilling meat on the breeze, and dream about what my life could be.

I start my unpaid work experience at Elliot's architect office two weeks later. I'm pretty certain Dad's just pleased that I'm out of the house all week long doing something constructive. I'm also pretty certain Dad wishes I was a boy. He has no idea how to deal with me, a headstrong, passionate, loud-mouthed teenage girl. He spent very little time with me when I was a kid, even less now.

I envy Elliot and Margaret's children, growing up together with a father who's interested in them, who shows them love and affection. I often wonder why Elliot and Dad are such good friends. I mean, they seem so different in the way they behave and how they think about family. I guess they've got plenty of other things to talk about and bond over besides their wife and kids. It might be different for me because I don't have any brothers or sisters. Maybe that's why I feel comfortable around adults, Elliot especially, because I'm used to having grown-ups for company.

It's shit-boring stuff I get to do, like filing and making hundreds of cups of tea and coffee, but Elliot doesn't treat me like a child or someone who's incapable just because I'm a woman. He lets me sit in on client meetings, and my secretarial skills come in handy taking notes and typing it all up afterwards. It also enables me to see the inside of running a busy architects' office. It's the meetings with the clients that interests me the most, and although I just greet them, take their coats and offer them a drink, I embrace the social side of the role. I know I'm good at making people feel at ease and welcome.

I settle into my two days a week working for Elliot, then the other three days at my secretary job where I'm actually getting paid. Having a pay cheque at the end of the month is exciting but I'm careful with it, putting most of it away and only spending a little when I'm out with friends. I'm on friendly terms with everyone in Elliot's office even though I'm the only woman there apart from Shirley who answers the phones and does admin. I've been helping her out loads. It gives me hope that I might potentially get a paid job in the end, if I ensure that I'm indispensable. There's more to it than my secretarial job, it's more interesting, and I like working with Elliot. I like the way he treats me as an equal, doesn't talk down to me like Dad does. He drops me home after work and we have time to chat in the car about so many things. No subject is off the table: politics, travel, hopes, dreams, work. I see another side to him, not just Dad's friend, someone I've known from afar for many years.

I've been there for two months when I tidy up my desk, say goodbye to Shirley and knock on the open door of Elliot's office.

'Everyone's already left.'

He looks up from his desk. 'Sorry Leila, I got snowed under with everything and lost track of time. I'm going to need to work a bit later. Are you okay staying, or do you want me to call your dad to pick you up?'

'No, don't call Dad. I'm fine waiting.' I start to go, intending to wait out in the main office, but turn back before I reach the door. 'Can I do anything to help?'

'Actually, yes.' He gathers a pile of papers together from his desk and hands them to me. 'If you wouldn't mind filing this lot for me, it'll save time tomorrow. And a coffee would be lovely. Make yourself one too. I probably only need another half hour or so.'

I switch on the kettle and start filing the plans. It's quiet in the office without Shirley tapping away at her typewriter, the phone ringing, and the other architects chatting amongst themselves. The kettle boils and I make a strong coffee and take it in to Elliot's office and set it down on his desk.

'You didn't get yourself one?'

I shake my head. 'Caffeine keeps me up at night.'

'Me too, but I tend to work at home later on in the evening.'

'Margaret doesn't mind you doing that?'

He picks up the coffee and looks at me. 'Oh she minds all right, but she likes our lifestyle so she appreciates that I need to work more than just office hours.'

'I'm almost done with the filing.'

'You know what, my head's scrambled. I'm not sure I'm going to be very productive for much longer. I think I'll take it home instead. Don't suppose there are any biscuits to go with this coffee?'

'Yeah.' I go into the main office, grab the biscuit tin and head back to his office. I hand it to him.

'Have a seat.' He indicates the chair on the opposite side of his desk.

He offers me the opened biscuit tin. 'Don't let me be the only greedy one.'

I take a chocolate digestive and bite into it. Crumbs fall on to my bare legs and I brush them away. When I look up Elliot's watching me.

'Your dad mentioned a while ago that you'd talked about going to university. You shouldn't let him stop you, if that's what your heart's set on.'

'Easier said than done. Anything I suggest to him, he brings me crashing back down with some crap about it not being suitable for a woman. Sorry, you're friends; I shouldn't be talking about him like this.'

'Don't apologise. Being good friends with him doesn't mean I have to agree with his views, particularly about women. I've got two daughters for God's sake. I want the same for them as I want for my son. If they choose to get married and not have a career, that's fine. But if they want to be say a lawyer, I'll support them the whole way.'

'It's so good to hear you say that. Most the time I feel Dad just wants me to disappear, be the easy daughter, find a nice young man to settle down with – a doctor, an accountant, an architect,' I grin at him, 'and have kids and look after the home like Mum has.'

'And that's not for you?'

I shrug. 'Not now, maybe one day though. Right now I want to work, have fun, meet new people. Dad's stuck in the past.'

I want to hug him for being on my side. What with the opportunity he's given me with this job and the confidence I've gained, I believe I can do what I want, apply to university and go, escape my parents, be free and forge a career for myself. If a husband and kids happen at some point, well, that's fine too, but I want time to be me first.

His hands are clasped around his mug of coffee. He's watching me. When I was growing up he was just Dad's friend, but as I've got to know him over the last few weeks,

I'm thinking of him differently. He's always well dressed, clean-shaven. Girls at school used to laugh at a boy in our year with red hair, calling him a carrot top, but Elliot's hair is a deep reddish brown and he has the most mesmerising green eyes that makes you believe you're the only person in the world when he's focused on you.

My cheeks flush. I glance away and pick up a biscuit crumb from his desk. I've caught myself looking at him over the past few weeks, really noticing him. The warmth of his personality, how friendly he is with everyone, how handsome he is despite being old. Well, he is older than me, but not *old*. He has striking features, a strong jawline, those smiling eyes. Not like who I've gone for before, skinny young hippies, smoking pot.

'You can be anything you want to be, Leila. There's something about you, I don't know what it is, that thing some people have, when you notice them the moment they walk into a room. You've got that special something.'

My throat's gone dry. A reply eludes me. My palms are sweaty, my heart thumping, playing his words over and over... *He's noticed me.* I'm more than just his friend's daughter; I'm someone he can talk to on the same level, someone with potential, someone he wants to spend time with.

I run my palms down my short dress, neatening it as I stand up. 'We'd probably better get going if you're finished?'

Something's changed between us but I'm not sure what. My mind's wandering into dangerous territory.

He downs the rest of his coffee and places the mug on his desk, gathers together his coat and folder and joins me.

'I hope you don't mind me talking to you honestly? I had a father who used to put me down – for different reasons than yours does – and I can see Henry doing it with you. His heart's in the right place, I just don't think he realises he's doing it, or the damage that kind of negativity can have.'

I look up into his green eyes. The way they bore into me,

as if he's drinking me in. 'Seriously, it's refreshing to be able to be so open with someone. Someone who gets me.'

We're so close, warmth radiates off him despite us not touching. I don't know if I'm the one who falters, but the gap between us closes and he leans down. His lips find mine.

Feelings I've never known shoot through me. Emotions fight against each other, clashing with wanting more, knowing this is so very wrong.

Shock. Lust. Excitement.

I kiss him back. His stubble grazes my skin. If he's conflicted, I sure as hell can't tell. He drops his coat and folder on the floor. He reaches for my face and holds me, moving me closer as he kisses me more passionately. His hands travel downwards, skimming over my dress just enough to make me long for his hands on my skin. I ignore the little voice in my head telling me to stop.

I want more.

He does too.

He backs me up across his office till I'm pressed against the wall. His hands dipping beneath my dress give me permission to touch him. His chest is firm beneath his ironed shirt, not the body of a wiry seventeen-year-old. His hands run up my thighs, his thumbs slipping beneath the edge of my knickers, tugging them down. I close my eyes and lean my head against the wall, as my fingers work on his belt buckle, loosening it, then the button of his trousers. He lifts me like I'm as light as a feather. I wrap my legs around his waist. He grinds himself against me, pushing into me, kissing my neck. My heart thud thud thuds to his rhythm as we have sex against his office wall.

'No one can know about this. About us.'

About us. That makes my stomach do funny things. The idea of me and Elliot as an item. A couple.

We're two roads away from my house, parked at the end of a cul-de-sac with just trees in front. There are no street lights at this end of the road, no houses overlooking us. I know what we've done is wrong and I understand his worry. I'll keep it a secret like my life depends on it. I breathe deeply, sliding my hands down the creases of my dress. My heart beats faster and faster at the memory of what just happened in his office. My parents can never know.

'No one will find out,' I say, 'don't worry.'

'Are you on the pill?'

'I can be.'

'Oh fuck, Leila. What are we doing?' The worry in his voice is betrayed by his actions. He cups my face in his hands and kisses me. I close my eyes, losing myself again in the smell of his aftershave, the scratch of his stubble against my skin, the taste of coffee and cigarettes. He's a man compared to the two boys I've been with, one the same age as me when we were both sixteen, then Duncan, older at twenty, but still, a boy compared to Elliot.

I pull away from his kiss and look at him, every part of me tingling at the excitement.

'You'd better drop me home before my parents wonder where I am.'

'Yes, of course.' He starts the engine and turns the car round, drives the short distance to my road and pulls up outside our semi. I thud back to reality. Before we'd even touched each other in his office, he'd managed to make me feel special, believing in me, giving me the confidence that I can be so much more than my parents' expectations.

He slides his hand over mine and nods towards the house. 'I'll see you in the morning.'

'Not tomorrow, I'll be in on Friday, though.' I slam the car door shut and walk up the path to the front door, sensing his eyes on me the whole time. He waits until I've closed the door behind me, and I lean against it, listening as he drives off up the road.

I can hear the TV from the front room, so I quietly head for the stairs.

'You're back late,' Mum calls out.

I take a deep breath and poke my head around the living room door. Mum's knitting and Dad's watching a game show. 'Elliot needed to work late. I told him not to bother calling Dad to pick me up.'

Mum nods but doesn't look up from her knitting. 'Dinner's ready, we were waiting for you. Go and get freshened up; it'll be on the table in five minutes.'

With flushed cheeks I retreat from the room, relieved that neither of them bothered to pay me any attention. I lock myself in the bathroom and look in the mirror. I run my hands through my hair, smoothing it down where it's tangled from rubbing against Elliot's office wall. I clean my teeth, ridding the taste of Elliot and splash cold water over my face. I lean on the edge of the sink and breathe deeply, calming my nerves at the thought of sitting at the dinner table and making polite conversation with my parents after having just fucked their best friend.

I don't start taking the pill. I don't get round to seeing my doctor, knowing that I'll get a lecture about sex before marriage and the risk of pregnancy, blah blah blah blah. Our family doctor is a man and ancient with outdated views, a bit like Dad. The trouble is, we're not careful. Protection isn't something Elliot thinks about because he probably doesn't think about it with his wife, and to be honest I'm pretty certain they rarely have sex. With me, well there's not always time to think about it. I naively think getting knocked up is something that's not going to happen to me.

Norfolk, 2006

'Eek! You're here!' I hook my arm in Jocelyn's and lead us towards the house, her suitcase bumping over the gravel behind us. 'I can't tell you how grateful I am.'

'It's my pleasure. You know how it is, since the kids left home I have time to do things like this. And Alan's quite happy to spend a week playing golf while I get to come and see you and help out.'

I push open the front door. 'Well, I can certainly do with some help. If you think the garden looks a mess, you should see inside.'

I've managed to strip out most of the brown threadbare carpets but the tobacco-stained flowery wallpaper remains, along with the 1970s kitchen, although I've scrubbed it to death with a load of antibacterial spray. I've been living off microwave meals, takeaways and the occasional meal I can cook in one pot on the stove. There's now a ruddy great big skip on the driveway that's nearly full and I'm desperate to strip back the cottage to how it would have looked originally and then improve it bit by bit.

Jocelyn's quiet as I show her around. Just having the carpets taken out has made a huge difference and although the wooden floorboards need sanding and staining, at least it doesn't feel like I'm walking in decades' worth of dirt, smoke and grease.

'It's going to be stunning,' she finally says when we reach the kitchen.

'Going to be…'

She laughs.

'And trust me, it's looking better than it did when I got here.'

I lead her out into the garden. It's the perfect time of day. The sun's beginning to go down, sending a magical glow across the horizon. The bottom of the garden is framed by trees, and two horses are silhouetted against the low orange sun.

'Oh wow. There are no words.' Jocelyn stands on the step and looks past me. I grin like a crazy person, happy to finally show her one of the reasons why I bought this damn place.

'Not bad is it.'

'Not bad? It's heaven.'

'Cup of tea?'

'I'd love one.'

I leave her to enjoy the sunset and the birds flying between the trees. I nip back inside and put the kettle on. I'm filled with pride at having my first friend to stay, knowing that feeling is going to grow as the cottage improves. I like the seal of approval from Jocelyn especially in Sophie's absence. It makes me sad that she's not been involved with me moving here.

I make the tea and take the cups and a tin of biscuits outside and join her on the step. Us sitting together gazing out at the garden is reminiscent of my first conversation with Robert. It's also a reminder that I need to buy some bloody patio chairs. Even in the depths of winter I can still imagine myself spending time out here before retreating to the warmth of the living room.

I shiver. 'It's a bit cooler over this side of the country than it is in Bristol.'

'It's that breeze off the North Sea.' Jocelyn takes a chocolate digestive and dunks it in her tea. 'To be honest, I thought you were mad when you said you were thinking of moving out here. I never thought you'd really go through with it.'

'What did I have to lose?'

'Your friends.'

I gently knock my shoulder against hers. 'The distance isn't going to stop us being friends, it just means we'll have to spend quality time together and make more of an effort to see each other. Like we are now.'

An owl hoots in the distance and ducks fly over, black shadows against the pale blue sky streaked with amber and gold from the fading sun. The field at the end of the garden leads to another and then another, rolling green stretching to a horizon of trees and a church spire. Beyond that is Blakeney, marshes, and eventually the sea. I imagine I can taste the fresh saltiness of it in the air. Having lived in a city for years, being this close to the countryside and the sea is revitalising. I don't feel contained or stressed any longer. Even the prospect of having to do this place up and the amount of work and money that it's going to take doesn't faze me at the moment, not even the thought of having to build my own business and make a success of it.

I hook my arm in Jocelyn's. 'I feel alive again.'

We drain our tea and retreat inside. I light the fire in the living room. Despite the room consisting of bare floorboards, one sofa, a sideboard and no curtains, it's quite cosy. Dinner is takeaway fish and chips from Holt, and then it's an early night for both of us. I have a spare bed, Sophie's old double from her room in Hazel Road, which Jocelyn sleeps on in the spare room. It's the only room where I've stripped the wallpaper, but even bare plaster is better than the flowery monstrosity that covered the walls before.

We get things done over the next few days. We strip the wallpaper off all of the other walls and fill the skip. I make phone calls and book an electrician to put in more sockets, and plasterers to redo the walls. It feels good to peel away the old layers. The fireplace in what will be my study has been blocked up. I take a lump hammer to it and smash away the brick to reveal an old fireplace, perfect for a wood burner. Just one more thing to add to my ever-growing list.

Halfway through the week, we take a break. I drive the short distance through the next village and park on the side of the road that leads to a ford. We get out of the car and watch a black Labrador bound after a stick straight into the water. The ford is wide and deep in the centre, the bottom rocky with large pebbles and flint. Two boys sit next to each other on the narrow bridge that crosses the ford, swinging their legs, each munching on a packet of crisps. The dog emerges from the water with the stick in his mouth and shakes himself, sending water spraying everywhere. The two boys squeal and protect their crisps from a soaking.

I catch Jocelyn smiling as she turns and follows me in the opposite direction.

'It's nice to see kids enjoying spending time outside.'

'Wait until they're teenagers, there's always a battle to be had then.'

'I'm sure it must help living in the country rather than a city to encourage kids outside.' Jocelyn sighs and shoves her hands in her coat pocket. 'It was never easy with my two when they turned teenagers; if they could stay in the warm and dry and play computer games or watch TV rather than get out and do something, they would.'

We only have to walk a short distance along the narrow road before turning off on to a grassy path that edges a meadow. We follow the river, our walking boots pounding the damp grass. The path is only just wide enough for us to walk side by side until it narrows and we walk in single file, as brambles and stinging nettles swipe against our jeans.

'Do you know, I was really worried about moving here and having to survive winter doing up the place, but I love it.

Although I know when summer arrives I'll be like, thank fuck for summer! But I do love autumn.'

'Me too. At least I enjoy being outdoors and in the fresh air as long as I can get warm and cosy back home.'

Getting the chimney swept in Salt Cottage as soon as I moved in was a bloody good idea. However grim the place is, even dirt and mould look hellishly better in the soft flickering light of an open fire.

We keep walking and stay warm despite the cool breeze. I haven't quite resorted to wearing a hat and gloves, but I have a thick woolly snood and layers underneath my khaki jacket.

The path meanders alongside the river. The clear water rushes over rocks making fronds of greenery sway beneath the surface. It's been ages since I took time to enjoy the simple pleasures in life – and I mean different pleasures than fancy meals out or lazy morning sex. This is what I've missed with life racing away at a hundred miles an hour: the gleam of sunshine through patchy clouds, open space with no houses in sight; just fields, trees, water, and fresh air with the scent of pine cones rather than exhaust fumes.

I like how Jocelyn and I rub along together not needing to fill every moment with chatter. We're just as comfortable in silence taking in our surroundings as we are talking about the millions of things we always find to gossip about.

The river forks away from the path and we climb over a stile and head into a wood, the soil damp underfoot and mushy with fallen leaves. A little further ahead is a shady car park and the welcome sight of the cafe, our reward for a cold morning's walk. We reach the entrance and I stop, a lump in my throat choking me up.

'I don't know what I'm going to do when you go home.'

Jocelyn shakes her head. 'You'll be fine without me. You moved to Bristol on your own while pregnant. If you can do that and make a huge success of your life, then this will be a piece of cake.'

'But I had you back then.'

She takes my hands. 'Yes, and you've still got me on the end of the phone, anytime. Don't go soppy on me, Leila, it's not your style.'

The cafe garden is peaceful, particularly during term time. By all accounts the summer holidays are busy, it's both the appeal and downside of living close to the sea, but for now it's mostly mums with toddlers and a group of elderly ladies out for afternoon tea enjoying the autumn sunshine.

We sit by a rock garden with a view of a border packed with plants and bushes. I order us each a hot chocolate with all the trimmings. One of the waitresses brings it out and I stir the cream and marshmallows in. I sense Jocelyn watching me.

I lick the teaspoon and relax into the wooden chair. 'I know what you're going to say.'

'What am I going to say?'

'That I've changed.'

'What because you've ordered us hot chocolate in the middle of the day instead of gin?' She laughs. 'You've mellowed, that's for sure, but only a touch. I bet you anything you're going to insist we going out tonight for a meal and a bottle of wine or two.'

'You know me too well.'

Jocelyn sips her hot chocolate and her lips are left coated with melted marshmallows. 'To be honest I'm glad we're going out to eat. Don't get me wrong, I love the house and its potential but I don't fancy eating anything cooked in that kitchen.'

'You and me both. I've managed pasta but I'm not even going to contemplate attempting to clean inside the oven. Roast dinners are going to have to wait until I have a new cooker – and a whole new kitchen.'

'Where are we going? The pub in the village? It looks nice.'

I scoop a half-melted marshmallow on to my spoon and eat it. 'Yeah, it is bloody nice. Really good food and a friendly landlord too. He was the first person in the village I met. He came over not long after I moved in with a bottle of wine and biscuits.'

'I bet that went down well with you!' Jocelyn looks at me over the top of her mug as she takes a sip. 'How old is he?'

I know what she's fishing for. 'I dunno. Late fifties maybe? He's a widower. And a grandfather. Not my type.'

'Perhaps that's a good thing; the last thing you need is a distraction when you've moved here to focus on you.'

'That's true. He's a nice guy though. I'm sure you'll meet him tonight.'

'Have you met anyone else?'

'A few people. They all seem lovely and welcoming. I think Robert – he's the landlord – is a bit worried about me moving across the country on my own and being lonely. I've assured him a bit of my own company for a while is exactly what I need.'

'He's sounds like a gem.'

I gaze out over the border at the varying greens of lush succulents and lavender mixed with pockets of colour. The leaves on the trees beyond are a bright yellow and are falling heavily, coating the ground with a colourful carpet. 'No one's ever going to replace you and Kim, but it's good to get to know someone here.'

All too soon it's time for Jocelyn to say goodbye. A week of having a familiar face around has been so good. She's been there for me during both the good and bad times, and it's a great feeling to share my new adventure with her. The two of us working on the house has helped move things forward.

I stand by the open gate and wave until her car turns on to the main road and is out of sight. She's driving the 240 miles back to Bristol where my old life was. Tears stream down my face. I feel silly because my gut is telling me I've made the right decision. I feel at peace here, calmer than I've done for years. I wipe my face and close the gate. I know there's still lots about my life I need to fix, like my relationship with Sophie, plus I need to get my wedding planning business up and running to make it viable living here, but I feel optimistic and have a renewed energy.

I literally shake the sadness of saying goodbye to Jocelyn out of my system. I stand in the middle of the drive, hands on my hips and gaze up at the blue sky streaked with white clouds. The air is cool and fresh and smells of the country: damp grass and soil, the sweetness of roses mixed with the occasional stronger whiff of manure drifting across from the lane. A horse snorts and birds fly over. It's everything I've longed for. I know it's going to be good for me, being away from the distractions of city life and the bad shit that went with that. Too much drinking, too much flirting, too many wrong men, too much meaningless sex. Not that I want to abstain from all that completely.

Sheffield & Bristol, 1978-79

It gets increasingly difficult to find time alone with Elliot. I go from unpaid work experience to being offered a job. I trust him when he says he's given me the job because he values my work and not because of our relationship. From that first time in his office in September, followed by occasional snatched moments mostly in his car, parked up somewhere dark and hidden before he drops me home, the time flies by. It's not like he can work late too often without arousing suspicion. It's secretive and dirty, and yet the thrill of it... I really don't care because I love being with him, I love how he makes me feel. I love him.

The Christmas party is torture, watching him from afar, Margaret there with him, their arms around each other's waists. They're seemingly a perfect couple, well-matched and stylish. I'm wearing wide-legged trousers and a boob tube, not at all sophisticated but I'm embracing being me. I catch Elliot glancing my way when no one's watching.

A family Christmas takes over and I endure a week in Northumberland, with a roast turkey dinner, the Queen's speech, board games at the dining room table, long wintry walks with my parents, grandparents and Aunt Pearl, my mum's unmarried childless sister who's about as much fun as a visit to the dentist. My cousins aren't even staying this year because Mum's other sister decided it'd be nice for them to go skiing instead. All right for some. So I endure it and torture myself with the thought of Elliot playing happy families back home.

The next time I see him is in the new year when we're back at work. It's busy with Elliot really having to work late, and our plans to be together are scuppered by Shirley offering to drive me home. I can hardly say no. A few days later when Shirley's off sick, Elliot takes me home, but first we head to our usual parking spot tucked away on the moors. It's fucking freezing in the car, even with the engine left running. The little bit of warm air pumping out does little to combat our icy breath, so we're quick about it. Our relationship has to remain hidden, so a quick shag on the passenger seat of his car when it's minus three outside is our only option, but it's so good to be back in his arms.

The worst of winter gives way to snowdrops and it's a relief to see trees beginning to bud. The greyness of winter retreats and lifts everyone's spirits. We're managing to muddle along together at home; I think my parents are pleasantly surprised that I've cut back on nights out and that I'm throwing myself into work. Most of all I think they're glad I'm not hanging about with any unsavoury blokes. Little do they know. I like seeing my bank balance grow too. Getting paid for full-time work makes a real difference.

I'm not thinking further ahead than the next time I'm going to be with Elliot. I ignore those niggling worries. My plans to apply to university have been put on hold and not just because of Elliot. Working and earning has given me new possibilities and I'm determined that with enough money saved I'm going to start the new decade by moving out.

It's a perfect plan until I realise it's been a long time since my last period.

Shit. My period's at least a week late, maybe even two weeks, I've not been keeping track carefully enough.

I've been locked in the toilet at work for too long. They're going to start wondering where I am. But the tingling pains in my stomach and light-headedness are making me unable to focus.

I could go to the doctors with a urine sample. They can tell me I'm not pregnant and everything will be fine.

Who the hell am I kidding. I know the truth without a test to tell me one way or another.

I'm stupid. I've been too swept up in love.

I can tell I'm pregnant. That icky sick feeling for the first hour or two in the morning and just the way I feel different, like my body already knows even if my head doesn't want to accept the truth.

At six in the morning when I'm retching my guts up in the downstairs toilet in the hope that Mum and Dad won't hear, reality hits. He's married and already has three children, he's thirty-eight, my boss and best friends with my dad. I'm nineteen years old, unmarried and pregnant. I'm so fucking stupid. I've had plenty of practise hiding stuff from my parents: attempting to get rid of the smell of smoke after being out with friends, covering up a love bite on my neck, proving I can walk in a straight line despite having had way too much to drink. But hiding the fact that I'm pregnant, that's a whole new level of deceit.

My future is whipped away like a leaf on a breeze.

I don't know how to tell Elliot. The next time he drives me home I make an excuse about not feeling well, not in the mood to have his hands on me, be intimate with him. It's a half-truth. The nausea is there constantly, draining me, a reminder about how much I've messed up.

I don't tell him until I miss my next period. There's no denying it then. I know I should be going to the doctor, acknowledging the tiny life growing inside me, but I can't. I convince myself that Elliot will know what to do.

~

I'm too young. They're all looking at me, judging me. How the hell am I going to raise a baby when everyone still treats me like a child?

I glance at the women sitting in a circle alongside me. I'm the youngest here. By a long way. Most are probably in their mid to late twenties. The other difference is they've all got their husband with them, sitting behind them, rubbing their backs. I have no one. No husband. Not even a bloody supportive mother. I don't know anyone in Bristol apart from Duncan, and he's my ex-boyfriend and I'm not going to ask him to join me. Too bloody weird.

The class passes by in a blur. The midwife is efficient but doesn't exactly make me feel at ease when she uses me as an example as I'm the only one without a partner. She isn't so tactless as to ask who or where the father is though, and for that I'm grateful. The reality is beginning to sink in. The bump is too big to pretend I've just eaten too much, and the pummelling from tiny fists and feet is too real to ignore. My back aches, I need to wee all the time, and watching the midwife push and twist a plastic baby through a pelvis makes me wish I'd kept my fucking legs closed.

We have three more weeks of this to feel prepared, but I'm not convinced anything's going to actually prepare me for giving birth in a few weeks' time and what comes after. That bit scares the shit out of me the most. How the hell am I going to look after a baby when I feel like I can barely take care of myself?

'That's it for this evening,' the midwife's soothing voice says. 'Remember to keep practising your pelvic floor exercises, and I'll see you all next week.'

Chatter starts up around the room as everyone gathers together their leaflets and coats.

'Hi,' a friendly voice says as I pick up my bag. 'It's Leila, right?'

I stand upright, my back aching, and turn to see a woman with short dark brown hair smiling at me. She'd been sitting opposite me with her husband. She was the only one who gave me an encouraging smile when it was my turn to introduce myself.

'Hi, yes, it is.'

'I'm Jocelyn, and this is my husband, Alan. It's difficult to remember everyone's names, isn't it?'

She has a warmth about her that makes me want to cry.

'Would you like a lift home?'

'I was going to get the bus…'

'Don't be silly, we can drop you off. It's dark and not to mention you're pregnant.' She laughs and for the first time that evening I actually feel at ease.

I walk out with them. It's strange; since arriving in Bristol, I haven't had any company other than Duncan's. I mean, I can't thank him enough for being decent enough for letting me have a place to stay, but there's an awkwardness about our relationship, the distance of ex-lovers turned friends, being civil to one another and trying to make it work. The bump's not helping. It's plain weird and I know he feels the need to explain it's not his when mates come over. I know they couldn't give a shit, but I'm conscious he might want to bring a girl home. The last thing they'd want to meet the morning after is his pregnant ex-girlfriend – even if it's not his baby.

I clamber on to the back seat, sheer relief at the thought of not having to wait for a bus and then walk the last few streets to Duncan's in the dark.

'There's so much to take in, isn't there,' Jocelyn says from the front passenger seat as her husband pulls out into the road. 'It's difficult to process it all. I guess it's inevitable – this baby's got to come out somehow.'

We drive the short distance to Duncan's through city streets bathed in the orange glow of street lights. Despite the antenatal class and learning the process of early labour and delivery I feel woefully unprepared. My stomach protrudes and I can feel the baby kick, but deep down I'm in denial. My life has been flipped on its head in a few short months, while

Elliot's life has continued without a blip, except that he's no longer getting to have sex with a nineteen-year-old. Talk about having your cake and eat it. He's got away with this and come out the other side unscathed, his family life intact, his wife unaware of his infidelities *and* my parents still being friends with him.

I release my clenched fists as I tell Jocelyn's husband where to pull over.

Jocelyn twists round in her seat. 'Are you doing anything tomorrow?'

I shake my head.

'Come over for a cup of tea, then we can chat properly. Eleven o'clock suit you?'

I nod; I have nothing else to do.

She writes her address on a scrap of paper and hands it to me.

They wait until I've closed the front door behind me before driving off, headlights gleaming through the frosted glass panel. The tears I've been holding back finally spill, emotion shuddering through me at their kindness, understanding and non-judgement about my situation. Jocelyn's going to make a great mum, I think as I make my way to Duncan's upstairs flat; she's already so motherly, more so than my own goddam mother.

Jocelyn and her husband live in Bishopston, which socially seems a world away from my temporary flat on the edge of Filton, although it's only a short bus journey. The stepped front garden reminds me of the care and attention my mum puts into our garden back home. Shrubs and plants neatly line each level, their flowers blooming in the summer sun. Reached by a few steps from the street the semi-detached house is imposing and inviting, a neat mix of red-brick and brown pebble-dash. It's going to be one lucky kid growing up here. In many ways it's a similar to where I grew up, a wide street in a relatively well-to-do area, and yet it feels far removed from my old life back in Sheffield.

Jocelyn greets me with a smile and a hug and it feels like we've known each other forever. I follow her through the light and airy hallway into the kitchen at the back of the house. It smells of baking. The back door is wedged open and fresh air drifts through. I'll be forever grateful to Duncan for putting me up in his spare room, but it's no place to live once I've had a baby, with dirty socks lying around, cigarette stubs and spliffs in ashtrays, and random friends of his sleeping on the sofa.

'What would you like? Tea? Coffee?'

'Tea please. The smell of coffee's still making me feel sick.'

'Oh poor you; I seem to have got off rather lightly with very few symptoms and no real sickness. It's funny how everyone's different.' She gestures for me to sit at the kitchen table and she sets about making us tea. 'Alan's out playing golf, so it's just us. I made flapjacks.' She brings a plate over and places it in front of me.

I'm relieved about her husband being out. I feel like I'll be able to talk to Jocelyn, but I didn't really want her husband eavesdropping.

She pours boiling water into a teapot and puts it on a tray with two china cups. 'Your accent's not from around here.' She joins me at the table.

'No. Sheffield.'

'What brought you to Bristol?'

'Do you want the long or short answer?'

'I don't want you to feel like I'm prying in any way, but if you fancy telling me it, then the long story.'

I rub my hands over my bump. 'As you might have guessed, this wasn't planned.'

'Who's the father?'

I look down at my hands. I realise I've not told anyone about Elliot. Not one of my friends back in Sheffield knew. Apart from my parents finding out, the only other person who has any idea is Duncan and I've told him the bare minimum. He's got no interest in prying further.

I look up at Jocelyn. She pours tea into the cups. 'Milk?'

I nod.

'Do you know who he is?'

'Yeah, I do. Although I don't know if it would be better for this baby if I didn't. You know, if he was a one-night stand, it might be easier.'

'Oh?' She slides one of the cups of tea towards me.

'I had an affair with someone much older than me, a family friend. He's married with kids.'

If she's shocked, she's hiding it well. She takes a bite of a flapjack and chews it. 'I presume he didn't want to know as you're down here?'

'All he wanted to do was protect his family; and my parents, well they wanted to send me away to my aunt's to have the baby and then give it up.' My throat's sore and tears well.

'Seriously?'

'Huh uh.' I sip the tea. It's not the usual tea that we have at home, definitely something posher. 'I mean, times are changing. I know what I did was wrong, but *he* was in the wrong too, yet I'm the one being punished. Fine, I've had sex before marriage, I've been naive at best but it's done, I can't change what's happened.' I slide my hands across my stomach. 'I'm not giving this baby up.'

'Good for you. I can't tell you how brave I think you are for standing up for yourself, and for your baby.'

'Really? You're not shocked that I messed around with a married man?'

She takes my hand and squeezes it. 'Who am I to judge? We all make bad choices at some point in our lives that we end up having to live with. Like you said, times are changing. How old are you?'

'Nineteen.'

'Well, ten years ago when I was your age, things were very

different. Yes it might have been the end of the sixties and free love and all that, but my parents certainly didn't feel it was appropriate to be having pre-marital sex.'

'And you did?'

She laughs. 'Shush, don't tell my parents. Then of course I met Alan and we got married in our early twenties and here we are having our first child. But ten years ago the expectation was for a husband to go out to work and the wife to stay at home. Now we have the first female prime minister. So what if you're unmarried and pregnant, even if it was an accident, it's still your choice to keep the baby and raise it on your own terms.'

I can't hold back my tears any longer. To hear someone be so un-judgemental about my situation is giving me hope that somehow, however hard the next few weeks, months and years are going to be, I'll be able to make it work.

She hands me a tissue and I wipe away my tears.

'Have a flapjack; you could do with one.'

'Thank you so much.'

'For what?'

'For being so nice.'

She waves her hand at me. 'It's the least I can do. Truthfully I just wanted to hug you at last night's antenatal class, you looked so lonely and lost. I thought you could do with a friend.'

And what a friend she ends up being. She helps me find a room in a house with a couple who work shifts in the NHS and who don't mind that soon enough I'll have a new born baby. Despite being eternally grateful to Duncan for his hospitality, it's such a relief to move out of his flat and into a cleaner, better-kept house with professional adults and a kitchen that doesn't have mould growing behind the cooker or a damp bathroom. Jocelyn helps me sort out maternity pay, plus I have the money I saved while working in Sheffield, so I'm able to buy the essentials I need to look after a baby. By the time I give birth to Sophie in late September 1979, Jocelyn is there with me, giving birth to her own baby son just over a week later. To think that someone who's only known me for a short while can be so supportive while my own parents do their very best to ignore the fact that they're now grandparents. And Elliot, well he doesn't even acknowledge that he's a father for the fourth time.

And I'm a mum.

Norfolk, 2006-07

I continue to do as much work on the house as I can, decorating my bedroom, the living room and the downstairs study once the plasterers have redone the walls. I manage to live with the kitchen and bathroom in the state they're in until after Christmas when builders transform them into spaces I actually want to cook in or enjoy having a bath without worrying about contracting some horrendous disease.

Despite the cottage being a building site, I have to juggle managing the build with my wedding planning business. The wedding I'd moved to Norfolk for takes place in February and then I have three more weddings lined up over spring and summer. It's starting to feel like I can really do this, make a go of my own business; I thrive on the pressure and no longer being tied to a desk, an office, or a boss.

With two successful weddings behind me, word of mouth begins to take hold and I start getting potential clients that way. Pamela is the mother of a young bride-to-be and invites me over to their house to talk through me organising her daughter's wedding. I say house, it's more like a mansion. It's in the depths of north Norfolk, reached by narrow winding lanes where I really don't want to meet another car let alone a tractor. It has a wrought-iron gate with Kingfisher Hall inscribed on it. They open automatically as I drive up, and wide-eyed I follow the gravel drive that curves through trees.

The house takes my breath away. The stonework is covered in dark green creepers that curl around mullioned windows, and there are plenty of them. The place is huge, not just the house but the grounds too. If there's this much garden to the front of the house I can only imagine what there will be at the back.

'Fuck me.' I pull up alongside a Porsche and switch off the engine. For the first time since starting my business I feel out of my depth – the thought of being in charge of organising a wedding for someone who lives in a place like this. I take a deep breath, gather my bag, notebook and laptop and scramble out of my Mini. It looks overwhelmingly inadequate next to a sports car.

The oak front door swings open and a petite lady clatters out in heels, a smile on her face as she greets me. 'Leila,' she says, taking my free hand. 'I'm Pamela. It's lovely to finally meet you in person. Come on in.'

We're about the same age, but her two daughters are younger than Sophie. She's bubbly and blonde, has been liberal with the fake tan (or too many exotic holidays), and my initial reaction is that I'm not going to get on with her.

I'm right about the back garden. We sit outside on the patio – I say patio, it's huge, more like a terrace, the pale grey stone slabs glint in the sunshine they're so clean and completely weed-free. It puts my wild garden at Salt Cottage to shame. The garden at Kingfisher Hall is landscaped. The lawn is so perfect it looks like a green carpet sweeping away from the raised border that edges the patio, down to a river lined by weeping willows and silver birches.

We sit in the early spring sunshine drinking cups of tea and talk through Pamela's daughter's wedding. I have nearly eighteen months to make it happen and the location of the reception has already been decided – a marquee in this garden. I just have to organise it and add the magic and sparkle. The budget is beyond my wildest dreams and it's exciting – and nerve-wracking – to be in charge of someone's big day with a serious amount of money to play around with. The possibilities are endless.

The bride-to-be eventually joins us after Pamela and I have talked through the basic details. She's wearing pink spotty silk pyjamas and from the state of her tangled blonde hair, she's just dragged herself out of bed.

'You've finally emerged.' Pamela rolls her eyes at me. 'Youngsters.'

I'm shocked by how young she is, barely out of her teens, still living at home, although I guess coming from a family who live in a place this beautiful and large, it's not really that surprising. She's older than I was when I had Sophie, but behaves younger than her years.

'So, Sylvie, what ideas do you have for your big day?' I ask.

She pours herself a cup of tea and tucks her legs beneath her on the chair.

'Well,' she says, giggling. 'I love pink and I have this idea for the marquee to have, like, stuff from a fairground, like candyfloss and popcorn…'

After Sylvie finishes talking through her ideas and retreats back inside the house to get dressed, I have a pretty good idea of what she wants: a pink-themed sparkly wedding, with live music and no expense spared when it comes to the special little details. I'm going to have fun with this.

I close my notebook which is now jam-packed with sketches and ideas from both Sylvie and her mum. Pamela pours us another cup of tea and settles back in her cushioned chair.

'It's absolutely beautiful.' I motion down the garden to the river. Birds fly between trees and a kingfisher dives into the water and soars back up, disappearing in the foliage on the other side of the river. 'I see where the house gets its name.'

'Yes, I feel very lucky that we get to live here.'

'Have you been here long?'

'A few years. We moved from London when Sylvie and her sister were in their early teens. They were already at boarding school out this way, and my husband and I were fed up of living in the city. We had a lovely house in London but the size and space you get for your money out here compared to central London, well, it doesn't even compare.' She picks up her cup, her pink nails gleaming against the white china. 'You've not been in Norfolk long?'

I shake my head. 'Seven months. I moved from Bristol, so left city life behind like you.'

'Are you married?'

'God, no.'

She laughs. 'For my sins I've been married since I was twenty, and it seems Sylvie is following in my footsteps by marrying young.'

'Well, as long as she's happy and it's her choice, I guess age isn't that much of a factor.'

'Oh she is, happy. And Matt is a lovely lad. They both need to grow up though. It's the only thing I regret, our children living such pampered lives that they haven't yet seen any of the real world or had to fend for themselves. My childhood and teens were very different. I was well aware of how cruel the world could be long before I met Raymond and he became successful.'

'I'm sure if you've had that background, then that grounding will have rubbed off on your daughters.'

'I do hope so.' She flashes an overly white smile. 'So, you're not married, but is there a man – or a woman – in your life?'

'Nope. For once, it's just me. That's one reason I left Bristol, to escape my bad choices in men and concentrate on me for a while. I needed a change in direction and a slower pace of life.'

'Well, you've certainly moved to the right place, sleepy north Norfolk. Apart from the summer months of course when the villages on the coast are overrun by tourists, but even then, despite all those extra people, there are still peaceful places to be found.' She puts a cool hand on my arm.

'I'm looking forward to getting to know you better, Leila.' She claps her hands together. 'I think we're going to have fun organising Sylvie's wedding!'

I drive away from Kingfisher Hall with a feeling of contentment, everything going in the right direction, my business flourishing. Pamela is a good person to know, and surprisingly someone I get on really well with, despite unfavourable first impressions. As each month has passed since I moved here, little things have confirmed I've made the right choice.

Sheffield, 1985

It's been over five years since I've been back to Sheffield, set foot on our street or walked through the front door of my parents' house. And it is their house, I don't even think of it as my old home it feels so long ago and so far removed from my life now.

They've never met Sophie. They've never forgiven me. I get their anger, but for it to take this long for them to meet their grandchild, that I'll never understand. Surely they must wonder about her?

The drive from Bristol to Sheffield in my second-hand Peugeot is long and tiring. Sophie starts moaning about how long it's going to take when we're only twenty minutes into the journey. I can't blame her really; we don't usually travel far from home apart from over the bridge for a day out at a beach in Wales and I don't think she quite understands who she's meeting. All she knows about her grandparents is getting a card from them on her birthday and at Christmas with a token fiver tucked inside. She's not met them, not spoken to them; the concept of a loving grandparent is lost on her.

We stop at services for the loo and to stretch our legs. Back in the car, the further north we drive the more stressed I feel. I can't even remember whose idea this was. Did I suggest visiting? Or did Mum mention it on our yearly phone call. It wouldn't have been down to Dad. I've not spoken to him since the day I left for Bristol.

Although I grew up in suburbia, we weren't far from the wild openness of the Peak District. I have a pang of longing as I catch sight of the lush green of rolling hills in the distance. I've loved living in a city and I've made my home there. Nothing would ever drag me back to Sheffield and my parents. Apart from Elliot, but the chance of that is remote. I often think about him though, particularly as Sophie gets older and I see him in her red hair, the shape of her face and her beautiful green eyes that light up a room.

My heart is thumping by the time I park in my old road, a little way down from my parents' house. It's utterly familiar and yet it's the strangest feeling in the world being here. I've got used to living in a flat of a terraced Victorian house, with cars parked bumper to bumper and only enough room to squeeze one car down the road. I'm now a bloody pro at reverse parking. Here, the 1930s semi-detached houses have driveways, the road is wide and uncluttered with cars. There's space, that's what I miss in Bristol, although for a city it has plenty of parks, a river, and beautiful views. There's little to complain about considering I ended up living there by accident.

Sophie wakes as the engine stills. I catch her through the rear-view mirror, yawning and rubbing her eyes.

'Where are we?' She strains against her seat belt to see out.

'At Grandma and Grandad's.'

She yawns again. 'I'm hungry.'

'Well, I'm sure Grandma will have something for lunch, although not yet awhile.'

'I don't want lunch; I want a snack.'

'I'll get you something when we get inside.'

Great, a grumpy, hungry five-year-old about to meet her grandparents for the first time.

I feel leaden as I unbuckle my seat belt, grab my bag off the passenger seat and open the door for Sophie. It's October half term and the air is deliciously cool, the leaves are turning shades of red, gold and orange, the ones already fallen brown and crunchy underfoot. Children's laughter and shrieks ring out from back gardens. The sound briefly reminds me of happier times when I was young enough to have no cares in the world apart from what I was going to play and who I was going to play with. Now I'm carrying the weight of my parents' brutal disappointment in me.

'Do you have crisps?' Sophie asks the moment she's out of the car.

She's wearing a blue pinafore dress and woolly grey tights. She looks adorable with bunches, so different to how she usually is, racing around at one hundred miles an hour or scrabbling about in the garden in dungarees.

'Yes, I have crisps.'

She catches me looking at her dress and she yanks at the hem. 'I feel silly.'

'You look lovely.'

She sticks her tongue out.

It's going to be a long day, and we've still got the drive home to get through.

Sophie follows me, kicking the fallen leaves and trailing her fingers along the side of the front garden walls. I reach my parents' house. There's a new car in the driveway. The border is as neat and well-maintained as it's always been. I ring the doorbell and think how strange it is that I no longer have keys and can come and go as I please.

It only takes a moment before the front door is pulled open by Mum. Her personality never really matched her dress sense. She's got a bohemian style, favouring colours and long tunic-tops, still clinging on to flares from the seventies. Mum's greyer and a little older than the last time I saw her, but I guess that's to be expected seeing as though over five years have gone by. I'm no longer a teenager, but heading into my mid-twenties, single-handedly raising Sophie while working damn hard to earn a living.

Mum's eyes rest on Sophie who is half-hidden behind me,

and I watch them widen. I know what she's thinking; how much Sophie looks like her father.

'Come in, come in.' She ushers us through the door. I wonder if she's worried about nosy neighbours peering out and clocking me with a young child.

We go through to the living room and memories flood back, thumping me in the chest, a disconcerting feeling that won't budge. I remember walking in on Mum, Dad and Elliot discussing the affair. From that point my life unravelled.

Dad's in brown cords and a plaid shirt. He stands when I walk in and Sophie, usually so outgoing and confident around adults, curls her arms around my legs. Maybe she senses my discomfort at being here.

'Leila.' That's all he says, no hug, no smile, not even a handshake.

Mum bustles in behind us. 'So, Henry, this is Sophie.'

She kneels down next to Sophie and smiles at her. At least she's trying, even if she's done bugger all to be in our lives until now. I'm not actually sure becoming a mother was anything she really strived for, it was what was expected of her, and she conformed. Maybe that's the reason she punished me for my affair with Elliot, because I couldn't give a fuck about conforming to anyone's expectations.

'Sophie.' I try to prise her fingers off my leg. 'This is your Grandma and Grandad.'

It's absurd that this is the first time they've seen her. I mean, it was wise for me to stay away from Elliot – although I wasn't given a choice – but they could have visited us in Bristol. I think Mum would have, but I'm sure Dad wiped his hands of me a long time ago. My cheeks redden at the thought of my teenage mistake, at succumbing to and inviting Elliot's advances, at sleeping with Dad's best friend. How has Dad remained friends with him? How has Elliot managed to move on with his life scot-free while I was the one blamed and punished for something *we* did.

'So, Sophie,' Mum says, still kneeling on the carpet.

'You've just started school. Do you like it?'

'Yes.'

'What's your favourite thing about school?'

'Don't know.'

'Are you learning to read?'

'Can't remember.' Sophie shrugs and wanders over to the window.

'She's the same with me when I pick her up from school, doesn't want to tell me anything. Although she ends up drip-feeding me stuff in her own good time.'

Mum nods and struggles to her feet. 'You were the same, although better when you were younger. As a teenager you never told us a thing.'

With good reason. I don't say that out loud though.

Sophie has her nose pressed to the window. She turns to us. 'Can I go outside?'

'It's rather cold out,' Mum says. She plumps up a cushion on one of the armchairs and invites me to sit.

'Oh please!'

'Well, perhaps later. After some tea and cake. You like cake, don't you?'

I sit down and catch Dad watching Sophie as she skips across the room. She slips her hand in Mum's and I instantly feel tears pricking my eyes at the gesture. 'Cake's my favourite.'

Mum laughs. 'Good.'

Sophie's chatter about the Care Bears cake she had at her fifth birthday party gives Mum time to disappear into the kitchen to make tea, while Dad and I are spared having to actually talk to each other. Mum returns with a tray laden with cups, saucers, a teapot and a large Victoria sponge, oozing with jam and buttercream. Sophie licks her lips and sits down on the sofa, waiting for Mum to pass her a large slice.

Our conversation remains on Sophie, school, where we're living and my job – all relatively safe subjects that don't focus on the past. Sophie begins to thaw out too, her usual confidence returning with a glass of juice and a piece of cake. I nip upstairs to the bathroom, leaving Sophie chatting incessantly about dinosaurs. My daughter was never going to be the kind of girl who loved dolls and dressing up.

The bathroom is exactly the same. A pristine white bathroom suite with blue and white tiles. There's even the same purple orchid on the windowsill.

I wipe my hands on the burgundy towel and leave the bathroom. I pause on the landing tempted by the sight of my old bedroom door. I used to have LEILA spelled out in colourful wooden letters on it when I was younger, replaced with a 'keep out' sign when I turned thirteen. I give in to my curiosity and creep along the landing and push open the door.

Any sense of me has been removed from the room. I took very little with me when I left, just clothes, books and a couple of photograph albums. It's been transformed into a spare room devoid of any personality. Gone are my posters and the blue walls I know my parents never liked. Cream and beige dominates, yet the view out of the window remains unchanged, the garden still carefully maintained, pockets of colour in the borders amongst the green shrubs and the grass leading down to that damn apple tree at the bottom of the garden. Apple crumble, stewed apples, apple chutney, apple cake… I got fed up of being force-fed apple on a daily basis. Dad's shed is still there and the fence, a little more weathered, but the houses opposite look exactly the same.

I'm glad I said no to us staying. It's a hellishly long drive from Bristol to Sheffield but at least I'll be heading home at the end of the day and won't be tormented by memories I'd rather forget, or sleeping in a bedroom that was once mine, in a house I will never call home again.

I don't want a house like my parents', but I am longing for somewhere I can call my own. It's been too long having to share a flat and a bathroom, and to pay rent to a landlord who doesn't even care about basic maintenance. A place of our own is what I dream of and why I'm working as hard as I possibly can to achieve that for us both.

I close the bedroom door silently behind me and make my way downstairs. I take a deep breath before entering the living room, preparing myself once again to make polite conversation with my parents.

Once Sophie starts getting bored, Mum lets her play in the garden. I watch her through the window, kneeling on the damp ground by the border, her fingers digging in the soil. I bet she's hunting for snails.

'I was going to invite Elliot so he could meet Sophie too…'

That's news to me. My chest tightens at the mention of his name. 'You were?'

Dad looks away, focusing his attention on the clock on the mantelpiece.

Mum clears her throat. 'But we decided not to in the end. There didn't seem a good enough reason to be able to invite him without Margaret.'

Even if they passed Sophie off as my daughter from a relationship with another boyfriend or someone in Bristol, the fact that she looks so much like her father would give the game away.

I get that they've been disappointed and angry with me, but to deny themselves the chance of having any kind of relationship with their granddaughter, baffles me. But then I never did get them and they certainly didn't understand me.

Sophie has no clue about the past and is oblivious to the tensions between us adults. As far as she's concerned we're meeting two old people who happen to be her grandparents.

Dad stands and goes over to the window. 'You'd better get that child of yours in. She's taken off her coat; she'll freeze out there.'

I clean Sophie up as best I can, scrubbing the mud off her face and from under her fingernails. There's not a lot I can do about the dirt smeared over the dress. At least the material's relatively dark and doesn't show it up too much. Why the hell am I worrying? She's a kid for God's sake. Mum's bloody influence, that's what it is, thinking I need to keep up appearances now I'm back in my childhood home. Mum always worried too much about what everyone else was thinking, while I couldn't give a fuck.

I know that's the reason why we don't go to the local pub when Mum announces we're going out for Sunday lunch. She spouts some crap about their local not being as good as it used to be, but I'm not stupid – I know she doesn't want to risk getting into an awkward conversation with anyone who recognises me. Plus we go much further away than another regular pub on the edge of the Peak District, the one close to where Elliot and his family live. No way does Mum want to go anywhere near where anyone might look twice at Sophie and think she looks familiar. Instead Mum suggests we go in two separate cars and we drive a good forty minutes away to a pub I've never been to before.

I'll give credit where it's due, it's in a stunning location, an old coaching inn surrounded by wooded hills with a view to die for, along with a roaring fire in the bar taking the edge off the chill of autumn. The Sunday roast is delicious and even Sophie eats everything, apart from the carrots. Stuffed full of roast beef and Yorkshire pudding, the last thing I want to do is drive home, yet the relief I feel at saying goodbye to my parents and driving in the opposite direction to them leaves me with a renewed determination to make a success of myself and a better life for Sophie. And hopefully, in the not too distant future, we can have a real home of our own.

Norfolk, 2007

The phone rings. I'm expecting a call from the bride-to-be of the wedding I'm organising on a boat. It's been one of my favourite weddings to plan so far, understated and down to earth, just like the couple themselves, and more along the lines of what I'd choose if I got married. Not that I ever will.

'Leila Keech Wedding Planner, how can I help?'

'Leila?'

It's definitely not the bride or the groom. I get palpitations from just hearing his voice. A voice so familiar despite years having gone by since I last heard it. His soft deep northern accent conjures up feelings I haven't felt since I was eighteen when I was head over heels in love with him.

'Oh my God. Elliot.'

'How are you, Leila?'

'Seriously?' I laugh. 'That's what you're going to ask after how many goddam years? How am I? Where do I even begin? I was waiting for a phone call from someone else. The last person I expected was you.'

'Look, I'm sorry, for surprising you like this. It's just I've been thinking about you recently...'

'No. You don't get to do this. You have no right to contact me out of the blue when I was told in no uncertain terms by both you and my bloody parents to *never* contact you.'

'I've never stopped thinking about you, Leila. Never stopped loving you.'

'Shut up, Elliot. Please stop. Your feelings are meaningless.'

'I know I hurt you. Deeply. And I'll never be able to make up for that…'

'You think?'

'But it's Sophie's birthday next week and I wanted to make sure you're okay. Anna said she's in Greece and may not have left on the best of terms with you.'

I place my free hand firmly on the desk, my fingernails digging into the dark wood.

'What the fuck is my mother doing telling you anything.' I try and control my anger but it bubbles beneath the surface, ready to burst. It's just as well he's not actually here in front of me, otherwise I'd jam the phone into his bloody mouth. That would shut him up. How can I love someone I feel so much hatred for? Conflicting emotions tear through me. I take the side of hatred, it's less complicated. 'What the hell are you doing phoning me? And how did you get my number. Don't answer that, my bloody mother. I have no idea why I bother to speak to her any longer.'

'Don't be like that, Leila. She cares for you.'

'She's got a funny way of showing it.' Leaves dance in the sunlight outside my study window. There are snatches of colour too from the rounded tops of purple rhododendrons poking beneath the bottom of the window frame. I don't like how Elliot has infiltrated my home. It's been my new start, escaping all that was wrong with my life back in Bristol and my past mistakes that led me there in the first place. I breathe deeply and repeat, 'Why are you phoning me?'

'You ignored my letters I sent to your Bristol address.'

I didn't even open them, apart from that fateful one on the night we were celebrating Sophie graduating when I was drunk and revealed who her father was. Not only did Elliot happily have an affair with me, abandon me when I was pregnant, but he's kept interfering in my life in little ways through letters, getting information out of Mum, deciding not to meet Sophie when he had the chance. He has no right to be in our lives in any way.

'I've never contacted you, never tried to stir things up with you or your family. I kept my promise, Elliot. To you and my parents. Please don't phone me again.'

'Leila, please. Don't go, let's talk.'

'I've got things to do.' I put the phone down. The silence in my study is eerie. His voice echoes in my head, like a ghost. Taunting, teasing me. I hate the way all these emotions that I thought I'd buried are floating back to the surface, making me question myself.

Maybe I should ring him back. He still loves me, he said so. And I've always loved him despite everything. My hand hovers over the phone. A blackbird lands on the window ledge, then flies off, dive-bombing across the front garden. I moved here for a fresh start, to change my ways, to get out of bad habits, away from the wrong sort of men. I can't go backwards. I remove my hand from the phone.

It's only four in the afternoon and I still have things to do, but Elliot's call has wound me up too much. I'm seething inside and can't concentrate any longer. I switch the answerphone on, close my laptop and grab my keys and bag from the sideboard in the hallway.

The fresh September air immediately soothes me. I close the front door and breathe in the scent of the countryside. September is one of my favourite times of the year. Not only is it the month Sophie was born, but I love the subtle changes between summer and autumn, particularly on sunny but breezy days like today. High white clouds scud across the watery blue sky; leaves are beginning to turn varying shades of orange, red and yellow, floating down to coat the ground in their crunchy lushness.

I relax my tense shoulders and stride across the driveway. I head down the lane towards the village. This time of year on the north Norfolk coast is one of the best too, after the summer holidays when schools have gone back and families have headed home. There are still holidaymakers around but it's quieter and the rush of summer is over, the stream of cars trying to squeeze past each other through the narrow village roads has eased, and the locals can have the beaches, cafes, pubs and countryside back to themselves.

I push open the solid wooden door of The Globe and it takes a moment for my eyes to adjust from bright daylight to the softer light of the cosy pub. The place is quiet; just a couple having a drink in the corner with their wiry dachshund lying at their feet beneath the table. There's a young guy behind the bar, quite new; I've only seen him a couple of times before, but he's friendly and welcoming.

'You look like you could do with a drink,' he says as I perch on a stool by the bar.

'That obvious, is it?'

He smiles. 'What can I get you?'

I glance at my watch. 'I should have a coffee, but that bottle of pink gin is taunting me.'

He grabs a glass from the shelf below the bar. 'With tonic and ice?'

'Yeah please, be generous with the tonic.'

He sets about making my drink and I glance around. There are a few more people out in the conservatory restaurant finishing off a very late lunch.

I turn back to the barman and hand him a tenner as he slides my drink in front of me.

'Thanks,' I say. 'Is Robert around?'

'He's upstairs, doing some paperwork I think.' He hands me my change. 'Do you want me to get him?'

I falter. 'No, it's okay thanks. Don't disturb him.'

I go through the conservatory and outside into the large garden at the back. It's a sun trap throughout the day and I head for the table at the top of the garden, away from the few middle-aged couples enjoying a glass of wine or a pint.

I should be working; I should be doing lots of things beside wallowing in self pity with a large gin on a weekday afternoon. But then it's not everyday the past disrupts my life. I rest back in the wooden chair and shade my eyes from the sun. In my rush to escape the cottage, I'd forgotten to pick up my sunglasses.

Elliot had been right about one thing – Sophie's birthday is coming up. She's been playing on my mind for days, wondering what to do about it. There's still time to send her a present. Or I could phone her, we've not spoken to each other since Christmas. I miss her like crazy. I gulp the gin, trying to contain my fear that things are beginning to crumble around me.

'Hey there. This is unexpected. You okay?' Robert appears in front of me, a looming figure momentarily blocking the sun.

I nod. 'I've had a shitty last hour.'

'Oh?' He sits next to me.

Over the eleven months since I moved to Marshton, Robert's become a friend and I've talked to him about lots of things, but I've never talked to him about this. It's about bloody time really seeing as though he's been so open with me.

'Sophie's father just phoned. Completely out of the blue. It shook me up a bit.'

'You've never told me about him.'

'It's complicated. I try not to talk about it. Sophie didn't even know he existed until a few years ago.' I glance at him. 'That's what drove us apart.'

'She didn't know about him at all?'

I shake my head. My cheeks burn telling him this, but I know so much about him that I'm desperate to share this. 'Her father, Elliot, was – is – married. He's much older than me with three children – although they're now grown up. I was eighteen when we had an affair and I got pregnant.'

'I knew you were young.'

'The worst bit is him and his wife are my parents' best friends. To cut a long story short, he came clean to them about our relationship and I'm pretty certain he twisted what happened so he got off scot-free.'

'He's still friends with your parents?'

'Yep. Plays golf with my dad every weekend. My dad's pretty much spoken to me fewer than a handful of times since I moved to Bristol and had Sophie.'

'My goodness.'

I lift my glass and swirl the gin around. 'They all made me promise to not only end the affair and any kind of relationship with him but to never contact him again.'

'But he's breaking that promise.'

I nod. 'Yep, and it's not the first time either.'

Robert leans forward and rests his elbows on his knees. That intensity is back, making me notice the blueness of his eyes. 'Do you still love him?'

It's a bold question, but that's what I've liked about Robert from the first time I met him when we had tea and biscuits on the steps of Salt Cottage. I like his openness and I feel comfortable confiding in him.

'Yes. But I don't want to *feel* love for him. I want to get over him. I don't want to be torn every time I think about him. And Sophie, she's always reminded me so much of him. Not just the similarities in the way they look, the same green eyes, red hair, but her personality too. Maybe if I'd never got pregnant and never had Sophie our relationship would have fizzled out. Who knows.'

'But because of Sophie you've always had a connection to him yet haven't been able to let him go.'

'That's it exactly. When Sophie was younger she'd often talk about having a dad – or not having one in her case. It was a secret I held on to for years, rightly or wrongly. I beat myself up about it, thinking of the harm I did for not telling her the truth, all because I made a promise a long time before to people who couldn't actually give a fuck about me and Sophie.

I worry that I drove her away into the arms of a Greek because she's clutching at a different life, needing to escape like I had to escape my parents.'

'She wasn't running away from you though, was she? From what you've told me, she moved to Greece because she fell in love.'

I shrug. 'Maybe you're right.'

'I think you're too hard on yourself.' He nudges my arm. 'But kids, eh. They're always a worry even when they've grown up and long left home.'

'What's happening with yours?'

'Nothing with Vicky, she's never been one for me to have to worry about. It's Ben. It's always Ben. He's taken it badly since him and Mandy separated. He's started drinking heavily again. His drinking used to be a problem when he was a student, which I put down to student life but it carried on for a good while afterwards, him living the good life rather than focusing on work. Then he met Mandy and things began to improve; he got married, had Fraser and Bella, and I don't know, he's not one for talking to me much, but him and Mandy, they never seemed particularly compatible. I'm not totally convinced he was ever truly in love with her, just went along with getting married because it was what all his friends were doing. You know, the next natural step – marriage and kids.'

'It's hard work raising kids; I can only imagine what a strain they can put on a relationship if you're in the wrong relationship to begin with.'

He sits back in his chair and smiles. 'I think I could do with a drink now.'

I place my hand on his. 'You're a good friend, you know that, right.' I laugh and he moves his hand so his fingers entwine with mine. My heart falters at the intimacy of his touch. I slide my hand away to grasp my gin, catching sight of his gold wedding band as I do. Our past relationships have been so very different; while he lost the love of his life in the cruellest of ways, the love of my life has had an impact on every relationship I've had, despite us being over for nearly thirty goddam years.

Bristol, 1986

'Why don't I have a dad?'

Sophie's question comes out of the blue and is as much of a shock as if she'd punched me in the stomach.

'Where's this coming from?' I ask, biding my time, thinking through how I'm going to answer.

'Candy has a dad who lives with them all the time, well apart from when he's away working. All my friends have dads, even Lisa who lives with her mum because her parents aren't together still sees hers. I don't have a dad.'

I've been waiting for this question since Sophie was old enough to talk. It's like the other expected question of 'can I have a brother or sister'; a question which Sophie never did ask.

I lead her over to the sofa and we sit together.

'You do have a dad; it's just we weren't together for very long...' I've played this moment over and over in my mind for years, justifying that it's for the best to not tell her the full truth about who her father is. 'So sometimes when two people love each other, a baby happens... well my love with your dad happened over just one night. So unlike Candy's mum and dad who have loved each other for years, I only knew your dad for a very short time. I didn't even know his name.'

Sophie leans back and folds her hands together in her lap. 'Oh.'

It's so hard lying to her, but she seems to accept it. She's never had a father figure in her life and introducing one who she can never have a relationship with because of the secret he wants to keep, hardly seems fair on Sophie. I try to think of it as less of a lie and more of a way of protecting her, which I know goes hand in hand with protecting Elliot.

He sends a letter that arrives on Sophie's seventh birthday. It's evident from what he writes and how much he knows about my and Sophie's life in Bristol that my parents are discussing things with him. We keep up the pretence of being a family with occasional phone calls with Mum, and I hate the idea that they're sharing our life with Elliot. I don't reply to the letter, after all, he was the one who told me not to contact him. And although I communicate with my parents, mostly for Sophie's sake so she at least knows about her grandparents, we haven't been up to visit them since Sophie was five.

I trace his handwriting with my fingers, knowing he's touched the paper and spent time thinking about us, about me. Despite how it ended, I can't help but remember those first blissful few months with him, when everything felt so right: the ideas we shared, the discussions we had, they way he talked to me like an adult. The way he touched me and made me feel... I fold the letter and shut it away in a box. There's no sense in chasing after a dream that can never be.

From the early days of house sharing, which was both a blessing and a curse, by the time Sophie's seven we've moved into our own flat. It's rented of course and doesn't have a garden, but it's affordable and we can be a family, just the two of us. We don't have to live around other people in an adult-centred environment that isn't the best for a young child.

Mum and Dad visit Bristol for the first time when we're in that flat. I think they're quite relieved that we don't travel up to see them and risk being seen by anyone who might know

Elliot and his family. We've only been up there once and that was two years ago now. I have no intention of visiting again anytime soon.

I'm surprised they suggest visiting us, and I know it's Mum's doing; I really don't think Dad could give a shit about seeing us or not. I'm past caring about me, but it kills me that he's not interested in seeing Sophie either.

'My goodness, haven't you grown.' Mum holds Sophie at arm's length and looks her up and down. I can see her taking in her red hair, clear freckled skin and green eyes. 'My, don't you look just like…' Dad coughs and Mum stops talking. She releases Sophie and I show them into the living room. It's blatantly obvious who Sophie looks like; she reminds me of him every day.

There's only one sofa, so I bring a wooden chair in from the kitchen and perch on that while Mum and Dad settle themselves on the sofa, Sophie squashed between them, wearing her favourite grey and red chequered dungarees. Apart from being a little older, Mum and Dad are unchanged. Mum's still dying her hair a chestnut colour but has it permed now, which doesn't suit her. Long straight hair's always looked good on her, suited her more bohemian dress sense which was perfect in the seventies, but eighties fashion does nothing for her. Dad remains stuck in the 1960s with greying hair, a darker moustache, grey cords and a patterned jumper. Sometimes I can't even believe that I'm actually related to them.

'How are you doing? You must be working?' Mum glances around the compact front room.

'I am, at an events management company doing marketing.'

'Is that full-time?'

'Yes, it is. I'm saving up to buy a house.'

'What about Sophie? Who looks after her while you're working?' I can hear the disdain even though Mum's attempting to keep her tone lighthearted.

'Sophie goes to after school club a couple of times a week, then my friend Jocelyn whose son's in Sophie's class picks her up and gives her tea the other evenings. Then I pick Sophie up from their house on my way back from work.'

'Your friend doesn't work then?'

'She didn't used to but she's recently gone back to work part-time to fit around her children.'

'Well that's nice.'

'It is, if you can afford to do that. She also has a husband who supports them.'

'And whose fault is it that you don't?' That's the first thing Dad's said apart from hello, putting me in my place not letting me forget my past mistakes without actually spelling them out.

I clench my fists and stand up, telling myself this will soon be over, they're only down for the day so I need to keep the peace for Sophie's sake. She's not stupid, she can sense the tension in the room; she squirms between her grandparents, looking as uncomfortable as I'm feeling.

'Who'd like a brew?'

I escape to the kitchen and Mum follows me. I take teabags and drop them into three mugs and grab a packet of Jaffa Cakes from the cupboard.

Mum picks up a tin of tea. 'What's this posh stuff?'

'Earl Grey. My friend Jocelyn introduced me to it. It's nice.'

Mum wrinkles her nose. 'Bet it's nothing like good 'ole proper Yorkshire tea.'

The kettle boils and I pour water over the teabags and make a juice for Sophie.

Before we head back to the living room, Mum places a hand on my arm. 'I think it's good Sophie staying at your friends while you're at work; it's good for her to have some kind of normality in her life.'

I'm so damn close to telling them both to fuck off. But I don't, for Sophie's sake. We have no other family, and I know

Sophie feels that we're different enough as it is without me breaking all ties with her grandparents. But I can't wait for them to leave.

Norfolk, 2007

I didn't have a house-warming party when I first moved in because the place was such a shit tip – although maybe that would have been the time to have one when it didn't matter if the place got trashed. To be fair, gone are the days when my friends are reckless twenty-somethings, boozing, smoking and taking drugs. Most of my friends are now in their fifties at least. Time seems to be racing away, and yet I don't feel like I've ever caught up with my age.

The thing with village life is friends are easily made. There's an immediate bond through simply living in the same place, unlike a city where you're lucky if you know your immediate neighbours. Marshton village life revolves around the pub, social events peppered throughout the year and the church – for those who go. I've made friends with people I never would have been friends with back in Bristol, but I like how uncomplicated these relationships are. I like not having to deal with office politics. Although at times I miss having colleagues and that office banter, I relish working for myself. I'm also enjoying not having to deal with men on a romantic level and all the bullshit that goes hand in hand with that.

But having friends over and celebrating my new life is long overdue, so nearly a year after moving in, I have an open house and pretty much invite the whole village, along with a few client friends I've made through my wedding planner business. Jocelyn can't make it but Kim drives all the way across the country to stay with me for a few days.

I meet Robert's son Ben for the first time too, in unfortunate circumstances though with Ben's marriage having broken down. He's a younger version of Robert, good looking, muscular build, looks like he works out and keeps himself trim. Having got to know Robert well over the last few months it horrifies me to think that at thirty-three, Ben's a similar age to most of the boyfriends I've had over the past few years.

But I'm a changed woman. Single, embracing the freedom and loving my new life.

'You have so landed on your feet,' Kim says, pouring gin into glasses and adding a splash of tonic. She hands me one and taps her glass against it. 'I also feel I lucked out by visiting you when the place is finished, unlike poor Jocelyn...'

I feel lucky too. My life is finally heading in a direction of my making. Taking control, running my own business and having a place like this to call my own is the pinnacle of everything I've worked hard for ever since I left home.

'I wish my parents could see this place; see what I've achieved.'

'Invite them here and rub their noses in it.' Kim hooks her arm in mine.

'Part of me would love to do that; the other part doesn't want them anywhere near this place.' I have more pressing issues than rubbing my parents' noses in my success, like repairing my relationship with Sophie. Honestly, I couldn't give a fuck what my parents think of me any longer, but Sophie... Sophie means everything, I think as we head towards the laughter coming from the living room.

I go into the kitchen a couple of hours later to grab another bottle of red wine, and find Robert standing by the sink, looking out of the window.

I go over to him. 'You okay?'

'He won't talk to me.' He nods towards the darkening garden. Ben's sitting on the patio table, his feet resting on one of the chairs, his back to the cottage.

Robert's talked to me a lot about Ben, after all, apart from the pub, his life revolves around Ben, Vicky and his grandchildren. Worry coats his words now like it does every time he's talked to me about him.

'It's probably still too raw; give him time.'

'The trouble is, the longer he leaves it to try and make amends, the harder it's going to be for them to fix their relationship.'

'Not everything can be fixed, you know.'

'I know.' He folds his arms across his chest; they're tanned and shapely against his pale linen shirt. 'I'm scared he's going to completely lose his marriage, his kids…'

I put my hand on his warm firm arm. 'Don't pressurise him, whatever you do. From personal experience – and I'm talking about an extreme version of being pressurised into doing something I didn't want – it'll only drive him away. Nothing is worth losing your relationship over. Go easy on him.'

'You're right.'

'I know I am.' I grin.

'Thank you.' He kisses my cheek, picks up his beer and walks out of the kitchen, back to the laughter and chatter coming from the living room.

My cheek tingles where he kissed me. I wipe away the sensation and head outside. The sun's almost retreated; only a smudge of colour remains against the horizon. It's a beautiful early-October evening and surprisingly warm too, so still and silent. I walk across the short dry grass to the patio table. The only light spills from the house and the handful of solar-lanterns lining the borders.

Ben doesn't look up as I sit next to him. I realise he's the aftermath of an affair, he's what's left when a wife leaves her husband. Although to be fair to Ben, he didn't cheat on his wife, the affair he had was with drink and that was enough to tear them apart. It's a joke that he's around the same age as the blokes I normally go for, considering I'm heading into my late forties. I don't behave or look my age though, never have done. It's an odd thing – when I was eighteen I had an affair with an older married man, and now I'm older, the men I go for are a good few years younger.

'You needed to escape, huh?' I ask.

'Yeah, not much in the mood for partying at the moment.'

'You didn't have to come, you know.'

'Try telling that to Dad; he insisted being sociable would be good for me.'

'Well, that's a crock of shit. Sometimes being sociable is the last thing that's good for us, and that's coming from someone who loves a party. Also, parents aren't always right.'

Ben turns, a smile breaking the serious expression he's had plastered across his face from the moment I first met him a few days ago. 'I like that no-shit attitude.'

'Sometimes it's harder as a parent to let go, particularly when your kids are adults themselves. Sometimes you just need to stand back and let them find their own way, even if it means watching them make mistakes or get hurt.'

'Is this coming from experience?'

'Yeah, kind of. I had to stand back and let my daughter Sophie make her own decision and leave behind everything she'd worked for here – and I mean everything, her job, her friends, me – and go live with a man she'd only known for a few days.'

'And how did that work out?'

'Well, she's still living with him out in Greece, so she seems to have proven me wrong and it's working out just fine. My point to your dad was for him to support you, but also to let you make your own decisions and to not interfere too much. Put his trust in you that things will sort themselves out.'

Ben smooths his hand down his jeans and twists the wedding band on his finger.

'I know he's disappointed in me, that I couldn't make my marriage work.'

'I know what disappointment looks like; trust me, your dad's not disappointed. Sad for you, maybe, but not disappointed.'

'He is about my drinking; it's spiralled out of control before.'

'Well, he must trust you enough to invite you to my party where I've got enough booze in to start my own pub.'

'Ha, yes, that's true, but you realise it's only because he's here to keep an eye on me.' He taps a cigarette from a packet and holds it between his lips while he searches for a lighter in his pocket.

'Mind if I scrounge one off you?'

'You smoke?'

'Used to. Only occasionally nowadays.'

He offers me the packet and I take one, leaning towards him as he lights it. The tip glows against the darkening sky.

'I smoked a lot when I was sixteen, seventeen years old. Just one of the many reasons my parents were disappointed in me.'

'What else did you do to disappoint them?'

I take a deep lungful of smoke and breathe out, watching it plume into the dusky night sky. 'You don't even want to know.'

'Oh, I think I do.'

'Let's just say there's nothing you can do to make your dad be disappointed in you.'

'Does he know what you did?'

I nod. 'Yep. Your dad's easy to talk to.'

'How old's your daughter?'

'Just turned twenty-eight.'

'I assume you getting pregnant with her was what disappointed your parents?' He takes a drag of his cigarette.

'Bingo.'

'That's shit.'

I can't finish the cigarette. I put it out on the table and breathe in the fresh night air.

'I was eighteen when I got pregnant, nineteen when I had Sophie. I made mistakes, like most teenagers do, but mine were on an epic scale. Although I wasn't the only one to make mistakes – it takes two to tango after all – my parents have never forgiven me and I don't think they ever will, certainly not my father. But your dad loves you and will support you unconditionally, you know that, right? Whatever shit gets thrown your way, he'll be there for you.'

'Thanks, Leila.' He clasps his hands in his lap. 'I worry about what my divorce will do to him. He's been through so much, we all have, losing Mum the way we did, I don't want to put any more stress on him. I worry about losing Fraser and Bella, and I know he does too. I can't put him through that.'

'And I'm sure you won't. He's just worried, that's why he's being so hard on you. If he wasn't supportive he wouldn't have suggested you come and stay here for a while to clear your head.'

'I don't even know where to begin to fix things with Mandy.' He grinds his cigarette out on the edge of the wrought-iron table.

'Do you want to?'

He leans his elbows on his knees and gazes out at the darkening field.

'I don't know. Maybe. For the kids.'

'I get that, but what about you? Is that what will make you happy? Will your kids be truly happy?'

'I have no idea. I think I need time to think. Being here helps.' He motions towards the shadowed field and the horizon softened by the purples and pinks of the retreating sun. 'Away from the chaos I've left in London.'

'Yeah, city life can do that to you without any extra emotional crap going on.' I nudge his shoulder with mine. 'He'll worry less if you tell him what's happening and how you're feeling. Warts and all. It'll be easier in the long run for him, no nasty surprises.'

'I'm glad he's got you. He's needed someone like you in his life.' He jumps down from the table and shoves his hands in his jeans pocket. 'I'm going to go find him. Thanks again, Leila.'

I watch him walk across the garden. What does he mean by 'he needed someone like you in his life'? Like a friend? I frown; Robert doesn't seem short of friends. I wonder what he's said to Ben about me. I've needed a friend like Robert in my life too. But he is just a friend. I hope Ben can see that.

Bristol, 1987-89

Apart from giving birth to Sophie, the proudest moment of my life is the day we move into our house on Hazel Road. Our house. After years of sharing and renting, we have a place of our own. The Victorian terrace is everything I dreamed about. I can't quite believe it's mine. At least with a hefty mortgage it is, but I know I can make it work. I have to make it work. We have a living room, a dining room, kitchen, downstairs toilet, upstairs bathroom, two bedrooms, plus an attic room with an en suite. It all needs updating and there's only one plug point in each room, but most of it's cosmetic. It has original sash windows, single glazed and draughty but I love them, and there are Victorian fireplaces in three of the rooms including my bedroom at the front. Sophie has her own room that looks out over our garden and across to the red-brick terraced houses opposite.

The moment I found out I was pregnant with Sophie, I dreamt about raising her in a little cottage backing on to the Peak District, a smaller and cosier place than the large and expensive house Elliot shared with his family. Of course, Elliot was part of that dream – no longer a fling, but mine, committed to me. We were a family, living together and raising Sophie. The cottage was thatched with honeysuckle climbing up the cream wall next to the front door, and the garden was filled with colour and the scent of summer. In my dream it was always summer, never raining, never cold, never miserable, and Elliot and I were always blissfully happy. Sophie was a perfect baby and a charming child, no tantrums, no sleepless nights. I didn't doubt my ability to be a good mother. But of course, the problem with a dream is it is just that. In reality I was a pregnant teen, disowned by my parents, having an affair with a married man with kids. I lived in a dream world because that was the only way I could cope with real life falling apart around me.

More than eight years after leaving home pregnant and moving to a strange city on my own, I get the keys to a house I can call my own. Blood, sweat and tears with a bloody great big dose of hard work got me here and it feels good. So good. I love doing the place up, stripping back the house to its original beauty, unblocking the fireplaces so they're restored to their former glory and injecting my personality by painting over cream walls with bold colours. The back garden is a decent size for the city, with a lawn for Sophie to play on, a patio area where I have countless barbecues in the summer with friends and where I can sit outside with boyfriends for a late night beer or two. I keep the front garden simple with a couple of easy-to-maintain evergreen shrubs and I plant a honeysuckle next to the dark blue front door. Dreams really do come true and they're even sweeter when you achieve them on your own through hard work and perseverance. Fuck that thatched cottage and dream of family life with Elliot.

I manage quite well for the first two years, working two jobs to pay the mortgage, but the bills go up and I have little money saved for when things go wrong, like having to replace the boiler or our car failing its MOT. Soon enough feeling stressed is an everyday occurrence, balancing working with looking after Sophie in-between school and her after-school activities. With no family, I rely on after school clubs, friends and neighbours. Panic builds, leaving me exhausted. I'm doing everything I can – I can't physically work any more hours, and without a miracle like a pay rise, my options are running out.

Was I reckless buying a house? Maybe we should have continued to rent, but then it felt like I was throwing money away each month all for nothing.

A week later my decision is made. I can't see another way forward. I needed to work late so Sophie goes over to her friend Candy's house. Sitting in the kitchen on my own, I'm dreading Sophie's reaction when she gets home. The key turns in the door and Sophie calls goodbye to Candy and her mum. I grab a tissue, wipe my eyes and blow my nose. I force myself to smile as she walks into the kitchen. She stands there with her He-man lunch box in her hand and her long socks creased around her ankles.

'Why's there a For Sale sign in the front garden?'

She looks at me, her eyes big through long eyelashes, her red hair framing her freckled face reminding me so much of her bloody father.

I can't hold back the tears.

'Because I can't afford this fucking house any more!' I slam my fist down on the work surface.

Sophie jumps and clutches her lunch box to her.

I immediately regret my outburst. Still holding my scrunched tissue in my fist, I go over and hug her.

'I'm sorry, Soph. I didn't mean to scare you.'

She pulls away. 'I don't want to move.'

'I know you don't. I don't either. But without more money there's going to come a point when I can't afford the mortgage. So I'm going to try and find us a cheaper place, probably a flat…'

'No garden?'

'We might not have a choice, Sophie…'

'What about school? What about my friends? Are we going to move far away?'

'I hope not.'

'So we're not going to move near Grandma and Grandad then?'

I frown. 'What makes you think we'd do that?' I run my hand down the side of her smooth cheek. 'I'm never going back there. We'll stay in Bristol, I promise.'

'Do you have to sell up?' Jocelyn clasps her cup of tea and looks across her kitchen table at me, her forehead creased. 'I mean, if there's anything we can do to help.'

I shake my head. 'No, seriously, thank you. Looking after Sophie is more than enough.'

'We can loan you some money – you can pay it back whenever you're able to.'

'Thank you, but no.' My fingers tighten on my mug of coffee. Jocelyn has helped me out so much over the years, the last thing I want is to be in her debt. 'A loan isn't going to help; I need a steady extra income and I'm already working two jobs. Unless I get a pay rise or a promotion, which isn't likely to happen any time soon, then I don't really have much choice. I'll have to sell up and find a smaller cheaper place or go back to renting or sharing a house with someone again.'

Jocelyn nods.

'It'll be fine, moving will be fine. Sophie hates the idea but I just need to find the right place. A smaller place won't be a problem, it's just it's home, you know. Mine and Sophie's home.'

We fall silent, both of us sipping our drinks and thinking.

'What about a lodger.'

'What about a lodger?'

Jocelyn leans forward. 'Your attic room, it's perfect to rent out. It's got its own bathroom, it's out of the way at the top of the house and you're in a popular area. That would be a regular monthly income. Perhaps you could rent it out to another single mum?'

Jocelyn's idea of a lodger plays on my mind all the way home. I pick Sophie up from Candy's house and barely listen to what she's saying as I'm too distracted by a new idea brewing, one that will allow us to stay in our home. Sophie goes up to her room and I head to the attic. The spare bedroom is a big L-shape with a small shower room next to it. It's sparsely furnished, just a double bed and a wardrobe but it only needs a lick of paint and it would be perfectly liveable. And Jocelyn's right, tucked away at the top of the house it might work. I'm not so sure about renting it out to a single mum and another kid. That feels like too much hard work, having to share our lives with another family, but it's an option.

I know Sophie hates people traipsing around our house, up and down the stairs, nosing around our bedrooms, eyeing up our video collection, peering through the bathroom window at the garden, measuring up our living room to see if their sofa will fit. She hides herself away in her bedroom, pretending to do homework, but I catch her evil glares at the retreating backs of prospective buyers.

She doesn't want us to leave, she doesn't want to go to a different school or move further away from her friends, and I don't want to move out of the house I've worked so hard for either. I haven't found anywhere suitable yet and I loathe the thought of wasting money on renting.

Another Saturday morning, and we have another house viewing booked in, the second one since my conversation with Jocelyn. The doorbell rings and I sigh. Sophie thumps up the stairs and I know she's going to hide away in her room, pretending to be busy, while keeping a close eye on who's looking around our house. I dump my half-eaten piece of toast back on the plate, wipe my hands on the kitchen towel, walk down the hallway and open the front door.

The young, overly-friendly estate agent beams at me. Behind her is a thirty-something man in white trainers and a woman wearing grey kitten-heels. The estate agent says hello, introduces the couple and I let them in, then retreat down the hallway back to the kitchen, my multicoloured flip-flops slapping against the polished wooden floorboards.

I let them get on with it, wandering around the living and dining room, heading upstairs to my room at the front, Sophie's overlooking the garden, the bathroom and the large attic room at the top of the house.

'I'll let you have a bit of time to look around on your own,' I hear the estate agent say from the hallway. 'I'll meet you outside.'

I look up from my toast and newspaper as the couple wander into the kitchen. The man smiles at me; the woman frowns as she gazes around at the navy walls and black and white tiles at the back of the cooker. The man looks out of the back door.

'Nice size.'

Kitten-heels joins him. 'Needs a lot of work,' she says quietly. But I hear her.

It *is* a nice garden and a decent size for being in a city. Yes, it may be a little wild, the grass full of daisies and dandelions, the paving chalked over with hopscotch and a race track for toy cars, but Sophie loves it… I drop my toast on to my plate, no longer hungry. What the hell am I doing uprooting us from a place we both love, the place I call home, the only place I've ever truly felt at home.

The couple close the back door. The man says 'thank you' as they walk past, back into the hallway. I stand and watch their retreating backs. I know they're not going to put in an offer. White trainers might like it well enough, but kitten-heels is going to have a final say and all she's done is sneer.

Kitten-heel woman wrinkles her nose as she pokes her head into the dining room again.

'The colour scheme's way too bright. Awfully garish.'

I bite my lip. At least I try to.

Clip tap clip tap clip tap kitten-heel woman goes as she walks down the hallway to the front door. I wait until she places her hand on the door handle.

'Heard of B & Q?' I shout after them. 'Go get yourself a big tub of fucking magnolia!'

Norfolk, 2007

The brief from the bride-to-be is: registry office wedding followed by a classy reception in Norwich, somewhere unique, with a jazzy vibe, cocktails, amazing food, tapas style is perfect.

I have two months to organise it.

I decide the easiest way to find the perfect venue after a little online research is to pound the pavements in Norwich. It's my kind of research, finding the perfect cocktail bar for an intimate wedding reception. It's a shock being back in a city, in many ways reminiscent of Bristol, with an appealing older quarter which is where I focus my attention. It's too early to try the cocktails – plus I need to be sober to drive home again, but I certainly have my caffeine fix for the day, trying espressos or lattes in four bars before I think I find the ideal place.

Tucked away down a side street, the cocktail bar is in the heart of the city, surrounded by historic buildings which I know will appeal to the bride. At first sight it's attractive if a little small, but the outside is deceptive as it's bigger than it looks. Inside, it manages to be spacious yet cosy with plenty of tables along with a couple of chesterfields in the corner. It has dark grey walls, a sleek wooden bar, and chandeliers hang from the ceiling, adding to the atmosphere.

I'm won over by the virgin mojito the barman makes after

I confess if I drink any more coffee then I won't be able to sleep for a week.

I take a sip and it's like a flavour-bomb's gone off in my mouth. 'Bloody hell, that's good. You sure you didn't put any alcohol in it?'

He winks. 'Just our special recipe.'

'Secret too, I bet.'

Sold on the cocktail and the surroundings, I hope I've found the perfect place – if it's available for private hire on a Saturday in December.

'Would it be possible to talk to someone about booking this place for a wedding reception?'

'Sure, you can ask. I'll get the manager.'

I swivel on the stool and people watch while I'm waiting. It's late afternoon, a funny time of the day, way past lunch and a bit too early for pre-dinner drinks, but there are a few people sitting at tables drinking coffee or wine. This has been a fun day. Although I was desperate to escape my job back in Bristol, I do miss the banter with colleagues. I know I speak to clients on the phone all the time and get to visit them at home to discuss their wedding plans, but today's been a bit different, visiting bars, chatting to strangers, flirting with the barmen. A bit like old times, reminding me of nights out in Bristol and the possibility of a new relationship. I've loved moving to Norfolk but there are parts of my life back in Bristol I miss.

'Hey there, I'm Darren.'

I turn back to the bar and look across at a smiling face with defined cheekbones and big brown eyes. His chiselled jaw has just the right amount of stubble.

'Leila.' I shake his outstretched hand. 'I love this place. Do you own it?'

'Co-own it.'

'I'd love to book it for a wedding reception in December.'

'Yours?' He holds my gaze. I know that look; I've seen it many times before and have acted on it plenty of times too.

He's exactly the type I go for. Thirty-something, tall and handsome.

'Nope. I'm organising it for my clients. I'm most definitely single.'

I catch the barman glance at Darren before his attention is taken up by someone else at the bar.

'We don't hire out the bar, I'm afraid, but we do have a private room upstairs that might work.'

'Okay, great, sounds promising. Can I take a look now?'

'Of course. Bring your drink if you like.'

I don't need to be asked twice. Picking up my cocktail, I follow Darren out of the bar and up the stairs by the entrance. The room upstairs is almost the size of the room below minus the actual bar. Four chesterfields fill the middle of the space around a large oak coffee table. There's cushioned seating and tables on two sides, and a large window overlooking the street below. The pot plants are decorated with twinkly fairy lights and there's a wood burner. It's ideal for a winter wedding reception: stylish and cosy.

'It's perfect.'

He perches on the back of one of the chesterfields. 'Do you need to discuss it with your clients first?'

'No. They've told me what they want and want me to find it.'

'And this is it?'

'This is it.'

'Great.' He rests his hands on his black trouser-clad thighs. 'I'm about to finish if you fancy working out the details over a bite to eat. If that's not too forward?'

'Oh, it's forward but I like it.'

We leave his bar and go to another one a couple of roads away. He's everything I've always liked in a man: that forwardness, not beating about the bush, young and sexy as hell. It's good to have that sort of male attention again; it's been a long time, through choice, but God have I missed the attention. I've needed the space over this last year to concentrate on me, renovate Salt Cottage and build my business, but now…

A drink turns into two, then dinner and a few more drinks after that. He insists on buying the drinks at the last bar we go to and when he opens his wallet I glimpse a photograph of two young girls and a thirty-something woman, pretty with sleek dark hair. I have little doubt about who they are and figure he's after a bit of fun. I could do the decent thing and walk away before it goes too far. And yet, he's my ideal type of bloke, someone who doesn't want a serious relationship, no chance of us moving in together or any kind of talk about commitment. I'm getting way ahead of myself and I know I've drunk too much. Way too much to drive back to Marshton.

The cold air hits us the moment we leave the steamy bar. It's like a slap in the face but not quite enough of a wake up call. His arm slides around my waist as we make our way along the street, my heels clattering against the cobbles. I lean into him, the heat and firmness of his body next to mine something I've missed being on my own this last year. I think this might be the longest time I've not been with someone.

We reach the end of the road and he tugs me to him, leans down and kisses me. I close my eyes but falter for just a moment, a brief second of thinking about the consequences of another relationship with a younger and probably married man. And then I kiss him back, lost to the thrill of his hands traveling across my back as he holds me.

'You can stay with me tonight, if you like.'

With my suspicions about him being married, that surprises me but I say yes, without thinking about it.

His flat's not far from the bar he co-owns and it's definitely a bachelor pad. Sparsely furnished with nothing personal, no photos, nothing on the dark grey walls. Part of me thinks he must have another place somewhere, a family home while he uses this one when he's working in Norwich, the perfect job and excuse to make it relatively easy to have an affair. I'm past caring by the time he's undone the buttons of my blouse and my clothes lie crumpled on the floor. I'm back to my old ways, sleeping with a younger man I've only known for a few hours... My head might be trying to tell me one thing but his body beneath his clothes is telling me something else. Fuck me. All sense goes out the window as he leads me to his room and we tumble into bed together.

'Can I see you again?'

Having spent a year waking up alone in my bedroom in Salt Cottage, it's strange waking up in another place, in an unfamiliar bed with a man I barely know.

Our legs are tangled together in grey sheets. My head thumps from too much drink. He's lying on his side looking at me, his stubble darker and more pronounced this morning. He strokes my hair, waiting for me to answer.

I roll on to my side, pulling the sheet up so it just about covers me. Not that he hasn't already seen everything, but in the cold light of day... 'Did we even finalise the details of the wedding reception?' I ask.

'We can sort that out over breakfast if you like.' His hand continues to caress me, moving from my hair downwards, smoothing across my skin, gently tugging the sheet that I've only just pulled up.

'Yeah, I'd like that,' I say as his leg slides between mine. 'And yes, I'd like to see you again.'

It turns out he is married, with two young girls, but it's too bloody late by the time he tells me the truth a couple of weeks later. We've already shagged each other a lot, already had too much fun, and it's his decision to make. I'm his first affair, he assures me, and part of me believes him, part of me doesn't give a shit. Whatever makes him feel better. Whether he's had just an affair with me or countless other women, it still doesn't erase the fact he's cheating on his wife. I've always been the other woman, never the cheater. When I'm with someone, I'm with them. I don't mess about. If there's ever been someone else that I like, I end the relationship with the person I'm with before starting a new one. But I've always been drawn to married men – maybe that's the influence of Elliot, that being in a relationship with someone who's married there's very little chance it's going to turn into anything more than a fling. It might also have something to do with me forever holding out for Elliot, despite that being a futile dream.

Darren lives miles up the coast from Marshton in a village close to the other bar he co-owns, a swanky pub with a gourmet menu and a picturesque beer garden. His flat in Norwich is just for ease, to stay over when he's working late in the city, but he has the ideal job for making it easy to have an affair too. So it becomes a regular thing, either me staying over in Norwich or him occasionally driving back to Salt Cottage.

It suits me fine, the freedom of living my life how I want to, no worries about having to fit around anyone else or live with someone. When we do stay over at each other's, sex is always on the agenda. I like the thrill of it being an illicit affair even though I'm bloody old enough to know better.

There are problems in his marriage, there always are, I've heard it before, the pressures of work and family life.

'I think we got married too young,' he tells me at breakfast, the morning after the wedding reception at his bar. We're at his flat in Norwich and he's about to head back to the bar for an hour or two, then go home to his family, and I'm going to meet a client on my way back to Marshton.

'Oh?' I take a bite of toast.

'It wasn't so much getting married in our mid-twenties that was the problem, it was having kids too quickly. We had no time to just be a couple.'

I'm not sure I really want to be having this conversation; I'm not his bloody therapist.

'Which is why you're having an affair with me?' I sip my coffee and watch him carefully. 'You want that excitement of a new relationship with no ties, no expectations?'

He looks across the table at me. He's in a smart jumper and jeans, silhouetted against the window, a grey December day outside. 'It's fucking selfish, isn't it?'

I drop my toast on the plate and shrug. 'I've been selfish my whole bloody life then.'

'You've never been close to marrying anyone or settling down and having kids?'

'I did the kid thing, but I was eighteen at the time.'

He frowns. 'You've got a child?'

'Well, a twenty-eight-year-old daughter, I'm that bloody old.'

'You're not old.'

'I guess I'm not, because I've continued to act like a teenager my whole adult life.'

He comes over and sits next to me. 'Are you bothered that I'm married?'

'The question should really be, are *you* bothered that you're married?'

He doesn't answer, but I know it plays on his mind. We continue to see each other though; the sex is too bloody good. And we talk, a lot, about stuff we can't talk to our families about, both of us selfishly taking from the relationship the things that are missing from the rest of our lives.

Bristol, 1989-94

It's weird to begin with, welcoming a stranger into our house, but it's this or move somewhere smaller and I've worked too hard to give this up, plus we've put down roots and Sophie's happy here. Although the lodger has their own bedroom and bathroom up in the attic, they have to cook in our kitchen, not that they cook that much. I didn't go with Jocelyn's suggestion of another single mum. Instead, I've pretty much opted for students; I figure they'll be out most of the time, at uni during the day, the pub in the evening and when they are home, I'm pretty sure the majority of students sleep most of the time. I don't want someone my own age, a career person or another mum, someone I have to behave around and feel like I need to be a proper grown-up. I know I have a nearly eleven-year-old daughter by the time we take in our first lodger and I'm heading towards my thirties, but I honestly don't feel any older than the nineteen- or twenty-year-olds who rent our room. It's quite nice having another person about the place, I like the idea of someone else in the house after Sophie's gone to bed even if they do stay up in their room. After a while they spend more time downstairs with me. I like being sociable but find it easier sharing my home with a man rather than another woman. I like the attention too, always have done.

As Sophie heads into her teens she picks up on this.

'Why do you always rent the room to men?' she asks me one day, after another prospective student looks at the attic space.

I shrug. 'I don't know. Seems less complicated than having another woman in the house.'

Sophie's thirteen and I know she's beginning to feel a little self-conscious with a bloke around. In the beginning she'd quite enjoy the occasions the lodger would play Monopoly or Trivial Pursuit with us on a Sunday afternoon. She was oblivious to the fact they were usually hungover, plus she liked the attention of playing with someone other than just me. I did wonder if she liked the idea of pretending we were a happy family, the lodger taking the role of surrogate dad.

She gives me a 'told you so' look though when our third lodger who we refer to as Stinky Pete because he smokes pot in his room, pisses in the hallway after getting confused about where the bathroom is after a big night out. While he's hung over and still stoned, I send him packing. It seems easier then to wait until September and the new intake of students before getting another lodger and I know Sophie likes having the house to ourselves again. Even though I've had a promotion, I like the added security the extra rent brings in, so come September, the room is rented out again and we get used to a new face about the house.

Owen is twenty-one and in his final year at Bristol University studying law. He moved in eighteen months after Stinky Pete left. Owen is six years older than Sophie and thirteen years younger than me, and bloody hell, is he hot. I mean, when he came to look at the room, his good looks were obvious but the way he flirts, his smile… he's a bit of a distraction to say the least.

It's been five years since we took in our first lodger and while they've remained the same age around nineteen or twenty, I'm older, no longer in my twenties but early thirties now, with a teenager too. My mum friends are now all in their forties and I still feel too young to be acting like a proper grown-up.

I slept with a couple of the lodgers when I first rented the room out, but it was nothing more than a one-night fling (or two). They loved that I didn't want a relationship and also showed no awkwardness the next morning. Sophie was still young enough to remain oblivious to what was going on but with Owen, she's older and is aware of us flirting. She rolls her eyes at me when a suggestive comment is made, something that a couple of years ago would have gone right over her head.

Sophie's eating cereal up at the breakfast bar and Owen's making himself some breakfast when I walk in to the kitchen one autumn morning. We've settled into life with Owen, school and university in full swing for a few weeks now and my routine of nine to five at work continuing as normal.

I reach into the cupboard for my muesli and watch as Owen butters a piece of toast.

I pour muesli into a bowl and glance at him. 'Toast. You only ever eat toast. Did your mum not teach you how to cook?'

'Nope. You can teach me if you want, though.'

I meet his grinning eyes and I grin back. I could definitely teach him a thing or two, but it won't be cooking, that's for sure.

Sophie dumps her empty bowl next to the sink and shakes her head as she walks out of the kitchen. I don't even have to say it out loud for her to know what I'm thinking.

I do catch Sophie looking at him in *that* way too. When she was younger she'd treat the other lodgers we had like her best friend, but she barely speaks to Owen, and when he asks her anything her cheeks flush.

I get it. Sophie's fifteen and as far as I know doesn't have a boyfriend, in fact she doesn't seem to be interested in boys at all, almost like she's clinging on to her childhood, the opposite of how I used to be. I also understand her embarrassment at being a teenager in a house with a hot twenty-one-year-old man. He's so far removed from the boys she knows at school. I catch Candy lusting after Owen when she's over for tea. Candy is less subtle than Sophie and I hear them giggling about him on their way up to Sophie's room. I approve of her Red Hot Chilli Peppers posters on her wall and playing loud music. I'm easy-going but there's never been a mention of a boy coming over. Maybe that's a blessing in disguise.

He's a decent guy though, Owen, clean and tidy unlike Stinky Pete, and being easy on the eye is hardly a negative. After a few weeks we settle into some kind of routine, with him home for breakfast, out most of the day, back for a bit late afternoon then often out again in the evening. Sophie and I have our routines too, particularly in the morning with me getting up first. Sophie's turning into a lazy teenager.

I wind a towel around my wet hair, put my dressing gown on and open the bathroom door. I almost reach my bedroom when Owen appears at the bottom of the stairs to the attic, in just his boxer shorts. I was pretty certain he had a six-pack hidden under his clothes, and the sight of his firm tattooed chest confirms my suspicions nicely.

'Morning,' he says, brushing past.

'Morning.' My eyes linger, meeting his baby-blue ones.

We've been flirting for weeks and I've been enjoying the build-up. As far as I can tell he's single. I'm pretty sure he has flings with girls at uni, but he's not brought anyone home. There have been a few times when he hasn't come back until the next day, but recently he's come home every night.

I know his eyes are still on me as I push open my bedroom door. I leave it open, my heart beating faster, knowing things between us have been leading to a moment like this. I wonder if he'll take my almighty hint. My bedroom door closes with a click and his warm hands slide across the silky material of my dressing gown then slip beneath it, caressing my skin. His lips find my neck. I watch him through the dressing table mirror, his hands moving in opposite directions over my body; he's grinning as he kisses me. I want to run my hands through his messy hair. He looks like he's just got out of bed and I want him back in mine. He meets my gaze in the mirror and tugs the tie on my dressing gown. It slips open and he pulls it off my shoulders letting it drop to the floor. Kissing my neck, he leads me to my bed.

Shit, I'm a bad mother, bad mother, bad mother, repeats over and over in my head in time to the headboard banging against my bedroom wall. Owen's twenty-one and could keep going for hours and at this rate I'm going to be late for work… But it's too bloody good to stop. I grip his firm back, the words *bad mother, bad mother, bad mother* on repeat as I tip my head back and close my eyes.

It's eight o'clock on a Thursday morning and I'm fucking the lodger instead of getting Sophie her breakfast. I mean she's fifteen and can make her own breakfast but that's not the point. I'm behaving like a teenager and I shouldn't be able to get away with this now I'm in my thirties. Even above Owen's grunts and the headboard hitting the wall, I hear Sophie's bedroom door open then slam closed. Her footsteps retreat downstairs.

I leave Owen in my bed and have another shower. My hair's still damp and tousled now, but I haven't got time to dry it, let alone make it look less like I've just got of bed. I throw on slim-fitting boot-cut black trousers and a blouse and go downstairs. Sophie's sitting at the breakfast bar munching her Weetabix. She doesn't look up when I walk in. She's put on a pot of coffee and I pour myself a large mugful giving myself time to think through what I'm going to say.

'You okay this morning?' It's the best I can come up with. What the hell else am I supposed to say? Sorry about the noise…

'I'm fine.'

'I'm going to drive instead of risk being late on the bus – I can give you a lift if you like?'

'You do realise if you didn't shag the lodger, you wouldn't be late.' She dumps her bowl next to the sink and picks up her rucksack from the worktop. 'You know how we can hear Ella and Ken arguing next door, well, imagine what I can hear from my room. I'll take the bus, thanks.' She stomps down the hallway and slams the front door shut behind her.

I perch on the breakfast bar stool, still warm from where she was sitting. I put my head in my hands. For a brief time I actually felt good about myself, but all I was doing was thinking about the hot body of a twenty-one-year-old. Sophie's not a little kid anymore. What the bloody hell am I doing?

'Everything okay?'

He makes me jump. I pull my hands from my face and meet Owen's gaze. He's leaning against the kitchen doorway wearing only low slung jeans. Lust betrays me. He's hot as hell. Thank God Sophie's already left for school, otherwise she'd have another reason to roll her eyes at me and storm off.

'We should have been a little more discreet.'

'Oh right, Sophie. She heard?'

I nod.

He comes over and slides his hands around my waist. 'Next time we will be.'

That's bullshit; the next time happens to be five minutes later up against the breakfast bar. And I'm late for work.

Norfolk, 2008

I hear the roar of an engine on the lane and peer out of the living room. A motorbike skids on to the gravel driveway. It takes me a moment to realise it's Darren. My heart drops at the thought he's having a mid-life crisis and he's only just turned thirty-five. An affair with an older woman and now a motorbike.

I head out into the front garden and reach the driveway just as he's taking his helmet off.

'You have a motorbike?'

'Yeah, don't use it often but the car's in the garage, so thought I'd take her out for a spin. You ridden a motorbike before?'

'Nope, and don't really want to.'

He places his helmet on the seat of the bike and slips his arms around my waist. 'Ah, come on. A ride along the coast on open roads. You'll love it.'

I should say no but like everything else this weekend I'm doing the opposite of what I know I should do. I could just tell him now that it's over and send him packing back to Norwich and his wife on his flashy motorbike. But I don't; I have other things on my mind like slipping into bed with him between cool clean sheets.

'We'll go out on it tomorrow, I promise.' I take his hand and pull him towards the house. 'I have other plans for today.'

Over the next few hours I question why I'm not going to see him after this weekend. But I know if we continue it'll all end in tears one way or another. His wife will find out, he'll be torn but will return to her and his children and I don't want it to get to that point for his sake and mine. It's another relationship that's going nowhere and I'd promised myself I'd be different once I moved to Norfolk. New start, new me, all that bullshit.

I adore spending time with him though. He's fun to be around and he doesn't judge me, he doesn't think anything of my age. It didn't bother me so much when I was younger, being in my early thirties with a twenty-year-old didn't seem to matter, but being in my late forties with a thirty-five-year-old, I'm noticing the difference. Plus he has responsibilities and a whole other life waiting for him back home.

With a rare weekend off from weddings, I make the most of having his company for the last time, and after an hour in bed we take a short ride up the road to Morston for a pub lunch. Afterwards we enjoy a walk along the coastal path and I almost believe that we're a proper couple, strolling hand in hand, enjoying patchy sunlight, sharing the view of sky and marshes with other couples, families and holidaymakers.

Dinner is olives, salami, bread and anything else I can find in the fridge, and then we curl up together on the sofa and watch a film. Not that we see much of it; my attention is soon taken over by him kissing me. His stubble scratches my skin, his hands undo my buttons and tug at my clothes. My hands fumble with his T-shirt and pull it off over his head. I was kidding myself earlier on our walk that we had a proper relationship. We end up in bed, him forgetting all about his wife, and me forgetting my loneliness.

I love waking up naturally in the morning with no need for an alarm, slowly coming round to the sound of birdsong, and sunlight creeping through the gaps in the blinds. I turn on my side and watch Darren's bare chest rise and fall. I'm going to miss this, but I know finishing with him is the right thing to do. I can't keep on having affairs with married men.

'Morning, gorgeous.' He shuffles closer, turning on his side so he's resting on one elbow. He looks at me, his deep brown eyes drink me in, his stubble framing his strong jawline, and I'm lost once more. I've dyed my hair so many times I'm not even sure of its natural colour, but it pools on my pillow and I know my skin is smooth and clear, and my blue eyes are one of my best features. I believe in growing old gracefully and naturally and I know I look good. I always have done, regardless of my age.

He kisses me, his lips lingering. His hands brush over the sheet, the only thing covering me. He slowly pulls the sheet down, teasing it lower to my hips. His fingers trace a circle on my stomach and every part of me tingles.

'Come on,' he whispers close to my ear. 'Let's go for that ride, how about heading inland and finding a new place to have lunch.'

'How can you tease me like that, then want to get up?'

He laughs. 'Oh, I'm up all right.'

He yanks the sheet all the way down until I'm completely naked and straddles me, his firm hot body pressing down, that desire ever growing like the thoughts that continue to invade my head. I wonder if his suggestion of not going along the coast is to minimise the risk of anyone he knows seeing us together. He manages a beautiful pub in a lovely little village along the coast but we never go there, and of course the reason is me…

It's a hot and quick morning shag and he leaves me with a kiss. He walks naked across my room and out to the bathroom. Why do I care what his reasoning is? After today what he gets up to will no longer be my problem.

It happens so fast. One second we're zipping along open roads, my arms around Darren's waist, the next moment a deer shoots in front of us. Darren's reactions are instinctive.

We swerve violently, catching something in the road: a rock or a pothole. We're going too fast. He loses control. We skid. The wheel hits a tree. Darren's thrown forward. I land hard on tarmac, pain ricocheting through my body, every part of me feeling bruised and damaged. Then blackness, and when I come to I hear sirens, see shadowy figures peering over me. Darren's lying on the ground, his still body twisted and bloody. So. Much. Blood. Paramedics are with him as I'm stretchered into the ambulance. I close my eyes and let unconsciousness take over.

'Morning, Leila.' A warm hand is placed on my arm.

They want me to wake up.

I don't want to face reality.

The warmth of the hand disappears. With consciousness the pain returns, a heavy ache on my side like every rib is bruised, a soreness everywhere.

I force my eyes open.

Daylight.

It's too bright, making my sore head thump even more. It takes a moment for my eyes to adjust. There are two figures at the end of the bed, one dressed in nurse's scrubs, the other familiar but so out of place, with red hair framing her lightly tanned and freckled face.

'Sophie?' It hurts to get the words out my throat is so dry and sore.

'Hi.'

The nurse gently lifts my head and wedges another pillow behind me so I can see better without having to strain. 'She flew in yesterday to see you.'

'Really? The accident must have been worse than I thought.' That's mean, I know, but Sophie being here shocks me. She bites her lip, and it's too late for me to take the words back. How much worse could the accident have been? I have no idea how long I've even been here and I don't think I could feel any worse if I'd been hit by a bus. The heavy feeling in my head intensifies as vague images flood my mind. The stain of blood on the grey of the road. The impact of the hard tarmac against my skin, the crack of bones…

'Where's Darren?'

'Dr Mantel is on his way to see how you're doing.' The nurse is business-like in her response, checking the monitors. Curtains surround the bed, enclosing us in a cocoon, suffocating, trapping me.

'Why are you here, Sophie?'

She flounders for something to say. The curtain opens and a tall, dark-haired doctor with rolled up shirtsleeves closes it behind him.

'Good morning, Ms Keech,' he says, picking up my chart.

'It's Leila.'

'I'm Dr Mantel.' He has an intensity about him, his eyebrows furrowed, the chart clasped to his chest. He's wearing an expensive-looking watch, must be in his mid-thirties, possibly older and has a plain gold wedding band. 'How are you feeling?'

'Sore.' I'm not good with this small talk bullshit. Sophie's standing awkwardly at the end of the bed, not knowing what to do with herself; the nurse is still here too. I feel the blood drain from my face as understanding dawns on me.

'I treated you when you and your friend were brought in after the accident.' It's Dr Mantel's turn to place his hand on my arm. It's smooth and warm against my bruised skin, but his touch makes me shudder. He leans closer, his voice low and steady. 'I'm so sorry, there was nothing we could do for Darren. He was pronounced dead on arrival.'

Deep down I knew, from the amount of blood, from his eerily still body that he had no chance. No fucking chance. Dr Mantel's face is a blur through tears. 'I was wearing his crash helmet. Stupid bastard…'

The nurse hands me a tissue and I wipe my face.

'He didn't suffer.' Dr Mantel's words give me little comfort. It was my own stupid fault for agreeing to get on the motorbike with him. Would I have done that if he hadn't offered me his helmet? Why the hell would he be so fucking reckless? To impress me? When all the time I was leading him on, enjoying one last fun and sex-filled weekend with him before telling him we were over. I scrunch the tissue in my hand.

'Does his wife know?'

Sophie gasps, even though she knows what I'm like. It shouldn't come as a surprise that I was having an affair, that once again I was the 'other woman'. Sophie's eyes drop to the floor and I catch the briefest of glances between Dr Mantel and the nurse.

Dr Mantel nods. 'We informed his family yesterday.'

'He's got two kids.' Sobs take over my body causing searing pain each time I breathe in deeply.

'I'm sorry for your loss.' Dr Mantel removes his hand from my arm, and I sense his disgust. 'I'll be back to check on you later today.'

'Can I get you anything?' the nurse asks.

'I want to be left alone.'

'Mum…'

I can't even bear to look at her. 'You too.'

I don't watch her leave but I know she does. The curtain slides closed again and I'm encased in my cocoon, my heart heavy with the many mistakes I've made when it comes to relationships, from the very start. That first stupid misguided affair with Elliot; meaningless sex with lodgers, with random men on nights out; losing Sophie through lies about her father; killing Darren because I was too selfish to tell him we were over. I deserve feeling this broken and bereft.

Bristol, 1994-97

There are six fourteen- and fifteen-year-olds in my living room. When the hell did I become old enough to have a teenage daughter? Except, when I really think about it, I am still only thirty-four. I shouldn't be so hard on myself.

It's fun having the house filled with teenagers. Although I had to grow up damn fast after getting pregnant, I took the responsibility seriously and worked my arse off to provide for both of us, I still think I have the mentality of a nineteen-year-old. I guess that might have something to do with not being married or even in a serious relationship. There have been plenty of men in my life since moving to Bristol, not least of all Owen who's managed to make himself scarce tonight, but there's been no one serious, no one I've ever felt passionately about. No one like Elliot.

Screeches and giggles come from the living room. I can't ever remember having a sleepover when I was growing up. My parents would never have tolerated having a bunch of teenagers over. Although it's noisy, I quite like the fact that this is an innocent girlie night in, and yes, I'm letting them watch a video that their parents might not approve of and have a bit of alcohol, but I'm hardly leading them astray.

I know they all love staying round here; their parents aren't so keen. Sophie's probably the most sensible of them all because I've always let her do what she wants. Instead of going off the rails and taking advantage of the situation, it seems to have had the opposite effect. To be honest, I couldn't be prouder of her. I have no worries about how she's turned out. Proud as punch. Talking about punch, I could make a big bowl of the stuff. I imagine she's rolling her eyes right now at the thought of me in the drinks cupboard seeing what I can concoct.

I take a tray of glasses, lemonade and the peach schnapps into the living room. Sophie's kneeling on the floor in front of the TV putting the video in.

'I've wanted to watch *Thelma and Louise* for like forever,' one of Sophie's friends says. 'But Mum won't let me while I'm underage.'

'You're nearly fifteen though?' I ask. 'Right?'

'Yeah, in two months.'

'Well, that's fine then.'

'Leila, you're the best.' Candy takes a glass and I pour her a generous shot of peach schnapps.

I do swap the alcohol for lemonade before anyone gets drunk and there are giggles and tears as they watch *Thelma and Louise* and lust after Brad Pitt. I watch Sophie. She has her legs tucked up on the sofa, her arm linked in Candy's as they watch the film together. I'm proud of the close relationship we have, so different to the terminally strained one with my own parents. I'm also proud of the way she's turning out; a kind-hearted, thoughtful young woman, level-headed, making this parenting of a teenager-lark a dream.

Unlike me when I was a teenager, Sophie doesn't rebel. Candy's mum, Saffie, freaks out to me about fifteen-year-old Candy drinking, smoking pot and having sex, and there's Sophie being the sensible friend looking after everyone else. I'm pretty certain she's still a virgin, and trust me, I'm flipping glad about that. I hope to God though my behaviour and warped relationships with men hasn't put her off for life. I mean, I'm relieved she's waiting but I don't want her to be forty years old and still living at home.

I shouldn't worry; things change a couple of years later.

I'm lying in bed, it's seven in the morning on a Saturday and Sophie's not come home yet. That doesn't bother me, she's seventeen after all and quite capable of looking after herself, but I do wonder who he is. I know she's going to say she stayed the night at Candy's, but I saw the outfit she went out in. I also know what I'd have got up to dressed like that. She dressed to impress a bloke, that's for sure.

I sit up in bed, unable to get back to sleep, wanting Sophie safely home. I'm well aware of what I'm like on a night out, and I suddenly feel sick at the thought of what Sophie's been getting up to. I mean, part of me thinks 'about bloody time', but worry gnaws the pit of my stomach. Fed up of sitting waiting, doing nothing, I throw the covers off and get out of bed.

I go downstairs and into the kitchen. The tiled floor is cold against the soles of my feet. I boil the kettle and make a cup of coffee and sit at the bottom of the stairs, my hands clasped around the steaming mug. A tiny bit of me senses what my mum must have gone through not knowing where I was half the time, staying out all night, smoking, drinking, hanging around with unsavoury boyfriends – in my parents' opinion at least. Once Sophie's home safely I know I'll be happy that she's finally behaving like a teenager, but until then I'm going to worry like my own mother did.

I've finished my coffee by the time I hear the fumbling of a key in the lock. Sophie opens the front door and closes it carefully behind her.

'You dirty little stop out.'

'Bloody hell, Mum.' Sophie clutches her hand to her chest. 'You made me jump. Why are you sitting there?'

'I've been waiting for you.'

'I said I'd be late.'

'This isn't exactly late, Soph, it's the morning after the

109

night before.' I know I shouldn't, but I'm enjoying teasing her. This has been me so many times, the walk of shame home from the night before or even down the stairs from the lodger's bedroom. I remember that feeling well, sixteen years old coming home way past my curfew, having lost my virginity to Sid in his bedroom while his parents were downstairs. They didn't give a shit what their son got up to, but my parents grounded me for being late, thinking I was at my friend Karen's house. If only they'd known the truth.

Sophie's make-up has faded, the lipstick gone – probably kissed away – her hair wavier than normal and she's still in the short black skirt, sparkly heels and a low-cut silver top that she went out in. Her cheeks are flushed and she looks bloody gorgeous. 'Was it good?'

She falters and glares at me. 'Mum!' She brushes past me, and I get a waft of stale smoke as she goes up the stairs.

'I'm sorry,' I say. 'That was out of order.'

She doesn't look back. 'It always is.'

I could have made a career on saying the wrong thing. Instead I've managed to forge a career on being a fucking good people person. My confidence shines through – I know I can come across as bolshie and in your face in certain situations, but at work it's been a benefit, determination and my personality helping me to climb the ladder to events manager. Organising, networking and getting things done are what I do. What you see is what you get with me and I'm straight talking – sometimes it gets me into trouble, but most people seem to like to know where they stand with me both personally and professionally.

I've grafted to get where I am, and it's not been easy juggling Sophie, school and work, with money worries always on my mind. Since leaving home, I've never had someone to support me, no parents, no husband, not even a long-term boyfriend I could share the stresses and strains of everyday life with. It's been through choice, but it's been harder over the years watching friends meet the love of their life, get married and have kids, while I'm single with a daughter nearly old enough to leave home and go to university.

Unlike me, Sophie does go to university and I couldn't be prouder. She's a fantastic artist. She likes drawing people or landscapes but when she's drawn buildings I can't help but think that without knowing who her father is, she's got his creativity and architect's eye for detail. My life in Bristol is settled with our house and friends, a good job, great colleagues, plenty of opportunities to go on dates either through people at work or via friends I've met on nights out. Sophie leaving for university unsettles me, the realisation that eighteen bloody years has flown by since I was heading to Bristol pregnant and alone. Now I've made a real life and success for myself, yet I feel bereft when I kiss her goodbye on the doorstep of her student house in Falmouth, leaving her with three housemates, two boys and a girl she doesn't yet know. She waves me off with a smile, the pull of a new life and challenge, freshers' week, booze, new friends, boys, sex and everything else that goes hand in hand with uni life, a bigger draw than living back home with me. My eyes are blurry with tears by the time I make it back to my car and begin the three-hour plus drive home to Bristol.

'Your Mum's a MILF.'

Sophie informs me that's what one of her male housemates has described me as when I drive back to Falmouth to pick her up at the end of the first semester.

'Don't you dare sleep with him,' she warns.

I don't. He's eighteen, and gone are the days when it was just about okay to sleep with someone that age. I'm thirty-seven and men Sophie's age are off-limits. I do shag Drew, a mature student, after a night out when I visit Sophie in her second year. When I say mature, he's actually only twenty-six but that's a decent age compared to a fresher.

Norfolk, 2008

I've had friends to stay, but no one has ever lived with me in Salt Cottage. It's strange to think that Sophie's been staying here while I've been in hospital. Despite longing to be home and escape the noise and nosiness of the other women on the ward, I don't feel ready to share my home with Sophie. I'm sure she has the same trepidation, and I'm glad of Robert bringing me home to ease the tension.

He helps me out of the car and it feels so good to breathe in the fresh air. I feel fragile, awkward on my crutches. My tunic top's too big, my long skirt's sticking against the cast on my leg. Robert guides me through the front door and helps me settle on the sofa. Tiredness washes over me. I hear voices in the kitchen, Robert and Sophie talking, before I drift off.

Sophie cooks dinner and we eat it outside on the patio. The early September evening is a perfect antidote to the last couple of weeks. Horses graze in the field, a slight breeze rustles the leaves, and the cottage gleams in the evening sunshine. I pick at the salmon and new potatoes. Sophie's really trying, I'll give her that. I wonder if she wanted to come back from Greece and look after me or if she felt it was her duty.

'Robert seems to really care about you,' she says, filling the silence.

I'm perfectly happy not talking, just sitting, eating and

watching birds flit between trees, and the horses rub their necks against one another.

I sigh. 'He's a good friend.'

'I haven't met his wife yet.'

'His wife?' I stop cutting a potato. 'She's dead.'

'I didn't realise. He wears a wedding band, so I thought…'

'She died when Ben and Vicky were teenagers.' I skewer a potato on to my fork. 'Why do you ask? Did you say something to him?'

'No, no, nothing like that. I was curious. It's me assuming too much.'

'He always wears his ring but rarely talks about her. It's not a good subject to bring up.'

'I won't.'

'Did you think I was having an affair with him as well?'

'You've taken me completely the wrong way.'

'Really?' I let my knife and fork clatter on to my plate, no longer hungry. 'But you wouldn't have been surprised if we were?'

'Truthfully, no.'

This is the opinion my daughter has of me, and yet I know I've given her good reason to think that way over the years. Darren wasn't my first affair and I have no idea if he'll be the last. Not that I've ever cheated on anyone, it's just the men I've tended to go for have been in relationships or are too young and unsuitable. Robert's a friend and a damn good one at that. Maybe he's the type of bloke I should have been going for, but his friendship means too much to mess that up.

Sophie clears away and I stay sitting outside, watching the sun go down until it disappears on the horizon, spreading red, orange and gold across the sky. I'm shivering by the time I make my way into the kitchen, feeling slow and heavy on my crutches, tiredness and aches creeping over my body.

Sophie helps me up the stairs to bed. I hate this feeling of being dependent on someone, particularly Sophie after everything that's happened between us over the past few years. Her touch is oddly comforting and yet my reaction when we reach the landing at the top of the stairs is to pull away. I have too much anger simmering inside to let her in right now. I have no idea how we can even begin to make amends but I know now is not the time, not when I'm feeling like this.

'Do you need help with anything else?' she asks.

There's a distance between us and it's not just physical; the emotional one will be harder to heal. A moth flits around the naked bulb above us, reminding me I need to get a new shade.

Anger stirs inside me, making my chest hurt. 'I don't give a shit about cleaning my teeth or getting undressed. I just want to sleep, in my own bed.'

I push open my bedroom door.

'I'll be next door if you need me.'

'I know where my spare room is, Sophie.' I close the door and lean against it, breathing deeply. There's a moment of silence and then Sophie's footsteps retreat to her room.

My face is hot, tears ready to spill. I need to sleep, without being disturbed by the snores of the elderly women on the ward. The duvet is crumpled and as I pull it back an image flashes through my mind of the last time I was in this room, in bed with Darren, selfishly enjoying a goodbye shag. Not that he knew that – he'd been clueless that I was going to break up with him. And then the accident happened…

His glass of water is still on the bedside table. A lump forms in my throat. I open the wardrobe knowing I'm going to see his shirt hanging on the back of the door, separate from my clothes, like our relationship – together but not quite together. My heart thumps at the memory of him lying in bed the morning before he died, the sheet pulled up to just below his belly button. He was lying on his side, looking at me as he circled his fingers over my bare stomach. I pick up his half-finished glass of water and throw it against the wall. It makes a satisfying thump as glass explodes.

Sophie's door opens and she calls out, 'Mum?'

I slump down on the end of the bed, my broken leg sticking out awkwardly. I bury my head in my hands and sob.

'Mum, can I come in?' she asks from the landing.

'Leave me alone.'

'Are you hurt?'

'Of course I'm fucking hurt!'

The door opens and there's silence. I lift my head from my hands and watch Sophie as she looks around the room, her eyes resting on the water trickling down the wall next to my dressing table.

'It's like he's going to fucking walk in any minute.' I wipe my eyes with the back of my hand.

'I didn't want to touch anything in here,' Sophie says quietly.

'I thought I was okay about him. I coped too bloody well. But coming back to this.' I throw my hands in the air.

'I'll clear up.'

'Leave it. Just leave it, Sophie. It's out of my system now.'

'Do you want me to help you?' She motions towards the bed.

I shake my head. I don't want to do anything apart from sleep and forget.

Sophie nods and backs out of the door.

'Thank you,' I say before she closes it.

It's done, there's no changing what's happened. I never got round to breaking up with Darren. Maybe that was for the best. I may not want to get married or even settle down but I need to stop messing around with men who should know better. Yes, I might be using them as much as they're using me, but his affair didn't just end his life. It ruined the lives of his wife and children.

I drag myself into bed and close my eyes, but all I can think about is Darren between the sheets, the fading scent of his aftershave on my pillows. I will the thoughts swirling round and round my head to stop and give me a bit of peace.

We muddle along for the next couple of days, both of us adjusting to living together again. It's been a long time since we shared breakfast or sat and watched a film together. I've got so used to my own company that having another person in the house is jarring, particularly another woman. I clear away everything in my room that belonged to Darren and wash the bedding, erasing his presence from my life. Robert comes over and it's good to talk to him. I know Darren's death is far removed from the loss he suffered losing his beloved wife, but he understands my grief and has never judged my decision to be in a relationship with a married man.

I throw myself into work, relieved that I have something positive to concentrate on, finishing organising everything for a wedding happening this Saturday. At least being busy allows Sophie and me the chance to communicate even if it is about my work and organising things around the house. I think she feels the need to keep busy too. It all comes to a head when the flowers arrive for the wedding. Working together surrounded by the heady scent of roses gives us time to talk. Talking might not be the right word, a verbal thrashing is more appropriate, me suggesting she should be married by now and her turning my throw-away comment around to question why I lied to her for so many years about her father.

'When you opened his letter that night, why did you destroy it?' Sophie asks.

I shake my head. 'I was angry with him. It was unexpected. I hadn't seen him since I left Sheffield, pregnant with you. I'd kept my promise and stayed out of his life and then he did something like that.' I snip the pink ribbon I'm holding. 'I wasn't going to write back. What was I going to say? Your daughter, the one you've never met, is doing fine. Finished university. Just graduated. I'm proud of her. Hope you are too. Waste of bloody trees.'

'You could have let me read it.'

'It was an accident I even told you that night. You know I was drunk. His unexpected letter shocked me into saying something.'

'Otherwise I'd never have found out?' Sophie looks like she's fighting back tears.

'By telling you that I didn't know who your father was made me almost believe it myself. Except he's always played on my mind. You remind me of him so much. The older you got, the more you looked like him.' I place the last couple of miniature roses into the circular display. 'He said in his letter how proud he was of you. He's never even met you. He's an architect. Well respected. Intelligent, creative, focused, impulsive. You're alike, I can't deny that. You're more like him than you are me.' I put the rose I'm holding on the table and look at Sophie, my eyes searching her face, for what I don't know. Forgiveness? I'm not sure I can expect that from her. 'When you walked out that night, I was devastated. I felt I'd failed you.'

Sophie moves next to me and puts her arms around my shoulders. I shiver but welcome her touch, the comfort of my daughter back with me at long last.

'Until you have a child of your own, there's no way you can understand the amount of responsibility, time and love they take. They're your life, your whole fucking world.'

Our talk clears the air. We needed to thrash things out, to allow pent-up feelings into the open and to acknowledge the hurt I've caused and the things we've both said through anger to each other over the years. I'm exhausted – a combination of doing too much while still recovering from my injuries and the impact of bringing up the past. I retreat to my room to lie down.

It's late afternoon by the time I wake up, my head foggy from sleep. I throw open my bedroom window to let in some fresh air. It's another perfect September day, fluffy white clouds in an otherwise blue sky, yet there's a coolness that hints at autumn.

I make my way slowly and carefully downstairs. My mouth waters at the smell of roast chicken and I can hear Sophie pottering about in the kitchen. I take a deep breath and push open the kitchen door. Sophie's leaning against the work surface, a cup of tea clasped in her hand, pots of thyme, dill, basil and rosemary behind her on the windowsill. The colour scheme's more muted than it was at Hazel Road. I've replaced navy walls with cream, but injected colour into the space with turquoise kitchen units. It feels more like home than Hazel Road ever did. My muddy walking boots prop open the back door. On the outside step a fork and trowel lean against a terracotta pot crowded with flowers.

'It smells good.'

Sophie's smile lights up her face.

'I thought we deserved some comfort food,' she says. 'I'm doing Greek-style chicken with lemon roast potatoes.'

'Sounds delicious.' Leaning on my crutches I go over to the open door and relish the fresh breeze filtering through. 'You know, I can't think of a more perfect place to be than here. I knew I wanted this house the moment I saw that view. I mean I loved our house in Hazel Road, it holds a special place in my heart, but I never thought I'd find somewhere I loved this much. Do you know what I mean?'

'I know exactly what you mean.'

'Is that how it is for you in Greece?'

'Alekos said I'd tire of watching the sun setting behind Olympus. I don't know how anyone can; the light and colours are different every day.'

'That's the artist in you.' I turn back and Sophie hands me a mug of tea. 'You were always nagging about us moving to the country when you were younger. Remember? Candy would always go abroad with her family every year. Where did they use to go?'

'Ibiza.'

'While you were quite happy going camping.'

'I loved our camping holidays.'

'So did I. Every time I eat fish and chips it reminds me of being huddled in the doorway of our tent shovelling greasy chips in our mouths while watching fat drops of rain plop on to the grass.'

'Why did we stop going?'

I sip the tea and look at her. 'You grew up.'

Sophie grew up and somehow I never did. I was forever chasing something I couldn't hold on to: my youth, or inappropriate men. History repeated itself so many times, and yet there's never been anyone I love as much as Elliot.

Bristol, 2001

The bus stop is at the end of our road, which is just as well because there's no flipping way I can walk far in heels after a few too many White Russians or whatever the hell kind of cocktails I drank too many of tonight. I get off the bus and ignore the wolf-whistle from the group of blokes outside the pub on the other side of the road. I consider giving them the finger, but a reaction is what they want, so I clatter up the road away from them instead, my feet sore in my heels. I pass our Indian takeaway and Andy's Newsagents on the corner of our road. Cars are parked bumper to bumper, packed as closely together as the Victorian terraced houses. The park at the top of our road is shadowed by darkness but the leafy trees glow eerily in the yellow street lights.

Our garden gate squeaks open and I close it behind me. I fumble in my bag for my keys and breathe in the sweet scent of honeysuckle climbing up the wall next to our front door. The blinds are open. The flashing light from the TV punctuates the darkness of the front garden, so I know Sophie's home already. I slot the key into the lock and stumble inside, closing the door with a bang.

'Sophie?' I peer around the living room door. She doesn't turn. She's slumped on the beanbag on the floor, a Baileys with ice clutched in her hand. She's watching Baz Luhrmann's *Romeo + Juliet*. Claire Danes and Leonardo DiCaprio are gazing at each other through a fish tank. I frown. 'You're home early.'

She glances at me. 'Actually, I thought I was late.' She turns back to the TV and flicks channels. Eddie Izzard is on. 'Where have you been?'

'I completely forgot I'd said yes to drinks with Stu from work.'

'You couldn't cancel?'

'I've turned him down too many times before.'

'I was out with friends I wanted to be with and managed to get home early.'

I kick off my heels, chuck my red-sequinned handbag on the armchair, squat next to her and kiss her forehead. 'Come on, don't be cross. I thought I was going to be the one waiting for you.' I take her hand and pull her off the beanbag. 'I hope you haven't eaten?'

'I had one slice of pizza.'

'Stu wanted to go to some fancy French restaurant but I plied him with cocktails instead. Said I was eating sushi with you when I got home.' I lead her along the hallway and flick on the kitchen light. 'He told me sushi was an aphrodisiac; I told him he wasn't getting any.'

'Getting any what?' Sophie leans against the work surface.

'Sushi of course.' I throw her a box of matches. 'Bloody gorgeous night out. Light the lanterns would you.'

Sophie heads outside and I open the window by the sink and pass her a handful of tea lights. I watch her dot them along the middle of the picnic table. I open the fridge, take out the plate of sushi I'd made earlier and pad outside in my bare feet.

It's a still night and clear, with only the glow from the street lights to taint the darkness. It's not peaceful though, even this late, with cars driving along neighbouring roads and the splash of frogs in the pond. I can hear the TV from next door filtering out through the open windows.

Sophie lights the tall lantern wedged in the flower bed and

I place the sushi on the picnic table.

'Are you going to see him again?' Sophie blows out the match and smoke curls into the night.

'Who, Stu? I work with him.'

'But romantically?'

'No. He's good looking and a decent-enough bloke, but so bloody boring.'

'He didn't invite you back to his?'

'Yes, but I told him I was going home to celebrate my daughter getting a First.'

'Was he shocked you've got a twenty-one-year-old daughter?'

I shrug. 'I couldn't give a fuck what he thinks. Champagne!' I throw my arms around her shoulders and we head for the door, bumping the sides as we try to get through it together. We giggle and I let her go ahead of me. I've missed spending time with her while she's been away at uni. I'm going to make the most of her being home again; it's like old times.

I take one of the bottles of champagne from the fridge and Sophie grabs two tall glasses from the cupboard. We retreat outside into the warm July night.

We sit either side of the picnic table and I aim the bottle towards the garden. The cork punches the air like a rocket and foam spills from the neck.

'How many cocktails did you have?' Sophie asks.

I pour bubbling champagne into our glasses and lick the foam off my fingers.

'Enough to make me merry.' I raise my glass and smile at her. 'Well done, you deserve it.' I tap my glass against hers.

'Thank you.'

I dip a piece of sushi into the bowl of soya sauce and pop it into my mouth. 'Bloody hell, that's hot,' I say through a mouthful of cool salmon and burning wasabi.

'You made them.'

I wash it down with a gulp of champagne but the bubbles

make my mouth burn even more. Sophie laughs and takes a lady-like bite of her sushi.

'Are you going to miss being a student?' I ask.

'I'm going to miss living by the sea.'

'You're okay about moving back in with me?'

'Mum, my life was like a student's even before I went to uni. Living with you is like having a housemate.'

'Thank you, I guess!'

She tops our glasses up. 'How's work? Do you still hate it?'

'Hate is a little strong. I'm bored. The people are boring.'

'You said Stu's boring.'

'Times him by ten and you've got the idea. I want to get my teeth into something. Feel passionate about work, like you are with art.'

'Then go for it.'

I knock back my champagne. 'It's not that easy. I've worked hard to get where I am, it's a good job, more than pays the mortgage. It just doesn't challenge me any longer.'

Sophie knows how frustrated I am at work and moves the conversation away from my job. With the sound of frogs splashing, the drone of the TV from next door, and the flickering candlelight, we talk about everything else: parties, university, her friends, my friends, holidays, sex... I guess we've always had an open relationship where we can talk to each other about anything. Sophie always used to joke I'd talk about sex the way other people discuss last night's *EastEnders*.

Everything's swimming by the time I stagger inside, knocking against the door frame, to get the bowl of strawberries from the fridge.

'You're a disgrace!' Sophie calls after me.

I wave my hand, tuck the squirty cream under my arm, grab the post from off the work surface and weave my way back outside.

'Is your head spinning?' I ask.

'No. Is yours?'

'A little.' I giggle and sit back down with a thump.

I shake the cream, squirt a pyramid on to a plate and dip a strawberry in. We eat in silence for a moment, the frogs' splashing the only sound now Ken and Ella have turned off their TV.

'You should slow down on the champers,' Sophie says.

I give her a look and take another sip. I thumb through the post. 'Bills, bills, boring, boring…' I stop at one with our address handwritten on it and tear it open. I unfold the letter and scan over it. My heart stops at the name at the bottom.

'Who's it from?' Sophie pops a strawberry in her mouth.

'Elliot.'

'Who?'

'Your father.' The words are out before I can take them back.

Sophie holds my gaze, a frown forming on her pretty face. She shakes her head. 'I don't understand. You know his name? I thought you had no idea who he was.'

I grip the letter tighter, scrunching the edges. My eyelids feel heavy; my head is spinning. I'm not sure what to feel or how to react to Sophie or to the words on the page in front of me. 'The bastard made me promise… He didn't want you to know about him. I couldn't tell.' I reach across the table and place my hand on her arm.

'You actually knew him? You told me he was a one-night stand, that you didn't even know his name.'

She's looking at me like I'm the devil. Her eyebrows and lips pinched together.

I crumple the letter into my fist. 'It's no big deal.'

She yanks her arm out from under my hand. 'I hope to God that's the alcohol talking.'

'He didn't want me to tell you.' My voice is rising with panic at my mistake for saying his name out loud, releasing a secret I've kept for twenty-one years. 'He was afraid…'

'Of what? Me?' Sophie stands and paces away from the table. She turns back, her hands on her hips. 'Who was he?

Why the hell didn't you tell me?'

'I promised I wouldn't. It was complicated... It wasn't just him who wanted it kept quiet. My parents...'

'Grandma and Grandad have known all this time too?'

Tears slide down my face and I shrug, not knowing what else to say.

'So you decided to lie to me about it all this time.'

'It was easier for you not to know.'

'Then why the fuck tell me about it now?'

'I didn't mean to. I cut myself off from him, cut myself off from my parents, and haven't seen him in twenty-one years and now this.' I unfold my hand to reveal the crumpled paper. Reaching across the table I hold it over one of the candles and watch as the flame licks at the edge and catches hold, devouring it. I drop it on to a paving slab when the flames get too close to my fingers. 'I'm not very good at hiding my emotions, Sophie. It took me by surprise.'

'But it's no big deal, huh?'

'Soph, calm down...'

'You tell me my father's name and you don't think I'd have something to say about it?'

'You know me, never one to fucking censor my words.'

'So, he wasn't a one-night stand?'

I shake my head.

'Who is he then? Why the hell couldn't you tell me?'

I look away and pinch the stem of my champagne glass. 'He was married and we were lovers.'

'For how long?'

'Ten months. I was eighteen.'

'How old was he?'

'Thirty-seven.'

Sophie whistles, raising her eyebrows and shaking her head. 'Does he have kids?'

After building a lie around the mistake I made for so long, it scares me to tell her the truth. 'Three children.'

'So I have half brothers or sisters somewhere. A whole

other family. How could you keep this from me?'

I release my grip on the glass. 'He chose his family over us.'

'No, he chose them over you. He doesn't even know me.'

I can't hold back tears any longer. It kills me the way Sophie's looking at me, her beautiful face twisted with anger, all directed at me. 'It hurt, it still does, but I respected his wishes. Do you know how hard it's been...?'

'Don't you think I deserve some respect too?' Sophie's voice is tight, like she's trying hard to control her emotions. 'You lied to me.'

I wipe away my tears with the back of my hand.

'Do they know about me?'

I look up at her and sniff. 'His kids? I doubt it.'

'Did they know about you?'

'His wife never knew. He ended it and I promised I'd never contact him. I hope he's been looking over his shoulder ever since. I wasn't expecting to hear from him...' I scuff my bare foot against what remains of the burnt letter. I stand and go over to Sophie, reaching for her.

She pulls away from me. 'Your timing sucks.' She storms across the patio and disappears inside.

I sit down at the picnic table and watch a moth flit around one of the smoking candles. I put my head in my hands and sob.

Norfolk, 2008

I'm glad of Sophie's help. When I said yes to organising a big wedding for a wealthy family I hadn't envisaged being injured and wiped out for a few weeks. Pamela, the mother-of-the-bride, has become a good friend and despite me stressing about how the hell I can deliver a perfect wedding, she's cut me some slack, kept me on and supported me in seeing through the wedding plan.

With Sophie helping me with the flowers we manage to pull it off. It's not really hard to considering the reception's taking place at their home, Kingfisher Hall. Pamela and her husband are loaded, and yet are the nicest people. Sophie and I are invited back in the evening to join in the celebrations. After living in loose-fitting clothes since being injured, it's nice to dress up in a pale-pink fitted skirt and a cream top. Glancing in the mirror I look more like me, apart from the bloody cast on my leg.

The jazz band are in full swing by the time we get there. Guests are dancing, spilling on to the grass from the open marquee. The trees around the edges of the lawn are lit with pink lights, sending a confetti-tinted glow into the clear night sky. Everything's come together perfectly, the pink theme matching the bride Sylvie's personality to perfection, with popcorn and candyfloss stands, and an abundance of pink champagne.

Pamela greets me in a hot pink dress and matching hat, and kisses me on both cheeks.

'Thank you,' she says, handing me a champagne glass filled with pink fizz. 'You've made Sylvie's dreams come true.'

I sip the champagne and watch the scene play out in front of me; tipsy guests dancing to the jazzy beat. Sylvie is standing with Sophie, giggling and chatting non-stop. She's young, and I hope she's making the right choice getting married at her age. All the money in the world doesn't guarantee happiness, but she looks happy enough tonight.

Pamela leaves me with another kiss on the cheek as she's whisked away by her husband to talk to other guests. Leaning on my crutches, I make my way across the spongy grass to an empty bench beneath one of the willow trees. The best man is snogging a pretty brunette by the river. I sigh. Young love. It's quite a spectacle though, my creation, the perfect pink wedding. I can hear Pamela laughing even above a sultry saxophone.

Sophie leaves the throng of people drinking and chatting outside the marquee and walks over. She sits next to me on the bench.

'Why do people throw ridiculous amounts of money into a wedding when it's clear it's all going to go wrong.' She gazes across the lawn to the party.

'You think so?'

'Yeah, she's a trophy girl for him. He's good-looking but sounds a bit of a twat.'

'Maybe it will last then.'

'I swear that rock on her finger is just a status symbol. She cares more about the honeymoon than she does about him.'

I move to the edge of the bench and point at the plaque in the middle, it reads: *For Pamela & Raymond. On your 25th Wedding Anniversary.* 'Some things do last.'

Sophie waves her hands towards the marquee. 'All these people, all this attention, the big dress, the money spent on this wedding, I couldn't think of anything worse.'

'Good, I'm glad.'

She frowns at me. 'You planned all this.'

'It doesn't mean I have to like it, I'm just good at my job. I organised one wedding reception on a boat. Now that was classy. They only invited twenty guests and after the actual service they all piled on to the, oh bugger, the name escapes me...' I gaze up into the pink-lit leaves of the willow. 'The Marauder, that was it. They went seal spotting, then moored up at Wells for a Lebanese buffet and drinks late into the night. It was low-key. The bride and groom would have been happy with bangers and mash as long as it meant being together.'

'I like bangers and mash.'

'So do I.'

I lie in bed and listen to the birds outside and Sophie pattering about the house getting ready to go out with Ben. I don't know how I feel about their blossoming friendship. Despite my brief warning to her last night when we got back from the wedding reception and found a letter from Ben inviting her out, I don't want to say anything else and risk straining our relationship just when we seem to have got it back on track. I like Ben but since his divorce I sense he's floundering and thinking more about his own needs than his children's. He risks bringing a wedge between himself and his ex that will distance himself from Fraser and Bella and break Robert's heart.

I hear Ben's car crunch into the drive. I wait until Sophie closes the front door, then I get up.

Robert turns up an hour later, when I'm hobbling about the kitchen in my dressing gown. I make us coffee and we go and sit on the sofa in the living room.

'How did the wedding go?' he asks.

I'm in desperate need of caffeine to combat the late night and the glass of champagne. 'I'm shattered, but it was a success. It was good to have some time with Sophie, doing something together. It felt like we actually made peace with each other. Less anger simmering off her when she's talking to me at least.'

'Ben went out early, said he was taking Sophie somewhere.'

'Yeah, about that…' I'm not sure how to broach the subject with him.

'You think there's something between them?' Robert frowns. 'More than friendship?'

'I'm just worried about Sophie making the wrong choice, like I've always done with men.' I place my hand on Robert's arm. 'Not that I mean Ben's a wrong choice exactly, it's just Sophie's with Alekos and from the sounds of it life's been difficult in Greece. Not all she thought it was going to be like. What I'm trying to say is she's confused, Ben's split with Mandy. It's potentially a recipe for disaster.'

'Or they could be good for each other – someone their own age to talk to, someone removed from the situation.' He nudges my shoulder with his. 'Not a parent.'

'You're probably right.'

I hope he's right. But they're out for a long time. Robert only stays for half hour or so, then heads to the pub to open for lunch. I get on with some work in my study, make a few phone calls, grab a sandwich, do some more work and then decide to make flapjacks. It's late afternoon and I'm sitting on the patio when I hear Sophie come in and go up to the bathroom.

I drum my fingers on the patio table, impatient for her to come down and to find out what they got up to.

'Hi,' she calls as she walks across the grass. Her greeting is too keen to sound normal.

I wave. She's got her hair twisted into a ponytail, she's fresh-faced but looks guilty.

'You look relaxed,' she says as she joins me.

I wiggle my drink. 'Fancy a G&T?'

She shakes her head and sits down. 'You made flapjacks.'

'I fancied getting off my arse. And I wanted something sweet to eat.' I glance at her over my sunglasses. 'Where've you been?'

'To see the seals and then we walked to Stiffkey.' Her cheeks flush.

I'm pretty certain she's fucked him. I take a sip of my G&T and choose my words carefully. 'Why are you getting involved with him?'

'I'm not involved. We've been to the beach and gone for a walk. What's the big deal?'

'What would Alekos say?'

'You're a right one to talk.'

Maybe she's right, who the hell am I to be giving her relationship advice? 'I just don't think you want to get attached to him and his problems.'

'Give him a break, his marriage has broken up.'

'Did he tell you why?'

'It's none of my business. Or yours.'

'Ben makes it everyone else's business. He's not the victim he makes out to be.' I rattle the ice in my drink, thinking I really should have a coffee to soak up the alcohol.

'Does Robert know you don't like his son?' Sophie asks.

'I never said I don't like him. Robert's fully aware of my feelings about Ben. He feels the same. Don't look at me like that. I speak my mind, Sophie. Always have, always will. I stuck up for Ben when he first moved here. We spent a lot of time talking and I defended him when Robert was being too harsh.'

'What changed then?'

'Him putting himself before his kids.'

'I turned out okay, didn't I?'

Once again I'm thrown by how easily Sophie's anger turns on me. We may have begun to mend our relationship but there's still a long way to go. Her unconventional childhood and my loose morals will always be ammunition for her. I'm worried about her following in my footsteps and throwing her life with Alekos away over a man who can barely function. Having sex and a bit of fun may be one thing but I hope to God she's not getting emotionally attached to him.

A few days later when Sophie goes out for a meal with Ben I just about manage to keep my mouth shut. It's more than complicated because Alekos is flying over later in the week for Sophie's birthday. I tell myself it's her life and not to stick my nose in. She's an adult, old enough to know her own mind. She needs to learn from her own mistakes, just like I've done. Plus, I know I'll get the gossip from Robert anyway.

'So, what happened?' I ask him two days later at the pub.

'I don't think anything happened. Mandy turning up early with the kids scuppered any potential for romance but I think that might be for the best. Sophie embraced the kids being there; I think Ben still wanted to go somewhere just the two of them.'

'Typical bloke.'

Robert shrugs. 'Yeah. It's difficult; Ben's heartbroken, Sophie's lovely and there's obviously a connection between the two of them but it's complicated…'

'Just a bit. You know Sophie's going to pick up Alekos from Heathrow tomorrow.'

'Yeah I know. I'm sure she knows her own mind though.' He places a warm hand on my arm. 'And I promise you, apart from having a meal and chatting, nothing else happened between them yesterday.'

I'm not convinced, but I don't tell him. I don't want to fuel the idea that there really is something going on between Sophie and Ben, but she's been quiet, not quite herself. I mean, I know we're getting used to being in each other's company again, but I sense something's changed.

Although Robert sort of puts my mind at rest in the pub, when I wave Sophie goodbye the next day, I sense an unease about her, like there's a heaviness weighing on her mind. Perhaps it's the thought of a long drive to Heathrow on her own.

I'm out in the garden when the phone rings five hours later and I curse as I hobble back inside to answer it.

'He arrived safely?' I ask.

'Yes. And his mum. Despina turned up too.'

'Oh.'

'I'll sort everything out when we get back. Despina can have my room. Me and Alekos can sleep downstairs.'

'There's a camp bed in the attic.'

'Great. Perfect.'

'You sound pissed off.'

'I am.'

'I hope she likes roast beef and Yorkshires.'

'I'm so sorry. If I'd known she was coming… This is the last thing you need.'

'I should have learnt some Greek.'

'We'll be home before eight.'

'Drive carefully.'

I put the phone down. I'm going to finally meet Alekos. And his mother. But who the hell thinks it's okay to turn up in another country uninvited?

Bristol, 2004

I find it weird, Sophie ringing the doorbell instead of simply waltzing on in like she used to. She's still got the house key but chooses not to use it ever since she moved out after *that* argument. It's my own bloody fault, I know, but I miss her and moving countries to avoid seeing me is taking things to the extreme.

I open the door on a hot July day, heat steaming off the tarmac. She's standing with one box by her feet and balancing another box on the wall.

'Bloody hell, how much stuff do you have?'

'It's only two boxes. You said it was okay to store it here. I can take it to Candy's if you like.' She turns to go.

'No, of course, it's fine. Come in.' I pick up the box on the path and walk through the hallway to the kitchen, my flip-flops slapping the polished floorboards as I go. I dump it on the floor. The front door slams shut and Sophie joins me in the kitchen. The back door's open letting in what little fresh air there is and I lean across the sink and yank the window open too.

I turn back to Sophie. 'Why are you really going to Greece? Is it because you're pregnant?'

'Really? That's the reason you think I'm going to live with him, because I'm pregnant?'

'Are you?'

'No.'

I take an open bottle of white wine from the fridge and pour myself a large glass. I imagine Sophie rolling her eyes behind me. 'You only met him six weeks ago and have only actually spent one week together. What do you expect me to think?'

'Is it too alien a thing for you to comprehend that the reason I'm moving to Greece is because I want to be with him? I love him.'

I sip my wine. 'Love is a strong word.'

'It's also the right one. Just because you don't believe in love at first sight doesn't mean I don't.'

'Oh, I believe in love at first sight all right, it's what happens after the initial honeymoon period that I'm wary of.'

'I don't need your negativity.' She pushes down the tape on the box nearest her.

I scuff the box next to me with my foot. 'I thought I'd got rid of all this when you moved out.'

'Well, I can't take it with me.' She takes a pen from her bag. 'Have you got some paper.'

I point to a used envelope wedged between the coffee and sugar jars on the black marbled worktop.

'This is the address in Greece.'

I take the envelope from her. 'It doesn't exactly roll off your tongue.' I set my wine down and pin the address to the noticeboard. 'I'm going to make a stir-fry. Do you want some?'

She shakes her head.

'The plane food will taste of plastic.'

She knows I'm right.

'Maybe a bit then.'

I start peeling an onion and watch Sophie out of the corner of my eye take the chicken fillets and vegetables from the fridge. Her hair is deep red and falls in waves against her shoulders. A hot summer and her week with Candy in Greece has accentuated the freckles on her face. She looks beautiful.

'Have you learnt any Greek yet?' I ask.

She slams the fridge door closed with her foot. 'A little.'

She dumps the food on the worktop next to me and reaches for a chopping board.

For a moment it feels like old times, us standing in companionable silence, preparing food together. But there's tension in her shoulders as she slices the chicken, and I know things between us will never be the same again. I don't know how to even begin to repair our relationship, and with her escaping to Greece, well it seems an impossible task.

'So,' I finally say, 'how are you going to get a job out there?'

'Same way as here, apply.'

'Don't be smart. You know what I mean.'

'The best place to learn Greek is in Greece. I want to start drawing again... I can teach English if I need to. I was thinking of setting up an artists' retreat.'

'You've high hopes.' I know I've said the wrong thing the moment it's out of my mouth. Why the hell don't I think before I speak?

Sophie stops slicing the chicken. 'What's wrong with that? I don't want to end up regretting my life.'

My cheeks clench. 'I may still have a lot of hopes, Sophie, but I've no regrets.'

'Are you sure about that?'

I drop a clove of garlic into the garlic press and squeeze it. 'You've known this Alekos for less than two months.'

'So what? Because of your lies, I don't know my father at all.'

It always comes back to this. Every argument we've had over the past few years. I drop the garlic press on the work surface and reach for my wine. 'I'll be the first to admit I made a mistake.'

'When have you ever admitted that?'

'What do you want me to say?'

'Nothing.' She turns her back on me and goes to the sink

to wash her hands.

I take a deep breath and steady my voice, not wanting to be angry or make it sound like I'm putting any blame on her. 'I care about you Sophie.'

'It's not the case of you caring, it's you expecting too much from me – the serious job you've never had. Try sorting your own life out rather than mine.'

I top up my wine. I pace across the kitchen and slam the empty bottle down on the draining board next to her.

'I'm not the one running away.'

Sophie wipes her hands on the towel and tucks it back on the rail. 'I'm not hungry any more.'

'Typical. Go on, avoid the truth. You're throwing away a good job and life here, Sophie.'

'You're so full of shit.' She grabs her bag off the worktop.

I follow her down the hallway. 'What if you don't find want you want in Greece?'

'I'm not going to find anything here.' Anger radiates off her as she glares at me. I stand my ground, arms folded despite wanting to hug her. I know another apology won't make a blind bit of difference because she's too damn cross. Her hand reaches for the door handle. 'I'll make do with plane food. Enjoy your stir fry.'

She opens the door and sunlight creeps into the hallway, making the dust dance in the light.

'If Alekos doesn't work out, you know where I am.'

'Fuck you.' She slams the front door so hard it makes the windows rattle.

I probably deserve that, but even so, it hurts. I can't help but think that she's running away from a decent life here. I get that she's pissed off with me, I understand she's bored with her job, God knows I've been there, but to throw all she's worked for away because she fell in lust with a hot Greek is something I'd do, not Sophie, and that worries the hell out of me.

The kitchen is empty without her. The two boxes are still

in the middle of the floor. She's really doing this, moving to Greece to be with a man she's only known for a few days. Maybe I'm being unduly harsh expecting her to come running home, her heart broken by a man after only knowing him for a week. I meant what I said though. Relationships are great in the beginning, the head-over-heels in love stage when it's exciting and sexy, until reality kicks in and the magic disappears. I gulp wine and glug olive oil into a wok. I wait until the oil is smoking before tipping in the chicken and vegetables, steam and sizzling engulfing the kitchen.

I eat outside on the picnic table. Early evening and it's still blazing hot and I can't help but think that this is going to be Sophie's reality now. Hot days and a hot man. I hope her expectations of life in Greece live up to her holiday fling. I pick at the stir fry, no longer hungry but knowing I should eat or the wine will go straight to my head. Roses entwine around the trellis against the red brick wall, and melted candle wax oozes down an empty Corona bottle. It's not often since I stopped having lodgers that I wished someone was still living in the spare room; I could do with a bit of company. I wonder what Sophie's doing right now. She's got the coach journey to the airport this evening, then tomorrow she'll be on a plane and into the arms of Alekos. I move the chicken and baby sweetcorn about my plate with my fork. It's an odd feeling, Sophie going to live with someone I've never met, someone she knows so little about. I've seen the photo of him that Candy's mum showed me and it's easy to see why Sophie fell for him. Dark haired and handsome with a deliciously tanned and toned body. I know with my history of men it's looks I always go for, but then I only ever intend to have a fling, not fall head over heels in love and want to settle down. From what Candy's mum's gleaned, Sophie's fallen for this Alekos hard – but good looks and great sex won't be enough to sustain a relationship long term. I've been there and done that more times than I care to remember.

I head inside and leave my half-eaten plate of food next to the sink. I need something or someone to take my mind off things. I take the cordless phone from the hallway and sit on the sofa. I put in a number and look at it, my fingers hovering over the call button. It's early evening on a weekday and he should have finished work by now. I haven't spoken to him in a long time, in fact the times I've seen him since he moved out we haven't done much talking at all. Other stuff, yes, but not much conversation. Maybe I should phone Kim instead, suggest an evening out or for her to come round to chat over a bottle of wine. That would be the sensible thing to do, but when have I ever been sensible.

The slatted blinds knock against the side of the open window, yet the breeze doesn't reach me on the sofa. The living room is perfect in autumn and winter with aubergine-coloured walls, an open fire, and plenty of throws and cushions, but in summer it feels too warm and cosy. I press call and bite my lip as the phone rings for what feels like an eternity.

'Hey, Leila.' Owen's smooth and familiar voice answers.

'Hey, I didn't think you were there.'

'I've just got home.'

There's a brief moment of silence.

'I've had a shitty day.'

'Oh?'

'Argument with Sophie, she's leaving the country tomorrow. I was kinda hoping for a bit of company, if you fancy coming over?'

'I can't, Leila, sorry.'

I realise I'm gripping my knee tightly, my knuckles white, the tips of my pink-painted fingernails chipped.

'No worries, it was only on the off chance. Another time.'

He coughs. 'When I said I can't, I mean not just tonight. I'm with someone…'

'You've been with someone before and that's never mattered.'

'I really like her. We're moving in together next month. So you know, no more messing around.'

I wasn't expecting that. We finish with an awkward bye and it's a weird feeling knowing I'm never going to speak to or see him again. He's been a part of my life for more than ten years and now it's over. We never loved each other, not like that at least, cared for each other maybe, fancied the hell out of each other but love, no.

Our relationship has only ever been based on sex. What did I expect. I know he's had girlfriends over the years, but no one he was serious enough about to ever say no to me. He's thirteen years younger. This moment was inevitable, him meeting someone he isn't willing to cheat on. He's grown-up, no longer a student or my lodger. He wants a serious and meaningful relationship, while I'm still chasing a quick shag with a younger guy to make myself feel better about Sophie leaving. I should have phoned Kim, but now I feel stupid, not wanting to see her, knowing the look she'll give me when I tell her about Owen and how he's moved on.

I wipe my eyes and put the phone back on its holder in the hallway. I pad out to the kitchen and take a second bottle of wine from the fridge – that will be my company tonight. Tomorrow is a new day, tomorrow Sophie flies off to her new life in Greece, but tonight I'm going to drown my sorrows and forget about the many mistakes I've made in my life.

Norfolk, 2008

Despina is something else. I mean, it's September and she's in a fur coat, hat and gloves. She's been travelling for hours and yet her make-up is spotless; her red lips so well defined they could be seen from space. I'm not surprised that Sophie's clashed with her.

The anger that simmers off Sophie is palpable, yet Despina seems oblivious, talking non-stop the moment she comes in to the house. I can't understand a bloody word. Alekos is as good-looking as the photos of him suggested. Whereas Despina doesn't seem to give a shit about the turmoil she's caused by turning up uninvited, it's evident in Alekos' quietness that he knows he's messed up. If there was a strain on his and Sophie's relationship before, the combination of Sophie spending time with Ben and now Despina showing up is not going to help.

We have a bizarre meal; my roast beef along with *spanakopita* that Despina's brought from Greece. She chews tiny mouthfuls of Yorkshire pudding, but I can tell she's not impressed. At least she's polite enough to keep eating. It's been a long day for us all one way or another so while I go up to bed and Despina heads to the spare room, Sophie and Alekos shut themselves in the living room. I'm hoping make-up sex will help ease the tension between them.

~

Evidently there was no passion on the cards last night. At breakfast the next morning the tension between them is unresolved and more intense if that's possible. Alekos barely says a word; Despina will not shut up, telling me all about where they live in Greece which Sophie begrudgingly translates. I put a couple more croissants on the plate in the middle of the table and Sophie reaches for the Marmite.

Despina takes hold of her hand and says something to Alekos in Greek. He mutters something back and Sophie replies. Despina frowns and places her half-eaten croissant back on her plate. '*Yiati ohi?*' she asks.

I sip my coffee and watch the three of them. I may not understand a word, but I sense the tone. Voices rise and then silence. Sophie's staring at her plate; Despina's fiddling with the gold cross on her necklace; and Alekos is leaning on the sink, looking out of the window.

'Um, does anyone fancy translating what's just been said?'

'Mum, really, you don't want to know.'

Alekos turns and looks at me. 'I asked Sophie to marry me last year.'

I turn to Sophie. 'You're engaged and you didn't tell me?'

She holds her hand up. 'Why I'm not wearing my engagement ring is what we were discussing.'

'And why aren't you wearing it?' I look between them. 'Do you love each other?'

'Yes,' they both say.

'Then what else matters?'

Despina pours coffee into her mug. '*Eiseh kakomathemenos,* Sophie.'

I frown. 'What did she say?'

'She said I was spoilt.'

'Spoilt?' I snort at Despina. 'That's one thing Sophie's not. Opinionated, passionate, angry, unforgiving, yes, but not spoilt.'

Despina stands and rattles something off to Sophie in

Greek. Sophie looks like she's about to cry. There's a vulnerability about her. Alekos takes his mum's shoulder and steers her out of the back door into the garden.

I reach my hand across the table and place it on top of Sophie's. 'It's your life; I'm not going to say another word. I can't understand half of what she says but I think Despina says enough for all of us.'

What a start to Sophie's twenty-ninth birthday. With the events of the last twenty-four hours I'm regretting agreeing to Robert throwing a birthday party at The Globe this evening. At least it gets us all out of the house, although Sophie looks like it's the last place she wants to be. I'm relieved though when we walk into the beer garden and are greeted by Robert turning sausages and burgers on a barbecue.

'Ah, the birthday girl!' he shouts across.

We walk over to him.

'Happy birthday, Sophie,' he says.

'Thank you.'

'Robert, meet Alekos and Despina.' I'm thankful to have Robert's warmth and friendliness to help ease the tension.

He shakes Alekos' hand and Despina kisses him on both cheeks.

'An English man cook!' she says in broken English.

He laughs. 'I can cope with hotdogs.'

'Don't put yourself down.' I touch his arm. 'Can we help?'

'Absolutely not.' He smiles and turns a skewer of onions and peppers. 'All under control. Help yourselves to a drink though.'

'I make salad.' Despina announces.

Robert frowns and looks at Sophie. 'Greek salad?'

'*To kouzina?*'

Sophie sighs. 'She means the kitchen.'

Robert points towards the doorway of the kitchen at the side of the pub. 'Our chef's still here…' But she's already set off across the lawn.

~

My relief at us not being stuck in the house together continues as the sun goes down. Lanterns wedged in the flower beds edge the garden and the coals of the barbecue glow. I have a pint and a plate of food; Robert's burger is slightly overdone but Despina's Greek salad is mouth-wateringly good. The Globe is inviting, warm light spilling from the now empty conservatory restaurant. Robert is grilling the last few burgers, and I've not seen Ben for a while. Sophie's been cornered by Despina and they're sitting together at a picnic table at the top of the garden.

Alekos is standing on his own, watching his mum and Sophie talk. I go over to him, marking the neat lawn with my crutches. 'It's not been easy for you and Sophie for a while then?'

He glances at me, then back to Sophie. 'You could say that.' He sips his pint. 'She's wanted us to move out for a long time. It's just not easy. We work there. Mama...' He shakes his head. 'I don't know.'

I remember back to the day Sophie left and the hopes she had for a new and exciting life with Alekos. I'd crushed her dreams, said harsh things; I'd take it all back in a heartbeat now to see her and Alekos happy.

'It was never going to be easy, though, was it? I mean, you two met and fell in love pretty quickly and then moved in together within weeks, Sophie to a new country and you back home. When I was living at home with my parents there was always loads of tension between us, and that was before I really gave them something to be upset about.'

Alekos nods, although I'm not sure how much of what I'm saying he actually understands. 'I just want to make her happy.'

'You'll get there, I'm sure. The time she's spent here has helped I think. We've certainly had time to heal our relationship. I'm sure the same will happen with yours.'

'You know she's missed you.'

'And I've missed her, more than I can...'

Sophie's in front of us, her cheeks red and clenched. She grabs Alekos' arm. 'Can I talk to you?' She pulls him away. 'What have you been telling your mum?'

'What is wrong with you?' Alekos says as Sophie leads him out of earshot.

Despina's still sitting on the bench at the top of the beer garden, watching them too. Alekos holds Sophie and leans his forehead against her. It's an intimate moment and I feel like I shouldn't be watching. I turn away and walk over to Robert.

'Well done,' I say. 'The food's gone down a treat.'

He wipes his hands down the front of his apron and picks up his glass of red wine. 'I'm all done now. About time we toasted the birthday girl.'

Before I can stop him he rattles the barbecue tongs against the side of his glass.

'Can I have everybody's attention?' he shouts. 'Let's raise our glasses to the birthday girl. To Sophie!'

'To Sophie!' I repeat along with everyone else.

'In the three weeks she's been here she's brought a breath of fresh air and Greek cuisine to The Globe, and, most importantly, she's been a great help to Leila.' He looks at Sophie standing with Alekos. 'I hope you can stay a while longer.'

Everyone claps. Alekos leaves Sophie and walks over to us.

'Everything okay?' I ask.

'It's no different to being home.' He swigs his pint and looks over my shoulder. '*Ti tis eipes?*' he says to Despina as she joins us.

Alekos has his back to the lawn but I can see Ben standing with Sophie. Alekos and Despina talk. I have no idea what they're saying but like earlier, I sense the underlying tension. Ben kisses Sophie on the cheek. I attempt to focus on Alekos, yet I catch sight of Sophie and Ben disappearing around the side of The Globe.

I should follow. Fuck that, Sophie's an adult and the last

thing she needs is me interfering. She's the one who needs to make a decision.

Robert removes his apron and joins me. 'I think everyone's enjoyed themselves.'

I love Robert's positivity. Whether he's sensed any tension tonight or not, I adore how he tries his hardest to make everyone happy.

I kiss his cheek. 'Thank you.'

'For what?' He smiles.

'For this. For everything you've done over the past few weeks. I've had a shitty time and you've made it a whole lot easier.'

'I think Sophie's had something to do with that too.'

Alekos and Despina's conversation is getting louder, staccato Greek snapping back and forth between them. Alekos throws his hands in the air, shakes his head and stalks off across the lawn.

Robert and I glance at each other.

Despina turns to us. 'It is… difficult,' she says, in broken English, her cheeks flushed.

'Tell me about it,' I say, 'things between me and Sophie haven't been easy for a long time either.'

She frowns.

Robert grabs a bottle of wine from the table next to the barbecue, pours a glassful and hands it to her.

I touch his arm. 'I'm going to see where they've all gone to.'

I feel mean leaving Robert alone with an upset Despina with no way to communicate properly, but I know he'll try his best. I'm more worried about where Sophie and Ben are, particularly with the mood Alekos is in. I just about reach the end of the lawn when Alekos appears, fists clenched, his handsome face pinched into a deep frown.

'You okay?' I ask.

He ignores me as he strides past.

Fuck.

Leaning on my crutches I go as fast as I can through the car park and out to the front of the pub. A passing car's headlights momentarily blinds me.

Ben and Sophie are sitting on the bench next to the door of the pub.

'What the bloody hell's going on? Alekos looked upset.' I stop in front of them. Ben's holding a blood-soaked tissue to his nose. 'Fuck me. Did he do this?'

'Apparently talking is a crime,' Ben says.

'You should get that seen to.'

'No.' He stands up. Blood trickles between his fingers. 'I'm going inside.'

He slams the pub door behind him. I turn to Sophie. Her eyes are rimmed red where she's been crying.

'You want to tell me what happened?'

'Where's Alekos?'

'Out back.'

'I should talk to him.'

'You need to talk to someone.'

'That someone being you?'

'Yes, if it helps. It's obvious what's going on. If you're trying to give Alekos an excuse to leave you, it's working a treat.'

Sophie shakes her head. 'I'm not doing anything. I don't have a plan. I wish I did. I wish I could see where I'll be in six months' time.'

'And who you'll be with?' I lean my crutches against the bench and sit next to her. 'Don't be like me, always running away from the good things in your life.'

'Maybe you should go and talk to Robert then.'

I don't know how to respond to that.

'Alekos,' she says, 'he's so… I don't know.'

'Nice. Handsome. Thoughtful.'

'Predictable.'

'Punching Ben was predictable?'

'No, and I'm almost glad he did it. At least he's showing

some kind of emotion. Anger is better than apathy.'

'So, there's nothing between you and Ben? Sophie, tell me there isn't.'

She shrugs. 'I don't know. There's something appealing about him. His energy and impulsiveness for life is how I wish Alekos was.'

I slide my arm in hers. 'Ben's in the wrong place emotionally to be getting involved with.' I brush away a hair from her eyes. 'And by the looks of things you are too. Don't turn into me. It doesn't make for a contented life. Go talk to Alekos.'

'You didn't think Alekos and I would last.'

'I've said a lot of stupid, selfish things. It doesn't mean I was right.'

'What do you think of Despina?'

'She's a character.'

Another car comes down the road, slows and beeps as it passes. I glance through the passenger window and wave at a friend who lives further down the coast.

'Alekos didn't invite her,' Sophie says. 'She insisted and he couldn't say no. Don't you think that's odd?'

'I wouldn't want to say no to her either.'

'But you know what I mean. He's thirty.'

'It's a different culture, Sophie.'

'I get that but you haven't seen the way she puts him down and destroys his confidence. He used to sing, play the guitar and write music, now he just works for his mother with very little thanks.'

I shiver; the temperature has dipped as the evening's gone on with the chill of autumn definitely in the air. 'Tell him how you feel.'

'I have done.'

'Tell him again.' I reach for my crutches and stand. With Sophie's arm linked in mine, we make our way slowly back round to the garden. Despina is sitting as close to the glowing coals of the barbecue as she can without setting herself alight, while Robert toasts marshmallows. There's no sign of either Alekos or Ben.

'I was wondering where everyone had got to,' Robert says when we reach him. He offers a toasted marshmallow to Sophie. 'Do you want one?'

She shakes her head.

'No Alekos?' Despina asks.

'No,' Sophie replies. She leans closer to me. 'I'm going to go find him.'

I watch her walk back across the lawn to the conservatory. I breathe deeply, worry gnawing at my insides that like me, she's going to lose the love of her life because she's chasing an unobtainable dream.

I turn back to the barbecue. Robert's watching me intently. Sophie's comment about him flashes through my mind.

'Everything okay?' he asks.

'I hope so.'

Norfolk & Sheffield, 2008

'I'm not going back to Greece with Alekos.' Sophie folds her arms. She's only just got back from taking Alekos and Despina to the airport; I assumed she'd stay another couple of weeks then go back too. Her legs are tense and rooted to the floor and I've seen this kind of determination before. It's like looking at myself. I know there's going to be no point in trying to talk her round but I'm not going to say nothing either.

'You're out of your mind. If you're not going back, what the hell are you going to do?'

'I don't know.'

At least she's honest. I shake my head. 'This is all very sudden, isn't it?'

'Not really, I haven't been happy for a long time.'

'But you're engaged?'

'We were, yes.'

'And the other morning, in this kitchen, you both said you loved each other.'

'Maybe that's not enough.'

I shake my head. 'You're throwing everything away.'

'No more than you did when you were pregnant with me.'

'That was totally different.'

'No it's not.'

I grip the edge of the work surface. 'I had no choice. I

150

couldn't have any kind of life in a place I wasn't wanted. I wanted to keep you. I didn't kiss goodbye to everything because I wasn't happy.'

'Don't trivialise my situation.'

'You can't always have everything. You have to compromise.'

Sophie frowns. 'I'm aware of that. Alekos needs to compromise too and he's never been willing to do that.'

I tuck my hair behind my ear and switch the kettle on. I lean back against the worktop and fold my arms. 'From what I've seen, Alekos is one hell of a decent guy. How can you walk away from him?'

'You've broken up with plenty of decent men.'

Have there really been lots of decent men? I know there have been plenty of men, but were any of them really that decent? Elliot, the married father of three; Owen, the lodger I shagged; then there were office romances, one-night stands, affairs with younger married men; and Darren, who wouldn't have lost his life if I hadn't been so fucking selfish.

Sophie sits down at the table.

'This isn't about me,' I finally say. 'I've messed up every relationship I've ever had and I've learnt to deal with that. I thought you were different. I thought you were crazy running away to Greece with Alekos but I understood you were in love. I'd have done the same for Elliot, dropped everything for him. But I had no choice. I couldn't be with him, even though I desperately wanted to.'

I drop a teabag in the pot and will myself not to cry.

'Did you get pregnant on purpose?' Sophie asks.

Did I? It seems a lifetime ago that I was eighteen and in love with a man who would never truly be mine. 'No. But I wasn't shocked. We weren't careful. I didn't care. I was in love.' I pour boiling water into the teapot and close the lid on the steam drifting into the dim light of the kitchen.

'Do you regret not being with anyone?'

'I'm always with someone.'

'You know what I mean. What about Robert.'

'What about him?' My hands tense where they're folded together on the worktop.

'You get on well.'

'Nothing's worth risking our friendship for.'

'But it might work.'

'I've never made a relationship work.'

'Maybe you haven't met the right person.'

I turn sharply. 'Your father was the right person.'

The lump in my throat intensifies and I can't hold back tears. Sophie scrapes back her chair, comes over and puts her arms around me.

'I didn't mean to upset you. I wasn't thinking.'

A sob catches in my throat. 'You haven't upset me. I'm just being stupid.' I pull away from her, grab a tissue and dab my eyes. 'It's pathetic. Thirty bloody years later and I'm still crying over him. And the truth of it is, I'd rather have had you, than be with him. He wouldn't have been happy if he'd left his wife. I'd have felt guilty. Guiltier. And I wouldn't have the life I have now.' I gesture around us at the kitchen and towards the garden. 'I was with a married man who happened to be my father's best friend. Either way it would have been a mistake.'

My conversation with Sophie plays on my mind for the rest of the evening. We have dinner, watch a bit of telly and go to bed early, but it takes me ages to get to sleep and when I do it's fitful, full of dreams. I wake early thinking about my many mistakes. I know what we need to do. I know it's about time to put all my demons to rest. I've finally made peace with Sophie, the next step is to stop holding on to the past.

It's been a long time since I've driven up north and I've never done the journey from Norfolk. The last time I drove to Sheffield with Sophie, she was five. Now she's twenty-nine. Where did that time go? We spend most of the journey in silence, lost in our own thoughts, Sophie concentrating on driving, while I gaze out of the window. We leave behind motorways and towns for countryside and the wide expanse of the Peak District National Park in the distance. Dark clouds charge across the sky, making the ground below a pattern of sunshine and shade. As soon as we pass Bakewell, Sophie tells me that she came up here once with Candy to see Elliot but bottled it when she saw him with his daughter and grandchild. I'm determined we're going to see him this time, so I ring Mum.

'It's Leila,' I continue without giving her time to make small talk. 'We're on our way to see Elliot. You might want to warn him. We'll wait outside his house. If he's home, he needs to make his excuses and then drive somewhere we can talk.'

'Sophie's with you?' Mum asks.

I glance at Sophie. 'Yes, she's with me. Tell him he's got fifteen minutes.' I feel great satisfaction at putting the phone down on her.

It's not long before the familiarity of the winding country road hits me, a road I've been along so many times before with my parents, either visiting Elliot and his family or going to a pub for Sunday lunch. I indicate to Sophie to pull over on a grass verge and she switches off the engine.

His house is up ahead, across the other side of the road, a beautiful detached period property with far-reaching views of the Peak District. Perfect house, perfect wife, perfect fucking family.

'He's lived in this same house for thirty-five years.' I stare out of the window, my eyes fixed on the driveway. 'He never liked change.'

'He was taking a risk trusting you not to come knocking.'

'If I'd wanted to I'd have found him even if they'd moved.'

'How long should we leave it?'

'As long as it takes.' I drum my fingers on my leg cast, nervous now at having to wait, and the thought of seeing him after so long. He's everything I thought I ever wanted in a man, and yet it's an empty dream I've been clinging on to for years. I've not being able to move on and have repeated the same mistake over and over, choosing unsuitable men, unable to commit because they're already bloody married.

Elliot. I grip Sophie's hand. He closes the front door and looks up the road. His eyes meet mine. Sophie starts the engine. Elliot gets into a silver Mercedes and backs out of the drive. My stomach's doing somersaults. He slows as he passes us and the enormity of what we're doing hits me when I realise that Sophie's going to meet her father for the first time.

I'm glad Sophie's driving because I'm in pieces as we follow him, zipping along fast winding roads, moorland spreading in every direction. I know he's driving somewhere we're not likely to be seen and eventually he pulls into a deserted lay-by screened by trees.

'Help me get out.'

Sophie comes round to the passenger side, her hair whipped by the wind. She gets the crutches off the back seat and helps me out. A cold wind whistles across the moorland swirling round us where we're exposed on the edge of wildness.

A car door slams and my heart thuds. Elliot walks towards us and we meet him halfway. His hands are in his jeans pockets and a thick grey jumper hugs his chest. He's achingly familiar and yet it's like I'm seeing him for the first time. His hair is a darker red than it used to be, and is flecked with a little grey and thinning on top. He's clean shaven and stockier than I remember but then he's in his late sixties now. He's weathered well and there's still a sense of the younger man I fell in love with.

He frowns and motions to the crutches. 'What happened?'

'I was in an accident.'

'Anna never said.'

'I never told her.'

This pathetic small talk is our first face-to-face

conversation in nearly thirty years.

'I'm Sophie.'

Finally he turns his attention from me. He takes her hand and shakes it. I want to pull Sophie to me and tell her how much I love her, to make up for the lack of warmth her father is showing.

'Well,' I say instead, 'this is about as comfortable as I imagined it would be.'

He looks between us. 'I'm sorry. You took me by surprise, Leila. It's a shock seeing you… both.' He looks at Sophie. 'I've wanted to meet you since you were born.'

I shake my head and clench my fists.

'I've only known about you for eight years,' Sophie says. 'I came up here when I was twenty-one, determined to meet you.'

'I know. Anna told me. I had no idea. She couldn't understand why you came all that way to meet me and then didn't.'

'You were with your family and I felt like a trespasser or a stalker or both.'

The wildness of the location is not lost on me. The howling wind ripples the moorland heather and grasses, adding to the intensity. The sun disappears behind a cloud and the temperature drops. I shiver. 'Are you mad we came?'

He shakes his head. 'God, no. I'd given up hope that you'd ever reply to my letters. I never expected you to come and visit.'

'Visit?' I laugh. 'That sounds like we were invited, and welcome.'

'You are.'

'Oh right, that's why we're standing out in the cold, miles from anywhere. You're ashamed. You were ashamed even when we were together. And you're sure as hell ashamed that Sophie looks like your daughter. That's why you can't let your family meet us. Because they'd know.'

He can't even look me in the eye.

155

'So why did you come, then?'

'To tell you I don't ever want you contacting me again. No letters, no phone calls. My mother should never have given you my new address, but she'll seemingly do anything for you. I've stayed out of your life like you and my bloody family asked; I lied to Sophie for years about you because I thought that was the right thing to do. I was wrong. It's up to you and Sophie what happens to your relationship but you leave me out of it. We haven't been together or had anything to do with each other for nearly thirty years and that's the way it's going to stay.'

I turn away and clump back to the car on my crutches, determined to reach it before I start crying or change my mind. Part of me aches for him, for us to be together as a loving, happy family, if only for a brief moment. I yank open the car door, lean the crutches against it and sit awkwardly on the passenger seat. I turn the rear-view mirror so I can watch them through my tears. They walk off a little way and stand rigidly next to each other on the edge of the moorland and talk. Even with the door open, I can't hear what they're saying. Their conversation is snatched away by the wind. I wonder what Sophie's telling him? She looks tense, her fists clenched, her face serious as they take it in turns to get off their chest whatever it is they've been wanting to say to each other. I may not be able to hear their words but I get a sense of what's being said, through the way Elliot moves his body from looking out over the moorland to blocking Sophie's words, getting defensive, raising his hands in the air. Sophie's getting in her stride, words pouring from her, jabbing her finger at him, attacking him with years' worth of hurt.

She makes to go and Elliot says something. She turns back to him and I can see the hurt on his face as he listens to her. Sophie stalks back to the car. He watches her struggle to open the door in the wind, slamming it shut. We sit in silence and I watch as he slowly makes his way back to his car. With a last glance at us he pulls out on to the main road.

I wait until his car is out of sight. 'How did you leave it?'

'I left it. He gave me a load of bullshit about family. He's not family. I don't even consider Grandma and Grandad to be family – when do I ever see or speak to them? Calling them my grandparents doesn't mean anything. Takis and Despina, now they treat me as part of the family…'

'He didn't live up to your expectations then?'

'I'm not sure what my expectations were. But no, he's not the man I imagined to be my father for twenty-one years. All I saw was a man scared of his wife finding out about a twenty-nine-year-old love child and an affair he wishes he was able to continue. I have no respect for him.'

'I'm sorry.' I wipe away fresh tears.

'Don't be. This is closure for both of us.'

Norfolk & Cephalonia, 2008-09

'I'm pregnant.'

We stop off for lunch on the way home from our windswept rendezvous with Elliot, and Sophie drops a bombshell like that. It's the last thing I expected her to say, particularly after she'd told me she wasn't going to go back to Greece with Alekos. At least our conversation on our drive back to Marshton changes from Elliot, to Sophie, Alekos, and an unplanned baby. It could be the story of a Hollywood movie.

It's a long drive to the Peak District and back again in one day, along with the emotional toll of seeing Elliot and talking to him face to face after all these years. I'm a different person now. I'm not sure I even recognised in Elliot any resemblance of the man I'd fallen in love with. Two years on from changing my life and moving from Bristol to Norfolk, I know I'm ready to move on from Elliot and the part of my life that has overshadowed every decision I've made for three decades.

It's a relief to get home. Every part of me feels drained and achy; I'm still healing from the accident and I know it's been too much today, emotionally and physically, despite not being the one to drive all that way.

Sophie pulls into the drive and helps me out of the car. I slam the door shut and take a deep breath of fresh Norfolk air. I realise I can breathe easy again; a huge weight's been lifted off my shoulders and I finally feel free. I look across the car at Sophie. 'You need to tell him, you know.'

'Tell who, what?' Sophie's looking at me like I'm crazy.

'Alekos. Who do you think? About the baby.'

She grabs our bags from the back seat. 'I know, just not yet. It doesn't really feel real at the moment.'

'Wait until you've had your first scan. Then it'll feel real, trust me.' I hobble after her to the front door and wait while she unlocks it.

She turns to me before going inside, her eyebrows furrowed, worry etched across her face.

'Seriously, Mum, you don't mind me staying with you for a while?'

'You seriously have to ask?' Leaning on one crutch, I hold on to her with my free hand. 'It'll be the perfect opportunity for us to make up for the years we lost not speaking to each other.'

Sophie may be shocked about getting pregnant by mistake, but I doubt she's as shocked as I am about becoming a grandmother. I mean, if you have sex then there's always a risk of getting knocked up. I learnt the hard way. Becoming a grandparent – unless the pregnancy is planned and the grandparents-to-be have been confided in, then you get no bloody warning.

I'm still clinging on to my youth and the idea of being someone's grandma is an alien concept, the image belongs to someone much older with grey hair, wearing a tweed skirt and sensible brown shoes. An outdated image, I know, and in this day and age an unrealistic one. But that isn't me. The same as I've never considered myself to be marriage material, I'm not grandparent material either.

Sophie scolds me. She says the image I have is old-fashioned and I know she's right. I find it strange, though, being younger than so many friends like Jocelyn who aren't yet grandparents themselves, particularly when I know she's longing to be a grandma. Her turn will come I'm sure. Although Sophie's ten years older than I was when I got pregnant, I shouldn't really be surprised it was an accident. It seems it runs in the family…

She's still not spoken to Alekos by the time she has her first scan. I know she's spoken to Despina about shipping her belongings over from Greece but from the little she's said, either Alekos hasn't been there when she's called or he doesn't want to talk to her. So I go with her to the scan and hold her hand while the nurse spreads gel over her bump. The black and white image of a tiny baby kicking and floating about is the most magical thing I've ever seen. I was scared and felt so alone throughout my pregnancy with Sophie, I didn't get a chance to enjoy it. I can't take my eyes off the grainy image of my grandchild, tiny arms and legs jerking about.

Tears roll down my face. Sophie looks up at me. Her cheeks are damp too.

'Pass me my mobile,' she says. 'I need to talk to Alekos.'

'How did it go yesterday?' Robert asks when he calls round early the next morning.

Sophie's still upstairs in bed but I close the kitchen door anyway so we won't disturb her.

'I'm going to be a bloody grandma, Robert.'

He laughs. 'It's only just dawning on you, is it?'

'I'm not ready for this.'

'Is Sophie?'

'She wasn't, but something clicked yesterday. I don't know if it was the reality of seeing that little baby on the screen but she finally phoned Alekos and talked things through.'

'Is she going back to Greece?'

I take two mugs of coffee and sit next to Robert at the end of the table.

'No, at least not yet. But it seems Alekos had news of his own.'

'Oh?'

'He's bought them a place on Cephalonia. It's a tumbled down shit-tip by the sounds of it, but he has plans to turn it into a home and business for them. He's working on doing it up before she goes over.'

'And Sophie knew nothing about this?'

'Nope, not a thing, just like Alekos had no clue about the baby.'

'Bloody hell, that was a bold and brave thing to do.'

'And exactly what he needed to do – step up and *do* something. I barely know him but I'm so bloody proud of him. And for Sophie taking the first step to fix their relationship. In their own way they've both come to the same decision that they want to be together and they want their independence from Alekos' parents – well, Despina at least.'

Robert taps his mug of coffee against mine. 'Being a grandparent is the best thing, you know.'

'Yeah okay, I'm sure the reality of it will be better than the thought of being old enough to be someone's grandparent.'

'You'll see.' He gives me a knowing look.

'Is Ben okay?'

'Muddling along, although Mandy's agreed for him to spend Christmas with her and the kids. I don't think it's going to fix things between them, but he was desperate to spend the holidays with Fraser and Bella. I'm going to miss seeing them though.'

I nod, biding my time, unsure how to ask and wondering how he'll take it. 'About that, I was wondering what you're planning for Christmas Day?'

'I'm going to be at the pub until about four helping with the Christmas lunches.'

'After that?'

'I hadn't really thought.'

'Come over here and join us.'

His eyes meet mine. 'Are you sure?'

'Of course I'm sure.'

We finish our coffee and say goodbye before Sophie makes it downstairs. She looks happier than she has for a long time, her skin flushed and healthy, brighter now the morning sickness has eased, and since speaking to Alekos. I know that feeling of relief, of clearing the air with someone, making a decision that enables you to move on with your life.

Coffee is still making her gag though, so I make her a cup of camomile tea and we sit together at the kitchen table just as Robert and I had a little while before, the chairs still warm.

'Robert just popped round, wanted to know how you got on yesterday.'

'Yeah, I heard him leave.'

'I thought we'd invite him over for Christmas if that's okay with you?'

'Of course it's okay, you don't need to ask my permission.' She cups the tea in her hands and looks at me. 'You really like him, don't you?'

'Yes,' I say, 'he's a good friend. Plus Ben's going to be in London so he can see his kids on Christmas Day, Vicky has a new baby and her in-laws over, and it's a long way for Robert to go when he's got the pub to look after too.'

'You really don't need to convince me it's a good idea.'

'To think one of the reasons why I left Bristol was to escape men, and here am I, two years later spending Christmas with the first man I met in the village.'

'Is he staying over?' Sophie raises her eyebrows.

'No. We're just friends.'

'Uh huh.'

'What does that mean?'

'You're really not sleeping with him?'

I look at her and shake my head. 'When would I have slept with him? Has he ever stayed over?'

'No, it's just… Be careful you don't lead him on. I mean if you don't like him in that way…'

'I… Sophie, I'm not leading him on. We're friends, really good friends. He knows that.'

'Uh huh.'

'Shit, Sophie, stop making that noise. It's annoying.' I put my arms on the table and glare at her. 'If you know something that I don't….'

She shakes her head and rubs her hand over her small bump. 'I'm just saying spending Christmas together seems like more than just friendship.'

'You're reading way too much into this.'

'Uh huh.'

The cottage is the perfect place to have Christmas. It's homely and cosy throughout the year, but now there's a Christmas tree in the living room window, decorations up, and lights threaded around the house. It's bitterly cold during the week leading up to Christmas, with frost coating everything, making the view from Salt Cottage a winter wonderland without there actually being snow. I love each of the seasons here and the changing colours of the landscape. Now in December my icy breath fogs the grey sky, while frozen puddles crack beneath my boots. Even better, I love the sight of the cottage coming into view on my way back from a walk, the tiny lights twinkling on the Christmas tree in the living room window and smoke puffing into the air from the chimney, promising warmth and cosiness once I get inside, kick off my boots and unwrap my scarf, hat, gloves and thick winter coat.

We have a proper family Christmas. After a lazy day with Sophie eating brunch at eleven, going for a walk by the sea, and coming home to cook Christmas dinner, Robert joins us and we sit together at the kitchen table tucking into roast turkey and all the trimmings, wearing colourful Christmas hats, and finishing it off by gorging on the Christmas pudding Robert brought with him from the pub.

I'm tempted to suggest he stays over, but I'm not sure how he'll take that and I'm not sure what I really mean by 'stay over', so I follow Sophie's advice of not leading him on. He heads back to The Globe late Christmas evening and returns on Boxing Day to eat leftovers with us and play Monopoly and Articulate. It feels right spending Christmas together.

Christmas rolls into the new year and while Alekos remains on Cephalonia updating us with progress – although I'm not sure how much progress he's really making on his own bar occasional help from friends – Sophie's bump continues to grow. My anxiety about becoming a grandma doesn't diminish, but that goes hand in hand with memories of my own pregnancy: the fear, loneliness, shame and uncertainty. I had such negativity at a time that should have been joyous, and those feelings flood back as Sophie heads into her third trimester and goes to antenatal classes on her own because Alekos is in Greece. At least she has Alekos, whereas I had no one. Apart from Jocelyn. And Sophie has me, and Robert, and an extended family in Greece, friends too; Candy comes over for a long weekend with her kids. Sophie's life is filled with love and support, and so, by the time we edge closer to her due date I feel calmer and almost ready to take on my new role.

Being there while Sophie gives birth though is a whole other matter. Bloody hell, it's a stark reminder of my own experience of childbirth, not so much the pain and the physical side of giving birth, but the emotional one. I'd do anything to take away the agony for Sophie. She has me, and I had Jocelyn, although in the darkest moments I'd have done anything to have had my mum holding my hand. I can't even remember if I wanted Elliot there or not. Would he have been any comfort? I doubt it. I wonder where he was and what he was doing during the thirty-six hours I was in labour with Sophie? Playing happy bloody families, no doubt.

It worries me that Alekos is missing his daughter's birth. I realise the connection gained by being there through the pain, the screaming, the determination, the final push, the relief, the immediate and overwhelming feeling of love. Alekos doesn't have that, not that I blame him; there was never any chance with Thea arriving early and relatively quickly for a first baby.

Beautiful Thea. My granddaughter. Robert was right, being a grandparent is the best thing. Those first six weeks with Sophie, Thea and me together, muddling along through sleeplessness, night feeds and nappy changes, I'll treasure forever. We also get baby snuggles, the best thing ever, and I get to see Sophie's happiness despite the tiredness. Alekos Skypes with them daily and is adamant the place on Cephalonia is ready for Sophie and Thea to join them. And so the countdown begins – six short weeks until the three of us are on a plane, heading to Cephalonia, Alekos, Sophie and Thea's new home.

Bristol, 1979

The hardest thing is being alone. Except I'm not alone. I'm never alone any longer. I stare at Sophie in her Moses basket. Her face is all screwed up from screaming, her tiny hands clenched into fists. She's been crying for so long she no longer has tears, just an uncontrollable sob that's made me cry too because I've no fucking clue what to do. I sit on my bed gripping the edge of the mattress and shiver. Moonlight creeps through a gap in the curtain, falling on Sophie's face. I've tried everything; fed her, changed her nappy, cuddled her, walked her round and round my room then up and down the landing, fed her again. I'm now leaving her to cry it out but it kills me, so I pick her up and hug her to me, feeling her chest heave against mine with each sob.

The couple I'm sharing the flat with are nurses and work shifts. They're on a run of nights, so I'm alone with Sophie and her screams. I can't phone Mum. I won't phone her. My parents wiped their hands of me and I told them that I could do this. Bolshie nineteen-year-old me, pregnant and fearless could do this. A dead-tired, scared nineteen-year-old new mum doesn't feel the same. All I feel now is fear. Fear that I can't do this, that I can't look after my own baby, pacify her, make her happy. I could phone Jocelyn, she said I could any time, even in the middle of the night, but I'm fearful she'll be asleep, her newborn son sleeping too and I'll wake them all up. So I'm alone.

I pace up and down the dark landing. Sophie's screams fill the narrow space. Tears stream down my face blurring my eyes until the combination of darkness and crying leaves me unable to see anything. I stop pacing and lean against the wall, my whole body trembling through cold and sobbing. Sophie's like something possessed against me, her screams heartbreakingly desperate.

I retreat into my room and sit with a thump on my bed. Sophie's tiny body jolts against me. Her screams ease for the briefest of moments before filling the room once more. I feed her again, the only thing I can do to ease her crying. I cuddle her in my arms and listen to the eerie silence of night, the only sound an occasional car passing by, headlights mixing with the moonlight through the curtains. I rock back and forwards trying to keep myself awake, scared shitless that I'm going to fall asleep and lose my hold on her. I've never known tiredness like it. In the middle of the night, I have no one to share my fears with.

I think of Elliot, asleep in his big beautiful house, his wife sleeping next to him, their three children tucked up in their own beds. Does he ever wake in the night and think about me? Think about the daughter he's not met? Wonder how we're doing, where we are… Why would he, what does he have to worry about? Still rocking, my thoughts elsewhere, I realise that Sophie's pulled away, her milky mouth open, her eyes closed, asleep and peaceful at last. My heart thuds, tension coursing through willing her to stay asleep as I slowly lean over the Moses basket and place her in it. I hold my breath and watch her chest rise and fall beneath her baby grow. I ease myself back on to my bed and cry myself to sleep.

With my flatmates back from work, dog tired after their twelve-hour night shift I leave the house, despite being as exhausted as they are. Sophie's asleep in her pram, her face serene, a world away from the distress she was in during the night. She seems to have no problem sleeping during the day and I know I should be sleeping too, but I need company. It's a couple of miles to Jocelyn's house but the cool air is revitalising as I push the pram along terraced streets and then along a main road busy with traffic. I take the route through the park in Horfield, the muscles in my legs straining as I push the pram up the winding path beneath trees full of autumn colours, and past the play area where a group of mums are chatting as they push their toddlers on the swings. This will be me and Sophie in a couple of years, doing things together. Laughter from the mums floats towards me as I reach the top of the park. I can't remember the last time I laughed.

Jocelyn's house in Bishopston is still as tidy as it was the first time I visited, apart from the addition of cloth nappies drying by the radiator in the hallway and baby bottles lined up on the draining board. Jocelyn looks in control, John snuggled in her arms, her maternity dress homemade but fitting her properly unlike the flowery monstrosity I'm wearing. Her hair is short and neat, her face make-up free and clear. She doesn't even look tired, just happy.

I leave Sophie sleeping in her pram in the kitchen doorway and sit at the table. Jocelyn makes us tea while holding John. I catch her watching me, her eyebrows pinching together. I must look a state. My long greasy hair's tied up into a messy ponytail, dark circles beneath my eyes, my second-hand maternity dress swamping me.

She puts the teapot and cups on the table, sits opposite me and pushes a tin of chocolate digestives towards me.

I take one and munch it, washing it down with a sip of scalding hot tea. I can't remember the last time I had a hot drink or even a hot meal, or anything that really resembles a meal at all. I've been living on toast.

Jocelyn places a cool hand on my arm. 'It will get easier, Leila, I promise.'

John is snuggled against her chest, dribbling on the muslin she's draped over her shoulder. She looks so together, so capable, a natural, while I feel a mess with no sense of style or a feeling of being me. I'm Sophie's mother and yet I feel a fraud. Less than a year ago, I was a fashionable eighteen-year-old, smoking, drinking, working hard, earning a living, and having an affair. I was in love with Elliot, the future was mine for the taking and there were so many possibilities. And now…

Jocelyn's still talking and I try and listen while I demolish the biscuit. 'My Mum, who's had four children, tells me the newborn stage will go so quickly that soon we'll forget all about sleepless nights and we'll have mischievous toddlers on our hands.'

I nod, unconvinced. It's been less than five weeks and it's felt like eternity and that I've aged a hundred years. I've lost weight and not just the baby-weight. I feel skinnier than before, a combination of breast feeding and not having time to eat or cook anything proper.

'I tell you what, why don't you go upstairs and have a shower. I'll watch Sophie. If she wakes, I can walk her around. John is quite happy lying in his basket watching his mobile for a while.'

My eyes fill with tears as I look across the table at her. 'Are you sure?'

'Of course I'm sure. I'll find you some clean clothes too – I'm pretty sure you'll fit into some of my pre-pregnancy clothes, and trust me, I won't be wearing them for a while.'

'Thank you so much.'

She waves her hand. 'It's nothing, Leila. The least I can do. And once you're all refreshed, how about having a little snooze and then staying with us for tea. Alan can drive you home afterwards.'

She may only be ten years older than me with a newborn of her own, but I feel mothered and looked after by Jocelyn, a feeling that's been missing from my life since I was eleven years old.

I stand in the shower, my tears mixing with the water

pummelling my body. I feel cleansed and refreshed at long last, and safe and comforted by Jocelyn, no longer quite so lonely.

Norfolk, 2009

I know I'm going to miss them like crazy, but Sophie and Thea being thousands of miles away in Greece, only really hits me when I get back to Salt Cottage. I've spent two weeks on Cephalonia looking after Thea and helping work on Birdsong Villas Creative Retreat. They're bloody mad taking the place on with a newborn when their home and business still pretty much looks like a building site, but as Sophie has pointed out to me many times before, no madder than a pregnant nineteen-year-old going it alone in a strange city.

I look in each room but it seems so empty without Thea's blanket draped over the back of the sofa or bottles for expressed milk cluttering the sink. I'm just about containing my emotions when I go into Sophie's room. She left the bed stripped. Thea's Moses basket is next to it, empty of Thea, her blankets and her cuddly teddy, one of the first things I bought her.

I sit on the end of the bed and sob. I held it together saying goodbye to them on Cephalonia, knowing if I let my emotions get the better of me I'd never want to leave. Looking back from the taxi at tiny Thea snuggled against Sophie's chest, Alekos with his arm around Sophie's waist, it felt like I was abandoning them. It was a perfect family scene, apart from the desolation behind them: the grey flaking walls of their house, the crumbling out-buildings, the weed-filled courtyard, the old olive tree the only surviving and beautiful thing amongst a huge amount of mess. I worry for their sanity, looking after a newborn and continuing with the building work after months of being apart, and the strain that will put on their relationship. It feels wrong to have left them there to live like that and work so hard, but my life and my business are back here. Two weeks off was all I could manage; I have back-to-back weddings throughout the summer. My wedding planner business is booming, and now I need to focus on it, after months and months of focusing on Sophie, her pregnancy and then gorgeous little Thea. I dreaded the idea of becoming a grandma, and now I am one, I can't think of anything better.

'They'll manage.' Robert's ever present optimism does little to lift my mood when I see him the next day, for a drink, a bite to eat and a catch up. 'It'll be the making of them. You wait and see.'

Life has a habit of taking over, pushing my emotions out of the way. They're still there in the background though. I miss Sophie and ache for cuddles with Thea, but I can function. I have work to focus on and friends to see, village life to navigate, countryside to walk through, weddings to organise. Life ticks on. Skyping with them in Greece brings them closer, sharing tears of tiredness and despair when nothing seems to be going right and Thea starts teething and not sleeping for more than an hour or two at a time. My own struggles as a new mum come flooding back, but at least Sophie has Alekos. I wish I could share the burden, let them sleep, help them build, paint, fix, and all the millions of other things they need to do. I share their successes too, when the villa has a brand new bathroom fitted, the roof goes on what will be the guest rooms, and Thea gets her first tooth. I book flights to visit them in spring of the following year. Knowing there's a countdown to seeing them again eases the heartache of being so far away.

Robert's my rock. He's my Norfolk version of Jocelyn. And it's strange because I've never been just friends with a bloke before. I catch myself wondering what he's up to, hoping he'll pop over unannounced, and looking forward to catching up with him for a drink at the pub. I've had plenty of friends with benefits before but never a male friend I wasn't sleeping with. He's no Jocelyn though. I mean that in the sense that my feelings towards him are so different than my friendship with her, with Kim, with anyone. I notice his smile, his vivid blue eyes, his broad shoulders. I notice *him*. I'm conflicted about what my desire to spend so much time with him means.

The year trudges on; Thea begins to babble at me through the camera, sitting up in her high chair, her face covered with food, munching on a cucumber stick. Summer's turned to autumn and now winter as we creep closer to Christmas. Last Christmas I spent with Sophie and Robert. One happy family. Almost twelve months later it feels very different, and I've not broached the subject with Robert yet, knowing he's got his own family with Vicky in Norwich and Ben in London.

A couple of weeks before Christmas Robert tapping on my office window makes me jump. By the time I go out into the hallway, the front door's open and he's standing on my doorstep, wrapped up in a coat, gloves and a hat, smiling at me. Cold air creeps in from the garden making me shiver in my boots, leggings and long-sleeved top.

'Hey there,' he says. 'My head is filled with Christmas music, Christmas bookings and talking to people about Christmas. I want to not think about mince pies and crackers for an hour or so. Fancy joining me for a walk?'

It's two o'clock on a Thursday afternoon and there are things I need to do, but what the hell.

'I'd love to.'

I swap my Uggs for wellies, slip into my winter coat and tug on gloves, a hat and scarf. I close the front door behind us.

The mud on the lane is solid and ridged with frost, the towering hedges on either side not giving the sunshine a chance to thaw it. We walk around the edges of the two fields that lead to the road and up to the Downs, our breath streaming into the icy air. I don't mention Christmas. Instead we chat about grandchildren – Robert's three and Thea. I still don't feel old enough to be a grandparent and despite Robert being older than me and the perfect doting grandfather, I don't think of him like that either.

By the time we walk up the sandy path to reach the Downs I've warmed up, which is just as well because higher up and exposed to the elements it's absolutely bloody freezing. No one seems to be about, not even the usual dog walkers. With the summer season long gone, it's just me, Robert and the birds soaring overhead.

'What are you doing for Christmas?' Robert asks over his shoulder.

I follow him along the single track lined by gorse bushes, their deep green leaves pinpricked with yellow flowers, a splash of colour on an otherwise cold grey winter's day.

'I thought you were fed up talking about Christmas?'

'I am, but I'm looking forward to Ben coming to stay and seeing Fraser and Bella on Boxing Day. Vicky's going to her in-laws. I just wondered if you'd like to join us? I wanted to return the favour of spending Christmas with you last year.'

'You sure it's a good idea me being there with Ben?'

Robert glances back. 'Leila, he adores you. Whatever happened between him and Sophie is in the past. It's done, isn't it? She's back in Greece with Alekos and Thea, and he's making the best of a bad situation here. We'd love you to join us.'

The path widens and I catch up with him, matching his pace. His long legs stride over the hard ground.

'I'd love to,' I say, remembering back to last year and my contentment with him sharing Christmas with us.

I stop before the path begins to weave its way down to the wood at the bottom. The wind howls around us and whips at the hair that's sticking out beneath my woolly hat. You can see in all directions from up here, the fields that lead to Marshton and beyond to the windmill at Clay, all the way to the smudge of deeper blue-grey of the North Sea on the horizon.

Robert realises I've stopped and walks back to join me.

I fold my gloved hands together and look up at him. 'What are we doing?'

'What do you mean?'

I breathe deeply and exhale frosted breath. 'We spend as much time together as we can, we spend holidays together, but the most I've ever got from you is a kiss on the cheek. So, I'm confused. Do you like me in *that* way or not?'

It's hard to make out his expression we're both so wrapped up from the cold. He glances away towards the distant sea. I bet it's even colder right on the coast, churning grey sea foaming on to pebbles.

'You've always been with someone…'

'No, I haven't. I've only been with one person since I moved to Norfolk and you know how that ended…'

He looks at me with his familiar intense gaze. 'Leila, I know what it's like to lose someone.'

'This was different, you know that. You know everything – I totally overshared with you about my relationship with Darren. He was married, it was only ever about sex and having fun and I was going to finish with him that weekend, before…' I can't say the words out loud. I wasn't in love with him, but I cared about him; the guilt I've felt over his wife becoming a widow, his children being left without a dad. I've beaten myself up about it frequently.

'What's made you think about this?'

I know exactly why my relationship with Robert has been playing on my mind. It started with missing him when I was in Cephalonia, the joy of seeing him when I got back, the *need* to see him, a desire to spend time with him. More recently I've been longing for a kiss on the cheek to be him kissing my lips, or him holding my hand to help me over a stile, his hands exploring my body.

'I don't know; I like spending time with you, that's all. Come on.' I start walking, carefully finding my footing down the stepped path that winds past the wood. 'Let's get back; I've still got work to do. I'm being silly, that's all.'

I know how I feel, I know what I want to say to him, but the words won't come out. Words I realise I've only ever said to one man.

We walk the rest of the way back to the village in silence, both lost in our own thoughts. I think I've confused things further by starting a conversation I wasn't willing to finish. We reach Salt Cottage and say goodbye.

Before pushing open the gate I turn back to him. 'Come over tonight for a meal and we can talk more.'

'Oh Leila, I can't tonight, I need to be at the pub, we've got a Christmas party.'

'Another time, whenever you're free.'

'Tomorrow night?'

'Perfect.'

He arrives clutching a bottle of wine and leftover apple pie from the pub. It reminds me of the first time I met him when he welcomed me to Marshton with a friendly smile, a bottle and a box of biscuits. I usher him in and he follows me into the kitchen which is filled with the warm spicy-scent of mulled wine. I've dressed up, unsure whether intentionally or not, but the amount of clothes I discarded points to me wanting to impress him. In the end I opted for a gold top that sparkles, a short black skirt, black tights and ankle boots. I take Robert's coat and notice he's made an effort too, with fitted dark grey trousers and a shirt that hugs his chest.

'Mulled wine?'

'Why not.'

I scoop hot wine into two glasses and hand him one. The lamb tagine has been in the oven for a couple of hours adding to the potent scent of spices filling the kitchen. All I need to do is make cous cous to go with it and open a bottle of red wine. I only half listen to Robert telling me about some incident during last night's Christmas party at the pub; my thoughts are elsewhere, working out what I'm going to say to him this evening – or if I should say anything at all.

We eat at the kitchen table, a candle between us, the under-unit lights the only other light in the room against the all-encompassing darkness outside. I stir my tagine letting the cous cous soak up the rich juice.

'You seemed to want to say more on the Downs?' he says after a while, moving our conversation on from family to what's been playing on my mind all evening.

I nod but take my time, sipping my wine and swilling it around my mouth. I swallow and dab my mouth with my napkin. I look across the table at him. We're playing at romance – the candle on the table flickering soft light over his face. He's handsome, and so familiar with his dark grey-flecked hair, deep brown eyes, strong jawline with just the right amount of stubble, clean shaven but not brutally so. The laughter lines at the corner of his eyes are one of my favourite things about him, that he's been able to find so much joy in his life despite the sadness he's had to endure.

'Yeah, I did, but I wasn't sure if it was the right thing to say. I don't want to change things between us. Mess up our friendship.'

He frowns. 'Why would you mess up our friendship? Tell me anyway.'

I meet his gaze. 'I love you.'

It's not so hard to say the words after all.

He sets his wine down on the table, his eyes not faltering from mine.

'You do?'

Oh fuck; he doesn't feel the same way.

'Sorry, that came out of the blue, I didn't mean to drop something like that on you, I…'

'Leila.' He reaches for my hands. 'What I meant to say is, I love you too.'

'Really?'

'For so long. You have no idea.'

Three simple words have opened up a floodgate of emotions. His eyes glisten in the candlelight and tears well in my throat at the relief of finally saying how I've been feeling for such a long time.

I slide on to the chair next to him. His hands encircle my waist. I lean in and kiss him and we stay like that for, oh I have no idea for how long, kissing and laughing and kissing some more, while the candle wax pools on to the wooden table.

'You don't have to go.'

I leave it for him to decide. Perhaps admitting that we love each other is enough for one day, acting on it might be a bit too much.

But he surprises me. He takes my hand and leads me upstairs. Slowly, we discard our clothes, no rush, no urgency. I've always jumped into bed first and then got to know the person after, but with Robert it's different; I know him so well. His face, his personality, his history. It's a revelation peeling away his clothes to the strong, firm body beneath. My desire on the Downs to have him kiss me, his hands exploring comes true, as we end up entwined together on my bed.

This is what it feels like to really love someone.

Grey lights pours in through the window, and it looks white outside, the tree branches frosted, the deeper grey of the sky heavy with snow. We didn't even think about closing the blinds last night, but there's no one to witness our bedroom antics besides the birds flying between the trees.

Robert's lying beside me beneath the covers, his arm lying

across my stomach, looking at me.

'Morning,' I say. 'I always knew you'd be an early riser.'

'So, you've been thinking about us spending the night together for a while, have you?' He grins and kisses me.

'Actually, no, sex with you was the last thing on my mind. Being with you is what I've wanted for a very long time.' I catch his frown and laugh as I realise what I've said. 'Sex with you is fabulous though. What I mean is it's being with you that I've wanted for ages.'

'Oh Leila, you make me laugh.'

'Some things are worth the wait.' I run my fingers through his chest hair, smoothing my hand up to his stubbly cheek. He rolls on to his back and I lean over and kiss him.

'It's taken us long enough to get to this point.' He stares up at me, caressing my cheek. 'I told Sophie that I loved you when we had that Greek night at The Globe. Do you remember, you came out through the kitchen and caught us sitting on the wall deep in conversation.'

'I remember. Is that the night she told you she was pregnant before telling even me or Alekos?'

'I'd guessed and asked her outright.'

'I should have known you'd be the one to ask. You always say things straight.' I stop, realising he's always been straight with me about everything apart from his feelings towards me. 'Which makes me wonder why it's taken us so long to end up together. Why didn't you ever say something?'

His chest is hot against mine where I'm lying against him, my leg resting on his thigh, the duvet pulled up over us.

'Because I was afraid you wouldn't feel the same way.'

I smile and slide on top of him, my lips finding his again.

Pembrokeshire, 2010

'Are you going to tell me where we're going?'

'Nope. It'd spoil the surprise, wouldn't it?'

I slide my arms around his waist. 'I like you taking charge like this.'

'What I can tell you,' he says, looking down, his arms encircling me, 'is we're going to be away for the whole week and it's quite a long drive.'

He's not wrong about that. It's like being on a magical mystery tour, trying to work out where we're heading. I rule out up north when we begin to head south; rule out London or the south coast when instead of getting on the A11 to head down to the M25, we continue along the A14, bypassing Cambridge and over the many roundabouts through Milton Keynes. We stop for lunch at Stowe Landscape Gardens and have a picnic beneath shady trees while looking over the lake with ducks flapping across, birds singing, and sunshine casting mottled patterns through the leaves on to the dry grass.

I begin to get a feeling of dread when our cross-country journey looks like we're heading to Bristol. Maybe we're going to Devon or Cornwall and so we'd naturally need to bypass Bristol to get there. We do stop, to break the journey up, but it's at a country pub on the outskirts of Bath. Although I've been back to Bristol to visit friends, it's a relief to not be staying there with Robert. Too many memories and too much history.

It's an epic drive, literally from one side of the country to the other, almost to the furthest reaches of the Pembrokeshire coast. It's a place neither of us are familiar with, a long way from north Norfolk, Bristol, London or Sheffield, a remote location and one that doesn't remind us of anywhere or anyone from our past. I like that about Robert, his ability to understand me, to know what I'd like before I even realise it myself.

Our holiday cottage, a one-storey converted barn with pale grey stone and blue woodwork, is reached via a long driveway. It's late by the time we get there, and the cottage and its surroundings are so still and quiet, bathed in the fading rays of the sun, casting a magical glow over the place.

Robert turns off the engine and we ease ourselves out of the car, stretching our aching limbs. The peace is all-consuming with only birds singing in the trees and the distant sound of the sea.

'It's stunning.' I go round to the other side of the car and slip my arm in Robert's.

'And ours for the whole week.'

We drag suitcases from the boot and Robert retrieves the keys from the locked box to the side of the door. We go inside and switch on the lamps to reveal a cosy cottage with a long open-plan space with a living area and wood burner at one end, a dining table in the middle and the kitchen at the end nearest the front door. On the other side of the entrance hall is a bedroom with an en suite bathroom.

Mid-autumn is the perfect time of year, the weather dry and sunny and not too cold. Crunchy leaves coat the ground and twirl down from trees like multicoloured snowflakes. We light the woodburner and the glow of the fire instantly warms the room. There's no TV but I like that. There is a cupboard stacked full of board games and books, and I adore that Robert's chosen a place like this where we can be together, talk, walk, eat, sleep, play games, make love in front of the fire, talk some more. Pretty bloody perfect.

After a good sleep following our insanely long journey, we get up early and pack rucksacks, pull on walking boots and hike along the coastal path. We have a picnic on a grassy hill with the view of the sea, and then head back along the same path. The remoteness of the cottage is what makes it so special. We turn off the coastal path and take the worn track around the edge of a field. The low building of the old dairy only just pokes above the stone wall that surrounds the property. It doesn't overpower, letting the beauty of the countryside and coast make the impact instead.

We reach the end of the field and Robert stops and rests his rucksack on top of the wall. He searches for something in one of the pockets. He's been quiet for the last part of our walk, and I've been happy to walk in companionable silence too, soaking up the view from the clifftop path, the sun straining through high white cloud making the sea glimmer. I drop my rucksack on the ground and lean against the wall, gazing down the field to the seemingly endless sea.

Robert puts his rucksack on the flattened grass and stands next to me. He places a small black box on top of the wall between us and opens it. I stare at a silver band with a small but perfect sapphire at its centre.

'I've been thinking about how to ask you this for so long. In the end I decided I wouldn't try and plan it, I'd know the right moment.'

My hands are clammy, my mouth dry. I'm suddenly very aware of everything around us like time has slowed; the thudding of my heart, the buzz of a lazy bee bumbling past, the roar of the waves hitting the shore at the bottom of the cliff.

'I love you, Leila, so much. Will you marry me?'

There haven't been many times in my life when I've been lost for words, but this is one of them. The answer I want to say gets stuck in my throat and the silence grows, accentuated by the peace.

'Yes.'

He throws his arms around me and holds me tight. I can feel his heart beating against my chest, the dampness of his tears where his head is buried in the crook of my neck.

'You're serious? You really want to marry me?'

He pulls away and holds my face in his hands. 'Yes, Leila. Yes. There's nothing I want more.'

The lump in my throat and the warmth in my chest makes me realise how much I want this too, despite never thinking settling down was for me. I'm crap at commitment, at sharing my life with someone else, and yet I can't imagine being without him.

He takes the ring from the box and holds my hand in his. 'Shall we see if it fits?'

He slides it on to my finger and it's strange to see it there, knowing what it represents.

We sit together on the stone wall, our fingers entwined, our legs dangling, looking out over the field rolling down the hillside to where the cliff starts and the sea takes over. The enormity of the moment is not lost on me and I want to stay here, out in the open, soaking up the view and allowing myself time to process the millions of thoughts and emotions racing through my head. Our shoulders touch, and I can feel the warmth of his skin through his T-shirt against my bare arm. My left hand rests on my knee, the silver band with its tiny sapphire glinting at me.

'When you went to Cephalonia with Sophie and Thea, I missed you like crazy; I kept thinking what I'd do if you decided to stay there. The thought was unbearable. I knew before then I wanted to be with you, but I knew then that I wanted to marry you.'

I remember feeling bereft when I left Sophie and Thea behind, like a lost soul when I arrived back in Marshton alone; it was Robert who made me feel capable of moving on with life. His positivity, his assurances that not only would Sophie be okay in Greece, but I'd be okay back in the UK too. I realise now, it wasn't just his words that made sense and comforted me, but him. And there wasn't sex or any relationship crap to complicate things back then; just me and him, friendship and I realise now, love.

I wipe away a tear with my free hand and slide my fingers tighter with Robert's. 'You know, it was risky, asking me to marry you. I've never wanted to get married.'

'Then why say yes?'

'Because I love you and I don't have any real reason to say no.' My hand tenses. 'That came out wrong. You know what I mean, right?'

He laughs. 'What you mean is you never met the right person until you met me.'

That's sort of true, but I don't say that. I thought I had met the right person, a long time ago. That's so far in the past now, my love for Sophie's father and desire to make a life with him a blur of conflicting emotions.

There's no one to tell our news to. I know Robert wants this week to be just about us – I understand his choice of remote cottage, lack of mobile reception, so that these few days can be about him and me, no one else. I'm sure he'll tell Ben and Vicky our news the moment we get home, but part of me wants to share. It's a monumental moment in my life, one I never thought would happen and I feel the need to talk to someone, for Sophie, Jocelyn or Kim to reassure me that yes was the right answer.

I pour myself a large glass of wine instead, the ring on my finger catching my attention as I do. It feels strange, so grown-up, despite me being well and truly old enough to get hitched. I'm a bloody grandmother after all.

'I'll cook dinner.' Robert catches my hand as I place a glass of wine for him on the work surface. 'You relax.'

I kiss him and leave him armed with a sharp knife and a

chopping board, beef, garlic, bok choi and noodles out on the side. It's warm with the wood burner pumping out heat, so I escape outside, leaving behind the sound of sizzling as Robert chucks sliced beef into a wok. The difference in temperature is startling and I wrap my woolly cardigan tight around me as my breath plumes into the air.

The wine is cold and sweet. I sit on the picnic table outside the cottage, my feet on the bench, my elbows resting on my knees, holding the glass in my hands. What a day. I mean emotionally, it's been a slam dunk. I'm engaged, something I dreamt about when I was eighteen, but to Elliot, and then I stopped dreaming when I was nineteen and pregnant, and then the reality of being a single mum kicked in hard.

The black sky is peppered with stars; the silence reminds me of Marshton, except here there's not even the sound of an occasional car passing by, only the faint rush of waves on to the beach. We're so far from anyone or anything.

Getting married has never been something I've longed for. I've lived by the mantra that I'm not the marrying type, and yet here I am, fifty years old, and I've just said yes. Yes, to a man who's already been married to and lost the love of his life, the mother of his grown-up children. Robert knows what I'm like. He was aware of my sordid and doomed relationship with Darren; he was there to pick up the pieces after the accident. How did I not see Robert then, the way I see him now? Did it take disaster and the loss of someone's life for me to see sense, for me to truly change my ways?

Tears stream down my cheeks, dripping on to my trousers. Robert's clattering about in the kitchen. The yellow glow of lamplight through the cottage windows is inviting. I wipe away my tears with the edge of my sleeve, down the rest of my wine, jump off the picnic table and head inside to Robert.

Bristol, 2005

'Have you spoken to her?'

'Who?'

Jocelyn shakes her head. 'You know exactly who I'm talking about.'

I clasp my hands around my cup of tea and gaze out of Jocelyn's conservatory window at the greyness of a damp Saturday afternoon. 'No, I've not talked to her.'

'At all?'

'Not a word since she left and told me where to go in no uncertain terms.'

'So you've no idea how she's doing?'

'Oh, I know. Sophie talks to Candy who talks to her mum and I get the gossip from her.'

'And is there gossip?'

'Not really. Although it seems I was wrong about it not lasting with Alekos. She's been over there a year now – at least she seems able to do commitment.'

'Is it strange you've not met him?'

'It's strange not having Sophie in my life.' I reach for a biscuit and take a bite of the crumbly shortbread. 'I'm estranged from my own parents; the last thing I want is not to have any relationship with Sophie but I have no idea how to make amends. I fucked up; I know I dealt with the situation badly. I should have been open with her about her father, like

186

we've been open with each other about everything else.'

'She'll come round eventually.'

'I wouldn't be so sure; I know how stubborn she is.'

'Well then, let's take your mind off things and have a good night. Kim will be over soon.'

I nod and bite my lip. There are other things on my mind besides Sophie, stuff I've been thinking about ever since she left.

Kim arrives half an hour later, clutching a bottle of wine, and wearing a little black dress beneath her faux fur coat.

'In or out?' She follows us through the hallway and dining room, back out into the conservatory.

'Have you seen how much wine Leila brought with her?' Jocelyn points to the bottles on the conservatory windowsill.

'I was hoping we could stay in tonight,' I say.

Both of them look at me.

'You feeling okay?' Kim frowns.

'I need to talk to you about something.'

'Oh God.' Kim grabs the nearest open bottle and pours red wine into three glasses. 'I get the feeling we're going to need this.'

Jocelyn takes a glass. 'Let's go into the living room; it's freezing out here now.'

The wood burner is glowing and pumping out heat. I've always envied how meticulously clean and tidy Jocelyn's house is. Bold and quirky are ways to describe my house; classic and stylish fits with Jocelyn's decor. She's lived in the same house ever since I've known her and I've had countless heart to hearts with her at her kitchen table. She's my go-to person when I need someone to talk to.

I know I've unsettled them this evening; I'm always the one eager to go out, clinging on to my youth. And I do feel like I'm clinging on. Kim likes to party and she's been my perfect companion over the years, particularly after the breakdown of her first marriage and before she met Tim.

Jocelyn never was one for nights out, although she would occasionally join us on someone's birthday or for a special occasion. She does enjoy a good night in though.

Jocelyn and I sit on the large velvet sofa and Kim sinks down into the armchair next to us.

'You're not pregnant or something crazy like that, are you?' Kim asks.

I place my wine on the coffee table. 'I'm forty-five.'

'I know, but it is possible.'

'Actually, considering I've not had sex for ten months, it isn't.'

'Really?'

'And you know what, the last person I slept with, I don't even remember his name. How bad is that? I'm in my bloody mid-forties and still having one-night stands.'

'This is sounding very much like a mid-life crisis,' Jocelyn says. 'You know it's up to you what you get up to, right?'

'You've always been too good to me.' I pat her hand. 'I know it's up to me what I choose to do, it's just I'm unhappy with how I'm behaving. I don't know, ever since Sophie and I fell out and since she moved away, I feel like I need to do something to change. Get out of my bad habits.'

'So what are you going to do?' Kim asks.

I breathe deeply. 'I'm going to move.'

'You are?' Jocelyn frowns. 'Where?'

'Norfolk.'

'Norfolk?' They both look at each other, then back to me.

Kim frowns. 'Leila, that's 'effing miles away.'

'Yeah, I know. I've thought it through. Let me show you.' I go out into the hallway and grab the papers from my bag. I spread the house details out on the coffee table. Kim moves across and sits on the sofa and Jocelyn puts her reading glasses on.

'Salt Cottage.' Kim picks up the top sheet of the estate agent details and stares at the photo of the flint stone-fronted cottage.

'It's gorgeous,' Jocelyn says, 'but it looks a little rundown.'

'It looks a mess.' Kim frowns.

'Oh it is a mess.' I take a large gulp of wine. 'But I've already put in an offer.'

'You've what?' They say in unison again.

'I went up last weekend to look at it. It needs everything doing to it, ripping out and starting again, but seriously, it's got so much potential. And the garden and the view, I can't even describe how right it felt.'

'But what about your job?' Jocelyn takes off her glasses.

'I'm going to quit. I've not been happy there for ages. I want a new challenge, to do something I truly love, something for me. So, I'm going to start my own wedding planner business. Don't laugh, Kim.'

'Are you serious?' she asks. 'You're dead against marriage, how the hell can you plan a wedding?'

'Because it's someone else's. I'm not against other people getting married, it's just I don't want to. I'm a romantic at heart and love the idea of making couples' dreams come true. Plus, I'm sociable, great at organising, am creative. I did make-up parties for years to earn extra cash, I've done a bloody flower arranging course. For God's sake I ended up being the event organiser at work. I can do this – I *need* to do this. Anyway, someone's already asked me to organise their wedding.'

Jocelyn picks up her wine and looks at me. 'I understand the job thing, but you'll be leaving so much behind – the home you've worked so hard for, all your friends…'

'There's only you two I'm really going to miss – I don't have anything in common with other friends any more, we don't spend time together. Plus now Sophie's gone…'

'It's the other side of the country, Leila. What the hell am I going to do without you?'

'You still have Jocelyn.'

'Yeah, but Jocelyn's not going to go out clubbing with me, now is she.'

'Don't you think we're getting a bit old for clubbing?'

'Oh my God.' She looks at Jocelyn. 'Is this really the Leila we know?'

'I've got to do something. I can't see how my life is going to change by staying here.'

'But moving that far away?'

Kim puts her arm across my shoulders. 'But why do you feel you need to change? We love you exactly as you are, don't we, Joce?'

'Of course we do.'

'Until a year ago I was still screwing my ex-lodger. The only romantic relationships I have are either with married men or one-night stands. My relationship with Sophie is non-existent. I need to get away from city life, from all its vices. I need to just be me, somewhere where there are less distractions, less men, less everything.'

Kim laughs. 'You do realise there'll be men in Norfolk too, right.'

'Most of them farmers.' Jocelyn taps her glass against mine.

'Exactly, not the type I normally go for.' I down my wine. 'It's not just about my shitty choice in men. I need to do something for me. I've worked hard to get where I am but I've always wanted to start my own business, be my own boss. You know this. I want to use the skills I've learnt over the last few years and make something of myself.'

It's a more subdued night than we usually have. I don't think they fully believe that I'm really going to go through with it and move to the other side of the country. The bright lights of Bristol aren't enough to keep me here. However convenient it is to live in a city with bars, restaurants and shops on my doorstep, I'm longing for a change and a new challenge.

Norfolk, 2012

I'll never get over how peaceful Salt Cottage is. It was the first thing that struck me on the day I moved in – that and the reality of what I'd taken on – and it still takes me by surprise six years later. I sit on the step by the back door and soak up the peace before it's shattered by Sophie's arrival, and then my friends from Bristol. It's perfect June weather with blue sky and sunshine and I adore how much fresher it is over this side of the country away from the humidity of a city. The garden is blooming, the grass, speckled with daisies, is a luscious green, the tall trees by the fence at the end shade the edges of the lawn. Red, white and pink flowers dot the garden with colour, birds flit between the trees, and butterflies flutter over a hebe. It's one of the best times of the year for a wedding and I've had to turn down planning one because I've been planning my own.

I've missed Sophie like crazy, and Thea, oh my God how I've missed her. Skyping isn't the same and although I get to talk to her lots, I miss our cuddles and reading her a story while she curls her sticky fingers in my hair. I'm beyond happy that Sophie found her way and realised before it was too late that Alekos is the love of her life, but I'm sad that their happiness has meant them living thousands of miles away from me. To think how close I came to losing Sophie altogether. Without that accident who knows if we'd ever have spent enough time with each other to talk, work through the past and repair our relationship.

The sun has crept higher and floods the step with warmth. The scent of honeysuckle is stronger now. It reminds me of our old house in Hazel Road and my dream of a country cottage with honeysuckle climbing the walls. Of course that dream included Elliot, but the country cottage at least has come true. He's my past, and Robert's my future.

The sound of a car on the lane snaps me from my thoughts. I jump up and head through the kitchen and into the dimly-lit hallway. I open the front door and stand on the step with my hands on my hips. 'About bloody time, Sophie. It's quite something that I have to be getting married for you to come visit me.'

Sophie and I slot together again like we've never been apart. Although I'm desperate to see Thea, it's good to have this time alone with Sophie. Robert can't wait to see her too and it's like a proper family reunion heading to the pub for dinner with him and Ben. I keep an eye on Sophie and Ben from behind my sunglasses. Although Sophie chose Alekos in the end, I'm not one hundred per cent sure what really went on between the two of them. Becoming stepbrother and sister in less than two weeks' time might be a little weird if three years ago they were having sex. There's something there, a closeness, an awkwardness that suggests they were more than friends, but as to how far things went, I'll give them the benefit of the doubt. We're grown-ups, we've all moved on, settled down. It'll be fine.

The arrival of Jocelyn, Kim and Candy the next day, puts me in the mood for a party. The bonus of getting married is a hen party and getting to see my closest friends. Sophie's surprise at the sight of Candy emerging from the back seat of Jocelyn's car makes all the planning worthwhile. Surprising her with her best friend is the least I can do after tearing her away from

Thea and Alekos to come party with me back in the UK. It all feels rather selfish and overkill for a fifty-something bride-to-be.

But fuck it, I decide to embrace having a good time and let my hair down with my friends. Sophie and I have Pimms on the go and I have a whole afternoon of festivities planned with a picnic on the beach followed by fun and games back here afterwards.

I want my hen night to be as much about celebrating what I've achieved over the past few years as it is about me getting married. Sophie and a handful of close friends is all I need. It feels right to do something a bit more sophisticated than I would have done a few years ago. Once everyone's settled in at Salt Cottage, along with my local friends, Pamela and Philippa, we head along the coast to Wells-next-the-Sea for an afternoon on the beach.

I've never been jealous of what someone else has. In the past I've longed for a house of my own but I think it's only natural wanting somewhere to put down roots. I was never jealous of Jocelyn's beautiful semi in Bristol; I'd have been happy with a tiny flat – as long as it was my own. I made things work my own way – no big house and husband to support us. I went for the more interesting option of working all goddam hours and having multiple lodgers (Sophie may argue, lovers) over the years.

I'll admit, I am bloody jealous of Philippa's beach hut, though.

I love the beach at Wells and the wide expanse of sand that stretches endlessly when the tide's out, backed by a forest of pine trees and a line of sky-blue, sunshine-yellow, bubble gum-pink and mint-green beach huts. They're bloody expensive painted bits of wood, but there's something magical about them. I like the idea of having one in winter, when a cold wind whistles across the never-ending expanse of sand, grey churning sea in the distance. But inside the beach huts, that's where the magic happens, being able to look out on a windswept beach from the comfort of a blue and white cushioned sofa, a hot chocolate cupped in my hands, a blanket around my shoulders. I'd have one with a wood burning stove. The warmth would be enough to keep the door wedged open to watch the wildness of winter on the north Norfolk coast.

But it's June. High white clouds give glimpses of blue, and although it may not quite be bikini weather, our conversation is fuelled by the heat and romance of Greece, and spiced up with sex-on-the-beach revelations from Sophie and Candy, a refreshing change from it usually being me the one to have got up to no good.

My head is swimming with too much wine mixed with sunshine and a huge dollop of laughter; I can't remember the last time I felt this relaxed and at ease with a group of girlfriends. Full of food and wine, we drive back to Salt Cottage and clatter along the path through the garden to the front door. I pause, listening to the chatter and giggles fade as everyone else heads into the house, while I steal a moment to myself, breathing in rose and honeysuckle scented air, the sigh of the wind in the trees noticeable once the front door closes.

Back inside, I'm enveloped in laughter again. Sophie and I sort out nibbles and drinks and join everyone in the living room.

I lift my glass and look around. 'Cheers everyone, and thank you Jocelyn, Kim and Candy for coming all the way over here to help me celebrate, and for those of you who are flying out to Greece for our wedding, I appreciate it.' I stop and grin. 'Bloody hell, I'm getting married!'

The wine and gin keep flowing and the games get rowdier and more personal, most of them centred around me, which I guess is to be expected. Although I'm a wedding planner, most of my clients have been younger than me. 'Bride' feels like a foreign word, something that happens to someone else.

We're playing a bride-to-be-themed Truth or Dare, the dare part being me downing a shot. With my head already spinning I'm trying my hardest to answer the questions rather than get even more pissed.

It's Candy's turn to ask a question. She rests her elbows on her tanned knees and looks at me intently. 'When did you fall in love with Robert?'

'Oh good question.' Pamela claps her hands.

I push the shot glass away. 'I don't remember there being a specific moment when I "fell in love", but I do remember where we were when I realised I was in love with him and had been for a while.'

'Go on, tell us then, Leila,' Candy says.

I glance at Sophie. 'It wasn't long after I came back from Cephalonia and I was missing Sophie and Thea like crazy. Robert had been a real presence in my life for a while by then. I mean he'd spent Christmas with us and days off together, but I guess I'd always thought of him as a friend, nothing more, despite Sophie suggesting he wanted more.'

'He'd never said anything to you?' Philippa asks.

I shake my head. 'No. Although I sensed he'd be happy if we were closer, but I wasn't sure, you know, because of his past, having lost his wife.'

Candy leans closer. 'So what made you realise?'

'We went for a walk up to the Downs, something we did quite regularly. We could see for miles over to the windmill at Clay, and I had this sudden overwhelming feeling of contentment. I wanted to tell him I loved him but I couldn't find the words, but the feeling I had here.' I touch the centre of my chest. 'Well, I'd only ever been in love once before and that was an all-powerful feeling based on passion and lust for all the wrong fucking reasons, and yet being there with Robert… I don't know, in that moment just looking at each other and talking, it was so intimate.'

Sophie wipes a tear from her eye and I can feel myself welling up too; it's something I've not told anyone about before.

'Had you slept together?' Candy asks.

'No, that was the thing, we hadn't. I'd always thought of love as going completely hand in hand with sex – so to speak – but I remember looking at Robert and just thinking, "I love you".'

'But you didn't tell him?' Sophie asks.

'Not then, no. I needed time to process it, but a day or two later I did.' I smile at the memory.

'And?' Pamela says. 'What happened then?'

I reach for the shot and down it in one.

'Oh, you tease!' Pamela says.

'I bet that's when you slept with him,' Candy laughs, 'wasn't it?'

I tap the side of my nose. The burning sensation of tequila slides down my throat. Bloody hell, I need to go easy and avoid any more shots.

'Your turn, Kim,' Sophie says.

Kim waggles her drink at me. 'I'm not sure how you're going to top that story, so, how about telling us how many men you've slept with?'

'Oohs' echo around the room along with a gasp from Philippa. I'm not sure if she's shocked at the boldness of the question, but I sure as hell know she's going to be shocked by the answer.

'To be honest, I'm not actually sure of the number.' I pick up another shot of tequila from the coffee table and down it. 'I lost track and there never seemed any point trying to remember.'

Candy refills my shot glass and pushes it closer to me.

'Last one,' I say, 'else I'll be sick.'

'So, you'll be marrying Robert,' Jocelyn asks, 'but when are you actually going to move in with him?'

Kim looks at me. 'Yes, Leila, I mean you're going to be husband and wife in less than two weeks.'

I wriggle in the armchair, every part of me tensing as I place my drink on the coffee table and fold my arms.

'I'm not selling Salt Cottage and he's obviously not going

to sell The Globe. We both live and work in our homes. Makes sense to me to keep both running and a shame to see either of them empty. Not that The Globe would be empty, it's just easier for Robert to live there particularly when he works long hours and late nights.'

I'm pretty bloody certain I've made everyone feel uncomfortable. Jocelyn fiddles with her bracelet and I know she's dying to say something. Kim downs her wine and Philippa's rigid next to me, her hands firmly on her knees. I avoid eye contact with anyone but I sense Sophie and Candy watching me.

'But you sleep together, right?' Pamela asks.

'Yeah Leila, you must end up staying at each others' when you want to, you know…' Kim giggles.

'Yes, we sleep together. Of course we do.' I feel the need to justify my and Robert's arrangement, despite not thinking I should have to. 'I've never lived with anyone – well, not in a romantic sense. I used to have boyfriends who stayed over, Sophie can testify to that, and we had lodgers for a long time when we lived in Bristol. But I've never shared my house with a man I was in an actual relationship with.'

'That's the problem.' Jocelyn nods. 'You're still thinking along the lines of "my house" instead of "our house". Getting married and committing yourself to someone means it's not just you any longer. You've got to think of you and Robert as "us" from now on.'

I love Jocelyn to pieces and she's my oldest friend, but part of me wants to slap her. I get where she's coming from, happily married for decades, never having to think of herself as a single entity, she's always been part of an 'us', unlike me. Her comments get under my skin, so strongly worded – although it's probably the alcohol making her sound harsher than perhaps she meant. But there's a truth in them, and I think that's what truly pisses me off, that deep down I know by marrying Robert we need to commit in a more practical way too, and not just by enjoying warming each other's bed on occasions.

I'm a little subdued for the rest of the evening but only Sophie notices. Tiredness and alcohol hide a multitude of sins.

It's pretty bloody late by the time Philippa and Pamela head home and the rest of us call it a night. I flop down on my bed, Sophie next to me, both of us still in our clothes and what's left of our make-up, not even bothering to clean our teeth. I'm dead tired, but I'm too giddy with alcohol and thoughts to actually sleep. I gaze at the gap in the blinds, glimpsing the dark night. I wonder if Robert had a good evening, playing cards with his friends and Ben.

'Have you invited Grandma and Grandad?' Sophie's question cuts through the darkness.

I hadn't even realised she was still awake. 'Do you think I should?'

'It's not about what I think. It would be a way to make amends, that's all.'

I shuffle on to my side, so I'm looking at her. 'It was their fifty-fifth wedding anniversary last month and they had a big party – do you think they invited me? Did they invite you?'

'No. I just thought the gesture of an invite might bridge the gap between you… Between us all.'

'My wedding to Robert is for close family and friends. On my side that's you, Alekos and Thea and what, the three friends of mine who are coming over to Cephalonia with us. Everyone I care about will be there.' I rest back against the pillows. 'Anyway, I have nothing to make amends for. I'm done with my parents punishing me for screwing around when I was a teenager. I'm fifty-two bloody years old, not a naive eighteen-year-old desperate to gain back their respect. I lost respect for *them* a long time ago when they sided with the man who was old enough to know better, rather than supporting their own daughter. I'm done with being a disappointment.'

'You really think they're still disappointed in you?'

'I wouldn't put it past them. But you know what, I don't

care.'

'Do they even know you're getting married?'

I let the silence between us grow. I pull the sheet up, suddenly feeling chilly. 'I phoned Mum on their wedding anniversary to congratulate them. She told me about the party they were having that weekend. She didn't have to tell me *he* was going to be there, but I knew that was the reason I wasn't invited. So I told her I was getting hitched. She sounded shocked, but I guess when your daughter is in her fifties by the time she gets married, shock is the natural reaction.'

Sophie sighs. 'I haven't spoken to Grandma since we went up to confront Elliot. They've never met Thea. I emailed them a photo but they never replied. I even said they could come and stay with us. I sent them all the details and left it up to them, but nothing. It's sad that Thea doesn't know her English great-grandparents.'

'There are a lot of things about our family that make me sad.' I take Sophie's hand and squeeze it. 'I hate how they're punishing you and Thea for my mistakes. But you, well I'm damn proud of you and how you turned out, particularly having me as a mother.'

'You shouldn't put yourself down,' Sophie says slowly. 'I may have had an unconventional childhood and you may not have been a traditional mother, but I wouldn't change it for the world. Except maybe that lodger, you know, the one who used to smoke pot in his attic bedroom. Oh and that other one – the two of you used to make the headboard of your bed bang against the wall a lot…'

Despite the darkness, I hide my head in my hands. I haven't thought about Owen in a long time. 'I was a nightmare – what the hell was I thinking? Seriously, how you turned out the way you have is a bloody miracle.'

'I think I rebelled against what I knew, so ended up being good rather than going off the rails. If you'd been a teetotal, happily married, calming influence I probably would have rebelled against that and been a nightmare teenager. I was always more worried about you and what twat of a bloke you were seeing.'

'And it's taken me more than fifty years to grow up.'

'And here you are, days away from your wedding to Robert. Definitely not a pot-smoking, horny twenty-something lodger.'

'He's about as far from that as you can get.' I laugh. 'I'm not sure he even smoked anything when he was young.' She turns to me. 'What the hell does he even see in me?'

'You seriously have to ask? You're a mature version of who you've always been – the best of both worlds. The same wicked sense of humour, feistiness, beauty. Crazy and lovable.'

'You've drunk too much.'

'Couldn't agree with you more. I need to sleep. This whole room is moving.'

'See, even on my hen do I'm a bad influence. We'll regret tonight with the hangovers we're going to have in the morning.'

'Just as well you stocked up on all that bacon and eggs.'

'Sophie please, shut up about food.' I gag at the thought and close my eyes. The room continues to spin beneath my eyelids. I focus on thinking about Robert, his booming laugh, that glint in his eyes, the firmness as he envelops me in his arms. My husband-to-be.

Cephalonia, 2012

Sophie, Robert, Ben, Candy, Jocelyn, Kim, Pamela and I, make the journey together to Cephalonia. It's a three-hour drive to Gatwick, followed by a nearly four-hour flight, and another hour's drive across the island to Birdsong Villas. I've been here four times now. The first was when I went over with Sophie when Thea was only a few weeks old. It's strange being here with other people, even stranger bringing Robert here and thinking this is where we'll be getting married. I get butterflies in my stomach at the thought. Is this pre-wedding jitters? I'm a bloody wedding planner, I hear about brides' nerves all the time, but still it unsettles me. This nervous feeling makes me doubt myself, reminding me that marriage is not something I've ever wanted. At least not since Elliot.

Yet seeing Sophie and Alekos back in each other's arms, Thea hugging their legs is enough to make anyone believe in true love. A picture of happiness against the backdrop of Birdsong Villas, all whitewashed walls, red-tiled roofs, with splashes of deep purple bougainvillea, pink roses and the green and browns of the olive tree in the courtyard. Add to that blue sky, endless sea and sunshine, and it's perfection.

The place is packed with people: my friends, Robert's family, Alekos' parents, larger than life Despina and quiet Takis, and there are more people to arrive later in the week. We're shown around and everyone has time to get settled, and while Despina makes frappes, Sophie and Thea show me to my and Robert's room.'

'Oh this is lovely.' I run my hands over the mustard yellow bedspread, a brighter version of the colour on the walls. The bed is piled high with pillows and cushions making me want to dive right in. A sofa faces the bi-fold doors that open out on to a small veranda overlooking the courtyard and sea.

'The best room reserved for the soon-to-be newly-weds.'

'Thank you, Sophie.' I slide my arm around her waist.

Thea clambers on to the sofa and kneels in front of us, her arms resting on the back of it. 'I picked the flowers from the garden.' She points to a vase filled with purple bougainvillea.

'Beautifully chosen. I can't believe I'm back here, and for my wedding too.' It doesn't seem quite real and the thought of '*my* wedding' is still an alien concept.

'It's going to be amazing,' Sophie says.

'So there's only this room up here?'

'Yep, complete privacy.' She leans closer and lowers her voice. 'No need to worry about the headboard banging against the wall.'

I slap her hand. 'Bloody hell, Sophie Keech, as if.'

She raises an eyebrow. 'Anyway, the communal living and kitchen area for the guest rooms is directly below, but this is separate.'

'Was this not done a year ago?'

'The bit downstairs was, and the other guest rooms, but not up here.'

'Well, it's beautiful, thank you.'

It is beautiful and I'm so proud of what Sophie and Alekos have achieved *and* that they've managed to work through their problems and come out the other side happy. I sense there's less stress for Sophie even with Despina here – not living under the same roof as Alekos' parents has obviously done a world of good for both of them.

We all rub along together, a wonderful mix of friends and family – a fusion of Greek and British. Dinner is a noisy and lively affair, all squeezed around the large table in the courtyard beneath the olive tree. Not long afterwards, one by one, people head to bed; Thea first, then Despina and Takis, Jocelyn and Pamela. Robert and I leave Kim and Ben having a smoke by the pool, and we wave to Sophie and Candy who are sitting together on the courtyard wall. We head up the steps to our room.

'Well, we're finally here.' Robert closes the door behind us. 'All the talk and planning that's gone into it and we're only days away.'

I switch on the lamp on the dressing table. Warm light spills across the flowers Thea picked. 'It feels like Sophie's done all the planning; we've just turned up to have a good time and make it happen.'

'It was a good decision though deciding to have the wedding here.'

'Neutral ground for both of us, makes sense.' I don't need to say more for him to understand what I mean. We're nowhere near my parents or my past, and being in Greece there's less chance of Robert being reminded of his wedding to his wife Jenny.

I sweep my hair back into a short ponytail and wipe my face clean of make-up. Through the mirror I watch Robert pull his T-shirt over his head, fold it and place it neatly on the back of the sofa. In the lamplight his chest is defined, his wedding ring on a chain nestled against his chest hair. He takes it off and puts it next to his book on the bedside table. He always takes it off at night; I'm not sure either of us would be comfortable with him wearing it while we're sleeping together, but I like the idea he keeps her close. It's a strange thing how the two loves of our lives are so very different to one another and how they've managed to keep a hold on us for so long yet in such different ways. He won't ever forget about Jenny or stop loving her, while the only way I've been able to move on was to let Elliot go.

My thoughts are interrupted by Robert kissing my neck. He meets my eyes through the mirror and slides his hand across my collarbone without dropping his gaze.

'If you're too tired, just say so.' He grins as he slips the spaghetti strap off my shoulder.

'I have a reputation to uphold. I'm no old married woman yet…' I stand and push him towards the bed. 'I've also had a bit too much to drink, so I don't really know what I'm saying.'

'I can tell.' He reaches for my hands and pulls me down on the bed until I'm straddling him, our faces inches away from each other. He kisses me and I kiss him back, unable to get Sophie's comment out of my head about the headboard banging against the wall…

I love everyone being here together. I've always been sociable and liked having people around, until my escape to Norfolk where the peacefulness was a tonic. Now I feel ready to embrace my sociable side again. The first couple of days fly by, a whirl of food, drink, laughter, lounging by the pool, sunbathing on the beach, more food, more drink. Sophie and Alekos, along with Despina and Takis, look after everyone, and I'm grateful that I get to spend time with Thea when she's here, and my friends and Robert when she's at pre-school.

I like how everyone is happy to do their own thing. On our third day when Robert's gone for a walk and Jocelyn and Pamela have taken a taxi to Omorfia, Kim and I grab a blanket and sit out in the garden, bare legs and arms on show, topping up our tans. After a while Sophie joins us. She dumps a basket of washing on the grass and brings a drink over for us.

'I must be getting old.' I sip refreshing sour cherry juice and look at Sophie. 'The thought of a few peaceful hours doing bugger all was far more enticing than traipsing around shops in this heat.'

'And quite frankly,' Kim says, 'I don't feel there's any need to leave this place. It's truly stunning, Sophie. Your mum was telling me what it looked like when you first arrived. Hard to believe really.'

'It's taken more than three years of hard work to get it looking like this, but yeah, it's a dream come true.' She looks at me. 'Remember thinking I was crazy leaving the UK for Greece to move in with a man I'd only known for a few weeks *and* scoffing at my idea of setting up a creative retreat.'

'I did and said a lot of things I wish I hadn't.'

'Me too.'

'I also had a rather negative view about falling in love so quickly and giving up everything for what I perceived to be just a holiday romance.'

'It was brave moving to Greece to be with Alekos,' Kim says. 'I'd never have had the guts to do something like that.'

'Sophie was properly in love. To be honest at the time I didn't believe you were really in love. I figured you'd had some great sex and had fallen in lust with a good looking Greek. I thought you were going to get your heart broken. I guess my experience of men and meaningless flings led me to believe that. I was very happy to be proven wrong.'

'Despite all my ups and downs with Alekos.'

'That's life. If everything was straightforward and easy it'd be boring.'

'True,' Kim says. 'I could do with some excitement in my life. Married for flipping donkey's years, kids at uni now and hubby can't be bothered going out, would rather spend the night in watching football. I miss you living in Bristol, Leila. I can't tell you how much I've been looking forward to this time away with you all.'

'Your husband didn't mind you coming out here on your own?' Sophie asks.

'Are you kidding? He couldn't wait for bit of peace and quiet for a couple of weeks. We're quite happy doing our own thing most of the time. It works fine for us.' She rests back on her hands and looks at Sophie. 'Do you and Alekos get to spend much time together?'

'Well, we work together so pretty much spend most of the time with each other.'

'I mean together when you're not working?'

'Not really.'

I put my glass down on the dry grass. 'You two should go out, make the most of everyone being here to look after Thea. Spend some quality alone time with Alekos.'

'Mum, this is your time before you get married to do what you want to do.'

'And I want to spend time with my granddaughter. You and Alekos too, and my friends of course, but mostly time with Thea.'

'Take the opportunity while you can,' Kim says. 'When was the last time you and Alekos had a night out?'

'Without Thea or anyone else?' Sophie frowns. 'I honestly can't remember.'

'Seriously, Sophie, take as much time out as you want this week – there are plenty of people here to look after Thea, not least of all me and Robert and Alekos' parents. Also, you've got Candy here and you two never get to spend time with each other any longer. I'm sure she needs the company after the year she's had with her cheating good-for-nothing ex.'

Sophie pushes her sunglasses down her nose and looks at me. 'Lack of company is not a problem for Candy at the moment.'

'What do you mean?'

'Really, Mum, you of all people haven't noticed what's going on?'

I shake my head.

Kim sits up and leans closer to Sophie. 'There's gossip we're missing out on?'

'Candy and Ben.'

'Oh I can tell they like each other.' I shrug. 'But then Candy has always been a flirt, it doesn't tend to mean anything.'

'It does this time.'

'They've slept together, haven't they?' Kim asks.

'They have?' I wedge my sunglasses into my hair and look at Sophie. 'And how do you feel about that?'

'Why would Sophie care?' Kim frowns. 'Oh do you mean because Sophie and Ben are going to be stepbrother and sister? Actually, I don't understand, why would that matter?'

'Sophie and Ben had a fling…'

Kim turns to her. 'You did?'

'A fling in the sense that we liked each other a lot, spent time together, got on well as friends, messed about a bit…'

'You really didn't do the dirty deed with him?'

'Mum, how many times do I have to tell you, we didn't have sex.'

I hold my hands up. 'Okay, okay, I'm sorry, I'm just making sure. There's such an awkwardness between you and Ben, and Ben and Alekos, it's easy to make assumptions.'

Her cheeks are flushed. She folds a piece of grass between her fingers.

'Well yes, that's because I did cheat on Alekos with Ben. We kissed, we had a bit of a fumble and I had every intention of having sex with him. I came to my senses in time when I found out I was pregnant with Thea. And of course there's going to be awkwardness between us all. Remember Alekos punching Ben?'

'How could I forget.'

'The whole situation was a mess but it was what pushed us into sorting our lives out. Not long after moving out here Alekos told me that without really thinking he'd lose me to Ben, he'd never have had the motivation to move out from home and buy this place. My ill-fated relationship with Ben was both the worst and best thing to happen to us. I just don't know how we can all move on from this awkwardness? I mean, Ben's going to be my stepbrother, which in itself is a messed up situation seeing as though our relationship started with us fancying each other… Alekos hates him, Candy is sleeping with him… I don't know how we can all get past the issues we have with each other.'

It is a mess, but only because Sophie's making more of it than there needs to be. It's in the past; time they all moved on. Knowing I usually say the wrong thing, I bide my time before saying, 'Go on a double date.'

Kim laughs. 'That is such a bad idea. Sophie, don't listen to her.'

'No seriously, it's genius.' I lean forward. 'I promise you the last thing Robert and I want on our wedding day is unresolved tension between our children. The four of you should go out, get drunk, have some fun. Maybe if Alekos and Ben got to know each other they could get past their issues.'

'Mum, a minute ago you were urging me to have a romantic night out alone with Alekos. Now you're suggesting we double date with my best friend who's shagging the man I briefly considered leaving Alekos for.'

'Well, when you put it like that…'

She folds her arms. 'How about this for an idea. We could wait until Demetrius and Katrina get here and all go out together. Then we can add extra tension by Candy having slept with Demetrius too.'

'Okay, now you're getting silly.'

'Is Demetrius the one Candy had the fling with when you met Alekos?' Kim asks.

'Yeah, he's Alekos' best friend. They were sailing a boat here when we first met them.'

'There's just too much gossip to keep up with.' Kim sighs. 'My life is so boring compared to yours.'

'Trust me, boring is sometimes good.'

'Maybe my idea of a double date is a bad one, but somehow you need to sort out the situation with Ben. Maybe it's a good thing he's with Candy; it can prove to Alekos that he's moved on. But Sophie,' I hook my arm in hers, 'why are you still feeling awkward about Ben? What happened is in the past and things between you and Alekos are good aren't they?'

She nods.

'You don't still have feelings for Ben, do you?'

'No.' Her cheeks flush redder. 'No, I don't. I don't even think I had real feelings for him back when I was living with you, but…'

'But what?'

'I don't know, it's just being back in Marshton for your hen do and seeing Ben again stirred up the past. It was a weird feeling. And the things he said and did…'

'Like what?' I ask. 'I knew there was something odd going on.'

'He still has feelings for you, doesn't he?'

'I think you've hit the nail on the head, Kim.' I turn back to Sophie. 'There's the problem; Ben isn't over you.'

'Don't be silly; if he wasn't over me, he wouldn't have slept with Candy.' She scrambles to her feet.

'Really? Not even to make you jealous?'

'I better get on with stuff.' She walks back across the grass to the basket of wet washing.

'Well, that was fun; I love a bit of gossip,' Kim says.

'You and me both.'

'Do you think she's telling the truth?'

'Who knows.' I watch her pull clothes from the basket and peg them on a line strung between two trees. 'I think she's tried so hard all her damn life to not be like me when it comes to men, I'm not sure she'd want to admit cheating on Alekos and having an affair.'

'You've never slept with Ben, right?'

I pull my sunglasses to the end of my nose and stare at her. 'Oh my God, Kim. What a question. No, absolutely not. He's Robert's son. I know I've made some questionable choices in the past when it comes to men, but there is a limit.'

She holds her hands up. 'I was just checking that nothing happened before you got together with Robert.'

'Before we got together we were friends.'

I know she's thinking what's the difference, after all I

shagged my parents' best friend. But that *was* different, I was so young. Whatever anyone thinks of me, I do have some standards now I'm older, lines that should never be crossed.

Cephalonia, 2012

It's a melting pot of emotions for Sophie, with everyone being together at Birdsong Villas, the past crashing into the present. I realise that once again I'm partly the cause, the same way I was the one to mistakenly reveal the truth about her father, my upcoming marriage to Robert is what's brought us all together. If Sophie does have unresolved feelings for Ben – and vice versa – they're having to work them out within the confines of the retreat and with the ever watchful eyes of parents and lovers on them. I think it's a good thing really; a chance for everyone to move on and put the past to rest. I manage to say the wrong thing again a day or two later when we're all relaxing around the pool and the conversation turns to men. Actually this time it's not totally my fault; Candy lets slip that Ben's been talking to her about what he and Sophie got up to – or didn't get up to more to the point. So together we manage to piss Sophie off completely. Her anger finally convinces me that she's been telling the truth all along about Ben and I need to stop asking her about it if she's ever going to be able to move on. Kick the past to the kerb where it belongs.

Alekos' old band turning up – my one request for the wedding – messes things up further as Alekos' past gets dragged up too. The lead singer, Aphrodite is, to put it bluntly, fucking stunning. I mean, I've always been pretty damn comfortable in my skin, but I'm jealous as hell of Aphrodite and her perfect hourglass figure, perfect skin, perfect hair and perfect bone structure. Everyone notices her, and I mean everyone. Men and women. Before things even kick off between Aphrodite, Sophie, and Alekos, I know without a doubt that Alekos had a relationship with her back when he was living and working on the island before he fell in love with Sophie.

The place is filled with gossip again, tension simmering as Sophie, Aphrodite and Alekos verbally thrash things out in the courtyard beneath the olive tree. We don't hear much from round by the pool, but Sophie and Alekos' friends Katrina and Demetrius fill us in on what's going on, and then Alekos comes and finds me.

'Everything all right?'

'Can we go somewhere quieter.'

I put my book down, glance at Jocelyn and Kim and follow Alekos to the edge of the pool.

'Sophie's talking to Aphrodite.' A frown pinches his dark eyebrows together. 'She overheard Demetrius and Aphrodite talking and got the wrong end of… What's the saying when you don't understand something?'

I smile. 'The wrong end of the stick.'

'Exactly.'

'We have some odd sayings. What did she misunderstand?'

'That I had an affair with Aphrodite before she came over here with Thea.'

'And you didn't?'

He shakes his head. 'No, I didn't.'

'But you were together before?'

He reaches for the cross around his neck and folds it between his fingers. 'Yes, before I met Sophie.' He gestures over the wall to the path that cuts down the hillside. 'I'm not sure what Aphrodite is telling her, but I hope it's the truth.'

'Well, as long as you're telling the truth, then I'm sure

she'll believe you, the same way you believed her about Ben, right?' It feels a little like I'm playing with fire bringing Ben up, particularly after some of the conversations over the last couple of days, but I now know Sophie didn't sleep with Ben and I hope to God Alekos believes her.

He runs his hands through his dark hair and nods, glancing to where Sophie and Aphrodite are, hidden by foliage on the hillside. 'Yes, I believe her.'

'Relationships are complicated at the best of times. But as long as you love Sophie, she loves you, and you trust each other, what else is there to worry about?'

With my history, I should be the last person giving relationship advice, but I guess Robert's changed me, and I'm nearly married. Maybe I do know my stuff.

Alekos nods but I'm not sure he's convinced that everything will be okay. 'Hopefully there's nothing to worry about, but that's why I want to do something nice for Sophie. I'm going to take her to the beach.'

'As in *the* beach.'

'To remind us of happy times.'

'I bet.' I raise my eyebrows.

'Not like that.' He grins.

'Yeah right.' I nudge his arm.

'I'm going to go wait by the car; can you tell Sophie when she comes back up to meet me at the top of the drive, please?'

'Of course.'

'Oh, and don't tell her where we're going. And Thea, will you be able to pick her up with Baba and look after her…"

'Alekos yes, I'll look after Thea, don't worry. You and Sophie need some time together. Go fix the misunderstanding and remember why you two got together in the first place.'

'Thanks, Leila.'

He hugs me and saunters off across the courtyard, his shoulders hunched, his hands in his short pockets, like the weight of the world is dragging him down.

I'm not good at waiting; too bloody impatient. I hover by

the gate to the pool so I can see the top of the hillside path. The moment Sophie appears I wedge my sunglasses in my hair and stride over, meeting her in the middle of the courtyard.

'I've been waiting for you. Alekos said you were talking to Aphrodite. Everything okay? Alekos seemed worried.' I realise I'm holding my breath, worry for Sophie and Alekos coursing through me too.

'Everything's fine. It will be fine.' Her eyes are red from crying and she looks as worried as Alekos did.

'Alekos said to meet him at the top of the drive. I'm going with Takis to pick Thea up later and I'll look after her this evening.'

'Okay great. Where am I going?'

'No idea, but Alekos said he's taking you somewhere special.' She turns to go and I catch her hand. 'By the way, I'm sorry about earlier, around the pool. I'm sorry I doubted what you told me about you and Ben. As you well know, I can be a dick at times.'

'I know,' she says with a smile which lights up her face. 'You don't need to tell me that.'

I kiss her cheek. 'Go find Alekos. Get out of here; I'll look after Thea.'

Thea's exhausted and in bed by eight-thirty. I know Sophie's had her issues with Despina, but she's a bloody saint feeding us all. While Sophie and Alekos are out for the evening rekindling their love on that beach, Aphrodite and the band pack up early and head back to their hotel in Omorfia, and the rest of us, once the kids are asleep, spend what's left of the evening by the pool, drinking wine and cocktails.

Robert's spent most of the afternoon and evening with Vicky, Ben, and his grandchildren playing in the pool, so I've not even had a chance to chat with him. It's late by the time he comes over and sits with me.

'Everyone's been talking about the commotion with

Aphrodite earlier.' He hands me a glass of something fruity and fizzy with a wedge of pineapple and an umbrella. 'Is Sophie okay? I've not seen her all evening. Or Alekos for that matter.'

'They've gone out. And it's all fine, a big misunderstanding by all accounts; nothing a romantic night out won't fix.'

My head is fuzzy from a bit too much to drink. The beat of Oasis' 'Supersonic' floats into the night along with shrieks from Vicky and Kim in the pool where Demetrius is attempting to teach them how to hit a blow-up ball like a volleyball. Now Robert's left them alone, Ben and Candy are on the far side of the pool snogging in the shadows.

'I'm heading to bed.' He touches my arm. 'You don't have to come up yet. Stay and have fun with your friends.'

'What time is it?'

'Nearly midnight.'

'That late? I thought Sophie and Alekos would be back by now.'

I get a stab of fear in my chest that something awful has happened to them, driving back along dark winding Greek roads. It's a long drive to their beach, particularly after the emotions of the day, and my imagination's getting the better of me thinking bad things happening instead of them having fun somewhere.

'I'm sure they're fine; probably snuck in earlier and headed to bed.' He slides his hand on to my thigh. 'You still fancy going to that winery tomorrow?'

'You bet.'

'We need to leave early. Do you think you'll be up and ready in time?'

I smile. 'I'll make this my last drink, I promise.'

Cephalonia, 2012

I struggle to wake up, my head a cocktail fog. Robert's annoyingly bright as a button, but I forgive him when he brings me a cup of tea in bed and doesn't hassle me to get up. His thoughtfulness is just one of the many reasons I love him. I manage to drag myself out of bed and blast my body with a lukewarm shower. I pull on a long white gypsy-style skirt and a burnt-orange cap sleeved top, slick on lipstick and mascara, towel dry my hair and leave it to dry naturally. By the time I emerge into sunshine and pull on sunglasses, I feel about ready to face the day.

Robert insists it's fine for Jocelyn, Kim and Pamela to join us. They're good company as we tour the vineyard. The lush greenness of the vineyard with the backdrop of tree-clad hills, contrasts with rocky outcrops, purple in the sunshine. We get to try plenty of the wine too. I have this weird sense of looking down on us, a feeling of total contentment that life can't get much better than this, standing in a beautiful location with Robert and my best friends, knowing Sophie's not far away happy with Alekos and Thea, their relationship back on track. The warm fuzzy feeling continues over a lunch of olives, bread, grilled cheeses, hummus and Greek salad, along with more wine.

We arrive back at Birdsong Villas and Robert closes the gate behind us. Laughter and chatter drifts across the courtyard as Kim, Jocelyn and Pamela head to their rooms, each carrying a bottle of wine, their sandals tapping across the paving.

Robert takes my hand and we wander towards our room. We stop before reaching the steps. I turn to him. 'That was a fabulous morning, thank you.'

'I thought you'd enjoy a wine tour.'

'You know me too well.'

He kisses me. 'I'm going for a siesta. You fancy joining me?'

'For a siesta or something else?'

He grabs my waist. 'Whatever you fancy.'

'I'll be up after I've seen Sophie.'

He kisses me again and I watch him saunter over to the steps that lead up to our room. Even though he's older than the men I've gone for in the past, he looks damn good with his salt and pepper hair and broad shoulders. He's muscular and fit, and a good bloke all round. A family man. I could pinch myself that after all these years of making bad choices, lusting after unobtainable men, I've finally found someone as wonderful as Robert.

He disappears into our room, and I push open the patio doors of the villa and step inside. It takes a second for my eyes to adjust from the brightness outside. Sophie's next to the fridge, clasping a glass of water, facing a woman standing in the middle of the room.

I frown. 'Sophie?'

She turns and knocks over the glass, splashing water on to the work surface.

'Where's Robert?' she asks as I close the door.

'Gone up to our room. I came to find you.' I look from Sophie to the woman. I step closer, confused at why she's so familiar.

'Sophie, what the hell's going on?'

The woman turns to Sophie. 'Will you please let me talk to your mum?'

'Oh my God,' I say slowly. 'You're Elliot's daughter, aren't you?'

'Mum, I'm so sorry, she turned up wanting to talk to you…'

I can't stop looking at her; she's an older version of Sophie, the same red hair, same features, same spitting image of their bloody father. It's like a ghost's walked in.

Sophie turns to Amy. 'You can go upstairs to talk.' Her voice trembles. 'No one will disturb you up there. My room's the last one on the right.'

With my heart thumping, I go past Sophie and walk up the stairs, not waiting for Amy. I feel like I'm in a dream, nothing's quite real, the edges of the landing fuzzy. I don't understand why she's here; she's the last person I expected to see the day before my wedding.

My sandals slap across the tiled floor of Sophie and Alekos' room. I stand in front of the bed, fold my arms and wait. It smells of Sophie's perfume. Warm air drifts in through the open window.

Amy closes the door behind her. 'I'm sorry for turning up like this…'

'Are you? Really? You seem to have pissed Sophie off.' And she's barely said anything to me and she's already pissing me off when I should be curled up in bed with Robert, sleeping off too much wine and tapas. 'Why are you here?'

Her cheeks are flushed and the confidence she had downstairs with Sophie has evaporated now she's alone with me. I'm only eight years older than her.

'Mum and Dad are getting divorced.'

It takes a moment for her words to sink in.

I shake my head. 'I don't understand.'

'Mum met someone else and they're moving in together. Dad's moved out and they're selling the house.'

I look at her, unable to fully comprehend. If I glance at her quickly I could almost believe it's Sophie standing in front of me, but their dress sense is different, and Amy's hair is shorter, her face older. She reminds me so much of her father. I clench my fists and fight back tears, wanting to, *needing* to hold it together.

'They're divorcing?'

She nods, her lips thin and tense, and I realise she's trying to contain her emotions too.

'It all happened suddenly, literally over the last few weeks. Mum decided she'd had enough; she'd met this new man a couple of years ago at the National Trust house she volunteers at of all places. He's a widower, was looking for love and Mum fell for him. It came as a total shock for Dad; I don't think he had a clue Mum was having an affair.'

I sit with a thump on the end of Sophie and Alekos' bed. 'You're telling me your mum has split with your dad because *she's* been having an affair?'

Amy nods.

I feel bombarded. Conflicting thoughts and emotions pummell me from every side, hijacking any reasonable chain of thought.

I smooth my hands down my skirt and stare down at my feet, nicely tanned from a few days beneath the Mediterranean sun. My toenails are freshly painted, a deep red against the pale grey tiled floor. I play her words slowly over in my head.

'You said she'd had enough? What do you mean?'

Amy meets my gaze, her green eyes bright with tears. 'Mum's always known about Dad's affair with you.'

I stand and pace across the room. All this time and she knew. All the time we spent hiding the truth, hiding Sophie and me, and yet she'd always known. I turn back to Amy. 'Why the hell did she stay with him for so long if she knew?'

'Why do you think? What else was she supposed to do? She had three young children, was a housewife, had no way of supporting herself, and she loved him. She told me that once she knew you'd left home and moved to Bristol, she felt Dad had made his decision to stick by her and us. That was enough for her at the time.'

The crazy thing is I've waited more than thirty bloody years to hear someone tell me that Elliot and his wife are getting a divorce. And now those words are being said, I feel numb.

'Your timing is beyond fucking awful.'

'I know, but I couldn't not tell you. All I've been able to think about these last few weeks is wouldn't my parents have been so much happier if they'd separated years ago. Mum's with someone she loves and who seems to unconditionally love her, and Dad, well he's lost without you.'

Her words slice through me, gutting me with their impact.

'*He's* lost without me?' I stare at her, every part of me tense and fighting a desire to punch the wall. 'I've been lost my whole fucking life, constantly in limbo with every relationship I've had because Elliot's always been there in the back of my mind.'

'I get that; I've seen the regret Dad's had over the past few weeks…'

'Regret for what? For losing me thirty years ago or ending up losing his wife after all?'

She shrugs. 'The only thing I know is he loves you. I wanted you to have the opportunity to decide who you love before it's too late.'

'Before it's too late? Are you for real? Get out,' I say through gritted teeth, conscious the window's open, unsure if anyone's outside and able to hear, but definitely not wanting Robert to catch any of this conversation or hear my anger.

'Leila, please.' She steps towards me. 'Just think things through; talk to my dad.'

'Did you not hear me?'

She puts her hands on her hips, her defiance reminding me of arguments with Sophie. 'Where do you want me to go?'

'I don't give a fuck where you go but away from here.'

Tears roll down her lightly freckled cheeks and a small part of me wants to wipe them away and hug her. Apart from her bad judgement of coming here, she's not the one who's to blame.

'How long have you known about me and your dad?'

She wipes away her tears with the back of her hand. 'A few weeks. Only since Mum broke the news to us that she was divorcing him.'

'You had no idea?'

She shook her head. 'We were just kids. I know you're not that much older than me, but at the time I was what nine or ten? I had no clue. None of us did. Apart from Mum.'

'Don't you dare go out through the courtyard; go out the back way, there's a gate to the lane at the far end of the garden.'

She nods and walks over to the door, pausing as she opens it.

'I'm sorry, Leila, for turning up like this. I'm sorry for everything.'

She closes it behind her. Footsteps retreat along the landing and down the stairs.

I go over to the window, lean my hands on the windowsill and look out. Kim, Jocelyn and Pamela are sitting at the table beneath the olive tree. I move away from the window before they see me. I have no desire to talk to anyone right now. I wonder where everyone else is? Where Sophie's gone? I hope to God Robert's been true to his word and is having a siesta.

Bloody hell. Robert.

I call a taxi. I need to be somewhere other than here. Despite the beauty and spaciousness of Birdsong Villas, it suddenly feels claustrophobic. My head feels like it's about to burst. My heart is thumping against my ribs, my chest is physically sore from the shock. Either that or a broken fucking heart.

Cephalonia, 2012

My first thought is to go to the airport, but it's not like I can simply jump on a plane. My heart is being torn apart. I need space to think. I get the taxi driver to drop me off on the edge of Omorfia. I walk; I don't care where, I just need to pound the pavement and let everything Amy's told me sink in.

The warmth of the sunshine and the sight of gleaming white villas and blue sea, mixed with splashes of colour: purple bougainvillea, mushroom-coloured cobbles, Aegean-blue-painted doors and shutters, conflicts with the desperation I feel. My white maxi skirt wafts around my legs, while a heaviness sits on my heart. Although I'm not focused on where I'm going, I end up weaving my way through the village, down narrow winding streets, each one leading closer to the beachfront and sea.

I don't want to think about the enormity of Elliot and his wife having split up. This moment is what I've been dreaming about since I was eighteen, certainly since the moment I found out I was pregnant with Sophie. I longed for the three of us to be a family, despite everything being dead against us. I don't know what to think, so I try not to. Instead, I focus on the little details as I walk: the Greek letters etched into the stone above the door of a church; an old lady dressed in black sitting on her doorstep; a tortoiseshell cat curled up on the narrow ledge of a wall; a cracked stone pot spilling with red flowers. Everywhere I turn there's beauty and a strong sense of Greek island life. No wonder Sophie loves it here so much.

Despite doing everything I can to take my mind off Elliot being single now, while I'm about to marry Robert, my thoughts revert back. Here he is, the day before my wedding, messing with my head once again.

I zigzag my way through the village. The sea's a blur by the time I reach the waterfront because I can't stop crying. Wandering aimlessly is doing me no bloody good.

I go to the fish restaurant on the beach; Sophie and Alekos' favourite. I'm glad of my oversized sunglasses, covering my tight damp eyes. Despite the delicious waft of grilled seafood, I'm not hungry. Less than two hours ago I was blissfully happy at the winery, tucking into tapas, with no worries in the world.

One of the waiters greets me with a smile and a 'hello,' followed by, 'a table for?'

'One,' I reply and he leads me across the decking to an empty table right by the beach.

'Can I get you something to drink?' He places a menu in front of me.

'I'll have a lemonade, please. But is it okay if I only have a drink, nothing to eat at the moment, thanks.'

He nods. 'Of course.'

I watch him walk back inside the restaurant. His white shirt fits nicely, his trousers snug around his bum and thighs. I take a deep breath and turn to the sea. What the hell am I like? I'd be better off single, it's always suited me, a casual fling with no commitment and no chance of my heart being broken. Or more likely me breaking someone else's. It's always been the thrill of the chase for me. I love flirting, I'm good at it. I've always known I'm attractive and exude confidence. I have no flipping idea where I get that from because Dad's as straight-laced as they come, and Mum got married and settled down with the first person she fell in love with. I've always questioned if Dad is actually her soulmate;

they've always seemed too different. I know there's a side to Mum that's dying to escape, a more creative, quirkier, more rebellious side that's been subdued for decades.

The heat wraps me in a hug and yet all I can think about is a drizzly day in the Peak District, meeting Elliot in secret and him enveloping me in his arms. That memory couldn't be more different to the blue sky, soft yellow sand, white and blue painted boats floating on the turquoise water here. It's perfection, and yet right this minute I'd swap it for that cold wet moorland.

The waiter comes back with my drink and places it on the table along with a bowl of crisps and the bill tucked into a shot glass. He leaves me with a smile and the realisation that ten years ago, there'd have been a strong possibility that I'd have left the restaurant with him.

I sip the lemonade and my thoughts travel across the sea to Elliot, free and single at last. I wonder what my parents think? I wonder if they feel relief at no longer having to protect him. Or perhaps they're feeling regret at choosing a relationship with him over a relationship with me, all for nothing when his wife knew all along. Were either of them ever happy, trapped in a marriage wrapped in deceit?

I don't notice Sophie until she pulls up the chair opposite, catching the legs on the ridged wood of the decking.

'You found me then.' I force my attention from the sea.

She looks so serious, worry etched in her frown and pursed lips.

She takes my hand. 'Mum, what happened with Amy? We thought you were still talking to her, not run off somewhere.'

I laugh, but it's hollow, as there's nothing remotely funny about the situation. 'If only I could run away. There's no point you being here, Sophie.'

'I've spent far too long fighting against my family. Don't push me away, not now.' She looks intently at me. 'You told Amy where to go I presume?'

I wedge my sunglasses into my hair, not caring if anyone

sees how much I've been crying. 'She gave me the news I've been waiting for since I was nineteen. That Elliot is finally single, divorcing and still loves me.'

Sophie squeezes my hands. 'Don't revisit the past, Mum. There's a reason it's in the past. He's not worth it. He's certainly not worth losing Robert over.'

'He was the love of my life, my soulmate.' I turn away from her, back to the sea. 'He was the wrong person for so many reasons and I shouldn't have touched him with a barge pole, but I fell in love and he encouraged me. I may have hated him over the years for abandoning us but I never stopped loving him.'

'So you don't love Robert?'

'I do love Robert.' I pull my hand from Sophie's and take a gulp of lemonade. 'You don't understand how I can love two men, can you?'

'Not when four years ago you effectively told Elliot to go fuck himself.'

I take a deep breath and lean forward. 'And that was the hardest thing I ever did. What if that was the wrong decision?'

'What if it was the right one? It took guts and enabled you to move on. It allowed you to have a proper relationship with Robert, something you'd never had before with meaningless boyfriends you had fun with but were never serious about.'

The waiter who served me stops at our table. 'Can I get you a drink?' He smiles at Sophie.

'*Ohi efharisto*,' she says, her focus solely on me.

'Sophie, for the first time in my life I really don't know what to do.'

She moves next to me and puts her arms around me. I cling on to her and can't stop the tears falling on to her shoulder. To think we wasted so many years being angry with each other. I don't know what I'd do without her now.

'Oh Mum, I really don't know what to say. Your friends loathe Elliot because of how he's treated you, and I know what I think you should do, but only you can make that decision. You have to go with your heart or your head or a combination of both.'

I lift my head from off her shoulder and wipe away tears with my fingers. 'But my goddam heart is pulling me in different directions. Part of me wants to fly back to England and run into Elliot's arms, the other half, well… It's Robert, the loveliest, kindest man I could ever have asked for and I don't think I deserve him. How can I ever live up to his wife?'

'Is that what you're worried about? You don't have to live up to her. You're you and he loves you because of who *you* are, Mum. He's not comparing you to his wife. I'm sure from everything that he and Ben have said about her, she'd like to see him happy, settled down and married again.'

'I don't think I can get married. I'm not the marrying type. I'm the screw-around with married, much younger than me, inappropriate men type of woman. That's not who Robert wants or deserves.'

'You don't think a person can change? That you can change? So what if that was you twenty years ago?'

'More like five years ago.'

'You're missing the point; it doesn't have to be who you are now. We all change, move on, grow up. Four years ago I was tempted to sleep with someone other than Alekos and I did cheat on him with Ben even if we didn't take things as far as I wanted to. And Alekos hadn't told me the truth about his relationship with Aphrodite until now. Ben kissed me a week ago when we were in Norfolk. Mum, we all have secrets and have done things that we want to forget ever happened. At the same time, they make us who we are.'

My fingers clench tightly around my drink. 'I can't hurt Robert and I'm scared to death that marrying him when I shouldn't would hurt him far more than walking away now.'

'Mum, you're risking so much. Trust me, I've come close to losing Alekos twice now through stupidity on my part, for thinking there's a better life for me with someone else instead of working through the problems we were facing. These last couple of days I've questioned his love for me, doubted him, assumed he's having an affair. I've been swept up in theories from well-meaning but blinkered friends all because they're dealing with their own relationship shit thinking that all men cheat, all men would go for the glamorous, beautiful woman over their own girlfriend.'

'My situation is different.'

'Maybe. But what if Robert is your soulmate? What if *you're* being blinkered by the past and the love you felt as a young, impressionable teenager, pregnant with a much older man's child? If you hadn't got pregnant, if you hadn't been tied to Elliot forever through me, don't you think you might have felt differently about him?'

'He's not with his wife any longer…'

'But that was *her* choice, not his. Mum, I'm begging you, don't throw your life with Robert away over a man who never had the guts to leave his wife. He didn't even come out here to try and win you back. His daughter's here on his behalf because he's hurting too much. Well boo fucking hoo. I'm only telling you what you'd tell me if it was the other way round.'

I stand up. 'I need time alone.'

'What am I supposed to tell Robert?'

'I don't know. Tell him I need time.'

'Mum, you're getting married tomorrow. Everyone's here, your friends, family…'

'I need time alone to think, Sophie.' I take my bag off the back of the chair and pull my sunglasses down from where they're wedged in my hair. 'This is the biggest decision of my life.'

'Where are you going to go?'

'I don't know. For a walk. Somewhere to clear my head where I can think straight.'

I walk away, across the wooden deck of the restaurant. I don't dare look back. I don't want to witness the look of disappointment, fear, worry on Sophie's face. I know it's not fair to leave her like this, for her to go back to Birdsong Villas with so much uncertainty, but I need this time on my own, to really think about what I want. About who I want.

I put enough space between me and the fish restaurant until I know I've disappeared among the crowd of holidaymakers. I head in the opposite direction to Birdsong Villas. My feet are aching as I begin the climb through the village, following winding roads snaking up the hillside to the old town. I pass the sand-coloured church and a cobbled square with a fountain in the middle, the trickle of water soothing and refreshing in the heat. I keep walking, until the road turns to a track and I'm heading for the pine forest.

I don't care how much it's going to cost to phone Elliot on my mobile. I can't fly back to England and talk to him face to face, not with the wedding tomorrow, so a phone call is the only alternative. And I need to talk to him. I need to find a way of unscrambling the confusion in my head. Within the space of a couple of hours it's all become such a bloody mess.

Pine forest covers the hillside surrounding Omorfia old town. I only need to walk for five minutes to feel like I'm on my own, miles from anywhere. The soil is soft and sandy beneath my feet. I find a log and sit out of the sun. The scent of pine fills the air. The view from this high up is breathtaking. The tops of pine trees clad the hillside before red-tiled roofs and whitewashed walls take over all the way down to the deep blue of the Ionian Sea glinting in the sunshine. I don't want to spoil the peace and quiet, but I can't do anything until I've spoken to him. I can't go back to Birdsong Villas or see Robert. It feels like I can't breathe, my chest restricted with panic that my life is crumbling around me.

I take my mobile from my bag and phone Mum. It feels like it rings for eternity before it's answered and a quiet voice says, 'Leila?'

'Hi, yes, it's me.'

'What are you doing phoning? Aren't you getting

married?'

'Tomorrow.' I breathe in the fresh pine scent. 'But Amy turned up.'

'Amy?' I can hear the frown in her voice.

'Elliot's Amy.'

'Oh.'

'So I need to speak to him and I need his number from you.'

'I don't understand.'

I sigh. 'I know everything. Amy's last ditch attempt to make her father happy was to tell me her mother's divorcing him, that he still loves me. I wish it was a fucking joke, but as you know too well, it's not. So I need his number.'

'Why didn't you get it off her?'

'For God's sake, Mum, who are you trying to protect? Everyone knows everything. Amy's decided to take it upon herself to mend her father's broken heart the day before my fucking wedding. I'm beyond confused and I need to speak to Elliot. I didn't think of getting his number off Amy because I was too bloody stunned at the time to think straight. I need to talk to him before I can go back to Sophie's. Before I face Robert.'

'Okay, Leila. Calm down. I'll get it.'

I fight the rage building inside daring me to shout down the phone at her 'don't you dare tell me to calm down!' But I don't, what bloody good would that do?

'I'll text it to you,' she says after a few seconds of silence.

We say goodbye and I spend the next couple of minutes staring at my mobile.

Ping.

I click on the text message from Mum. Just Elliot's mobile number, nothing else. I don't know why I should feel so disappointed that there's not a 'love, Mum', not even a kiss. I'm fifty-two years old and it's been decades since I've had any meaningful exchange of warmth or love from my mum. That's not going to change now.

My thumb falters over the number, my head telling me not to press it, my heart daring me to. I look up, sunlight making the pine forest a myriad of different greens, fresh against the deep blue sky. In such an inspiring location it seems a shame to revisit the heartache of the past. A shame, yet a necessity.

I press Elliot's number and wait for it to ring.

Cephalonia, 2012

I wonder where he is now, where he's living. The phone starts ringing and my body tenses. I grip the dry bark of the log. He's obviously moved out of the house he's lived in for the best part of forty years. He's seventy-one now and retired, that much I know. What an age to find yourself alone, the marriage he'd tried desperately to cling on to for decades yanked from him by his wife having an affair. Poetic bloody justice.

'Hello?'

'It's Leila.'

'Leila,' he says weakly.

'You know why I'm calling?'

He pauses momentarily. 'Amy.'

'You didn't even have the guts to come over here yourself, but sent your goddam daughter.'

'I didn't send her; I told her not to stir things up.'

'Well, you even failed miserably at that.' I release the tension in my fingers where they're digging into the bark. 'It's all true is it, your wife's left you?'

'If you're just calling to gloat…'

'There's nothing remotely funny about any of this.' I breathe in the scent of pine. I know now's the time to be completely honest if there's any way of making the right decision. 'I'm actually phoning because you no longer being

231

with your wife is news I've been waiting for since you got me pregnant and I realised how hard I'd fallen for you. But what I want to know is what do *you* actually want?'

'I want you; I love you, Leila. I always have done.'

'But it wasn't your choice to get a divorce. The only reason why you're now on your own is because she's left you. There's no way you'd have left her otherwise.'

His silence, his guilt, says it all. He's still as spineless as he was when he confessed our relationship to my parents more than thirty years ago. At the time I thought he was brave, admitting the truth and accepting responsibility, yet all he did was protect himself and paint me in a bad light: the horny teenager, unable to control herself around an older man, seducing him and getting *him* into trouble. It couldn't possibly have been the other way around. Or shockingly for my parents: mutual attraction.

I think back to what happened, the shame of it palpable even now. 'We fucked each other against your office wall. There was no romance, no love, although at the time and long after I believed we loved each other. We shagged each other in your car for God's sake. It was lust, pure and simple. My mum was right about one thing.'

'I loved you, Leila.'

'Why? I was eighteen, I had nothing to offer apart from sex. That was all it was.'

'No, it wasn't just that. We talked, about everything. Don't you remember? You were interesting, intelligent, ambitious. I loved how you were interested in the world, what I was doing, the creative side of being an architect. I never got that from Margaret. So you're wrong; it was more than just sex, whatever you or anyone else believes.'

'And yet you didn't have the guts to change your life; you settled for something you never wanted, avoiding conflict and difficult decisions.'

It's a beautiful temperature in the shade beneath the pine trees. The soft sandy ground is littered with dried pine needles and cones, the faint path I'd walked along meanders along the edge of the forest and back to the tarmac road leading to the old town.

'I don't blame Amy for coming over here. I mean her timing's shitty but I get it. She's been part of your lies for the majority of her life and now the truth's come out she feels compelled to do something. She must really love you, but then you did choose her over us, so maybe she feels like it's her turn to do something for you. She's misguided, but her heart's in the right place.' I smooth away the creases in my white skirt. 'I totally blame you though.'

'That's justified,' he says quietly. 'I've treated you appallingly, I know that, and it was all for nothing.'

'What, because you've lost out completely, on your marriage and having any chance with me?'

'That's not what I meant.'

'What do you mean then? Now's your chance. I'm fucking talking to you the day before my wedding, when I should be having a relaxing afternoon with my friends and family. Right now, you're stopping me from doing that.'

'You're really getting married?'

'Are you seriously asking me that?'

'I wasn't sure if it was something you'd just told your parents to get them off your back.'

'You really think my parents have any influence over my life any longer or if I give a shit about what they think?'

'It seems rather late in your life to get married, that's all.'

'You fucking piece of shit. So what if I'm fifty-bloody-two. Why the hell do you think I've got to be this age before settling down? I spent decades waiting for you. Despite staying out of your life, you wouldn't leave me alone, reminding me, taunting me with a letter, a phone call, so you continuously made me think about you. I was *never* allowed to get over you. You made your choice. You kept your wife, your family, and yet you couldn't leave me be. You wouldn't allow me to stop loving you.'

There's silence on the other end of the phone, like he needs a moment to process my words. 'If you love me,' he says slowly, 'then why are you marrying him, Leila?'

I don't know what to say to that. All I can hear is him breathing on the other end of the phone and the sea curling on to the shore in the distance.

'Come back to England and let's talk,' he says, taking advantage of my hesitation.

It's too beautiful a place to be thinking back on such unhappy times in my life, but the view is the perfect antidote to the pain ricocheting through me.

'I used to love you.' Fresh tears roll down my cheeks, making the view blur into a muddle of green and blue, spliced by red rooftops. 'My God, so much it hurt. And I held out hope for so many years that you'd finally leave your wife because you wanted to be with me and Sophie. I never got the chance to find someone to settle down with because I was holding out for you. I had relationships with married men, or much younger men who I knew wanted nothing more than a fling…'

I wipe my eyes with the back of my hand. An image filters into my head of Elliot in smart trousers and a jumper, sitting in the front room of my parents' house, a flowery china cup clasped in his hand after spilling his guts to my parents, *his friends,* about our sordid relationship and that I was pregnant. I was pregnant. He even took that from me, being able to tell my parents in my own good time. I could have lied for him, covered his arse by saying I'd got pregnant by someone else. I'd have been willing to do that, to protect him, but he cared more about protecting himself than us.

The image is replaced by Robert, popping his head round the front door of Salt Cottage the day after I moved in. His smile and his friendly welcome was perfection. I didn't fancy him, but I noticed him, his good looks, along with his warm personality shining through. He won my friendship with wine and biscuits and my heart through his sincerity and kindness. I wipe the back of my free hand across my face, my shoulders tensing with the realisation of how, despite never getting married, my life has been controlled by men. By Elliot. Every fucking decision I've made has been shaped by him and our brief but life changing relationship.

Elliot's deep voice in my ear shatters my thoughts. 'I still love you, Leila. I didn't think I'd ever get to speak to you again, not after what you said the last time we saw each other.'

The last time on that windswept moor, there was no possibility of us ever having a life together, but now… Now it's time for me to take control, for me to end this.

'I meant what I said four years ago about staying out of each other's lives. I still feel the same way.'

'Leila…'

'I used to love you. I used to want us to be a family: me, you and Sophie. But I have a new family now.' I look over the rooftops of Omorfia and along the coast, trying to work out where Birdsong Villas sits, nestled on the hillside looking out over the Ionian Sea. 'I have Sophie and Alekos, and my granddaughter, Thea. I have Robert and his children, Ben and Vicky, and their kids. I freaked out about becoming a grandmother when Thea was born, but now I embrace it.

'You have made me realise something, though. This commitment shit isn't me. There's been something playing on my mind leading up to this wedding and I realise now it isn't because I'm not in love with Robert, because I am, more than I've been in love with anyone, but I've been freaking out about the idea of marriage and being tied down. I've been fighting convention all my life. I've seen my parents' marriage and how stifled Mum's been; I've seen your sham of a marriage. I know it's not for me.'

I know this is the last time I'm ever going to talk to Elliot; that this is the last time he's going to have this kind of hold over my emotions.

'I hope the decision you made all those years ago was worth it.'

'Leila, wait.'

'Seriously, Elliot, I have nothing left to say to you.'

I press end call. I don't even say goodbye, because that feels too much like it's been a good experience and we'll pick up our conversation at another time. I know deep down that our connection is severed. Elliot and that part of my life is finally over. But I still have one more decision to make before I can face everyone.

I tuck my mobile in my bag and stand up. My shoulders and legs ache where I've been tense, sitting in the same position for so long. I brush bits of bark and dried moss off my skirt and throw my bag over my shoulder. I feel lighter as I follow the sandy path back out into the late afternoon sunshine. The dry heat warming my face is a tonic. I slip back to civilisation in the old town with the church gleaming in the sunshine, the water in the fountain glinting. In the background is chatter and the clatter of knives and forks from the cafes around the cobbled square. I'm not ready to go back to Birdsong Villas yet, to see Sophie or face Robert. I still need time to think, to make sure my heart is in the right place, that I'm making the right decision. So I walk, back down into the centre of Omorfia and out along the beach, climbing back up the path that leads away from the town, away from Birdsong Villas and my friends and family. I'm not running away, not any longer, but I do need this time to digest all that's happened today, in fact all that's happened over the last few years. Moving to Marshton and Salt Cottage has been life changing in more ways than one.

My sandals are beginning to rub the sides of my feet by the time I make it to the next village. My phone's been pinging all afternoon but I ignore it. It's quite a trek and although the heat of the sun isn't as intense as earlier in the day, I'm hot by the time I find a taverna by the sea and down a glass of water before ordering a white wine. I watch the sun set, pink and purple spreading across the horizon, and tuck into a plate of seafood.

By the time darkness descends and the twinkling lights of fishing boats out in the bay glint on the black water, I know what I'm going to do. The waiter calls me a taxi and I text Sophie, replying to one of the many texts she's sent over the last few hours. I know she must be worried sick, and I'm conscious of the stress I've caused her through my silence. I know from her texts that she's covered for my absence by saying we're on a night out with the girls so Robert doesn't suspect something's up.

I pay for my meal and leave a generous tip. Compared to the earlier walk, the taxi drive back to Omorfia is quick. I stare at my reflection in the car window; my chin-length choppy hair is windswept, my face looks tanned, my eyes red from crying. They still feel tight, although my head is clearer than it has been for a long time. The taxi driver drops me off at the top of the hill and I walk the short distance down the lane to the bar Sophie has told me they're in.

I spot them before they see me: Sophie, Candy, Jocelyn, Kim, Pamela. And Amy. So she didn't leave despite me asking her to. Not only does she look like her father, she takes after him too, thinking it's okay to interfere in my life. They all look deep in conversation, squeezed around a table, candlelight making everyone look tanned and healthy.

No one says anything as I reach them. I sit in the empty seat next to Pamela and look across the table at Amy. Everyone's watching me, waiting for me to say something. I'm all cried out, every single bloody emotion wrung out of me.

'I phoned your father and we talked. It's the first time I've spoken to him since Sophie and I drove up to see him before Thea was born. And it's only the second or third time since Sophie was born that we've actually had a proper conversation. That's insane, isn't it? Sophie's father, the man who turned my life upside down, the man who has continuously been there in the background for the last thirty-odd goddam years. We had a hell of a lot to talk about…' I rub my forehead and place my hands on the table, scrunching a tissue damp with tears between my fingers.

'What have you decided to do?' Amy asks.

I look at Sophie, then back to Amy. 'I've decided that I'm not going to marry Robert tomorrow.'

Cephalonia, 2012

I don't say a word all the way back to Birdsong Villas and no one dares question me further. I can't even bear to think how Sophie's feeling but I need to talk to Robert without risking anyone changing my mind. We're a subdued group by the time we reach the retreat, splintering off to our rooms as soon as we get through the gate.

I sense Sophie watching me as I make my way up the steps to the terrace outside my room. Every part of me feels emotionally exhausted. I place my hand on the handle, take a deep breath and push the door open as quietly as I can.

It's dark. Silent too; maybe he's not even come up to bed yet. I feel my way across the room, past the sofa to the end of our bed.

'Ben said you'd gone out with the girls and were staying with Sophie tonight.' Robert's voice cuts through the darkness.

I put my hand to my chest. 'Bloody hell you made me jump.'

He switches on the lamp on the bedside table. 'What's really going on, Leila?' He sits up in bed and looks at me. The sheet's crumpled around his knees. He's wearing pyjama bottoms and a white T-shirt, his arms folded, deep lines across his forehead. I've made everyone uneasy tonight.

'I've been talking to Elliot.'

'Wow, I really wasn't expecting that.'

'It's not what you think.' I drop my bag on the sofa, go over to the bed and sit on my side, sliding my legs beneath me.

'Then what is it, Leila? Something's going on; Sophie suddenly taking you all out, Ben's been acting weird, everyone trying too hard to make me feel at ease tonight.'

'Elliot's eldest daughter showed up. She's still here, in the villa with Sophie. It was completely unexpected, and to be honest I panicked. I just needed some time to myself.'

'What did his daughter want? Obviously important if she flew out here uninvited?'

I know being honest is best, however difficult this conversation will be.

'Elliot and his wife have separated. Her decision. Elliot moved out. She's always known about our affair, she just kept quiet for the sake of their children and because she loved him. Until of course she met someone else and so the whole truth about me, Elliot and Sophie came out. Amy took it particularly badly – I think she's always been closest to her father and so didn't want to see him hurting like this. She came out here to tell me that he still loves me.'

The words tumble from me, like I want to spit them out, get rid of a horrible taste in my mouth. They sound harsh and matter-of-fact in the silence of the room, when actually they're saturated with emotion for both of us.

I watch Robert. He seems impassive, his face unchanged as he looks at me, but I notice his hand bunching into a fist, the strong line of his clean-shaven jaw tense slightly. Despite never having met him, Elliot's played a role in his life too, a name bound forever with me. He knows every sordid detail; after all, Robert is someone I've always been comfortable telling everything to from almost the moment I met him, before we became more than just friends.

He finally finds his voice. 'And how do you feel about that?'

I look away from him at his clothes draped neatly over the back of the sofa, at my perfume on the chest of drawers.

'Be honest with me, Leila.'

'Honestly?' I turn back to him and take his hand, prising his fingers open until he relaxes. 'It's news that I've wanted to hear since I was eighteen. It's pathetic. I've waited my whole life and actually, instead of being excited and relieved to finally hear that he's free and still wants to be with me, it scared me shitless, because it made me question everything. It made me question us.'

'Do you still love him?'

'No. I really don't. And I'm not actually sure I was ever truly in love with him, even when we were together. I was so swept up in the thrill of our affair or what I perceived as romance, that I presumed I loved him, particularly when I found out I was pregnant. I was desperate for us to be together, to be a family. I was so fucking stupid and naive. My romantic ideal was in reality us shagging in the back of his car, because he was married and we were having a sordid affair. I mean the thought makes me cringe now. But every relationship I've had since, he's ultimately destroyed it because none of the men ever lived up to my perception of him.'

Robert slips his hand from mine, throws the sheet off and gets out of bed. He pours himself a glass of wine from the half empty bottle on the dressing table and downs it.

'Well, Leila, I really don't know what to say to that.' He puts the empty glass down and perches on the back of the sofa facing me. 'I know what he's meant to you, and I know you can't change the past. He's Sophie's father for goodness' sake. I understand the tie you have to him, but seriously…' He shakes his head. 'That man…'

'I phoned him. I was so pissed off with Amy turning up and stirring all these emotions in me, that I needed to speak to him.'

'You've been talking to him all this time?'

'Not all this time, no. I had plenty of time to think things through, and actually, in the end it was a reasonably quick conversation with him, because it's over between us.' I scramble across the bed and sit at the end of it facing Robert, my bare feet almost touching his. 'In hindsight it's been over since the moment he decided to break the news about our relationship and my pregnancy to my parents. It's been over since I was nineteen, and yet it's taken me until I'm fifty-two bloody years old to understand that, and to realise I'm not in love with him. I told him that, properly this time, that we are over. It's more that his emotional hold over me is gone, because for the first time ever he's single and not tied down by a wife and kids. I could be with him if I wanted to, but him finally being available made me realise that's not what I want. *He's* not what I want.'

Robert's eyes are damp. He wipes the back of his hand across them. 'Bloody hell, Leila. You're no good for my blood pressure.'

I stand and put my arms around him. His legs half-encircle me where he's resting against the sofa. His arms slide around my waist and he holds me closer, our breathing matching each others. I need to keep talking, tell him everything that's on my mind before I bottle it.

I lift my head away from his shoulder and rest my forehead against his. 'I love you, Robert. That's the truth and that's what I've been thinking about for the last few hours, but also that I can't marry you. It's been playing on my mind for days, actually weeks, maybe months. I don't know, probably ever since you proposed. Marriage isn't for me, it's not something that fills me with joy, and it's ridiculous because what actually fills me with joy is you. I can't tell you how much I want to be with you, but I don't think we need to get married for us to commit to each other in that way.'

He takes my face in his hands until we're looking at each other. 'This is why I love you. Your honesty, your guts, the fact that you know your own mind.'

'You understand that I still want to be with you, right?'

'I get that, you just don't need it to be official or a piece of paper to say so.'

'Yeah, exactly. Or people calling me Mrs Leila Thurston.'

'I don't think I've ever imagined you to be anything other than Leila Keech.'

'I can't replace your wife, and I don't ever want to, but us, spending our lives together, my God I want that so much.'

I've made him cry properly now. He lets go of my face as he sobs. I run my thumbs over his cheeks, wiping away his tears.

'Jenny would have loved you.' That's all he needs to say for me to lose it. I have no idea what the time is, but it's late, Birdsong Villas silent apart from the ever present sound of waves breaking on the beach. The intensity of today has broken me. Fresh tears stream down my face. 'You're very different; Jenny was always quite quiet, happiest with the kids or when we were all together. I think you would have been friends though, you'd have complemented each other. You'd have definitely brought her out of her shell. She had a good sense of humour and was loyal. She wanted me to find someone. All the time she was ill, she was worrying about me and the kids, how we'd cope. She didn't want me to be lonely. It's a strange thing being given permission by your wife to find love with someone else, when at the time I didn't think there was any way I could ever love someone as much as I loved her. And there wasn't, not until I met you.'

Curled up together on the bed we talk, almost until dawn. We talk about everything, it seems the right thing to do, talk until we can no longer keep our eyes open. And then we sleep, wrapped in each other's arms until sunshine creeps through the half-open blinds, and birdsong stirs me from a short but deep sleep.

Our wedding day.

I'm immediately panicked that I left Sophie and everyone else in turmoil last night, not understanding my meaning behind me not marrying Robert.

I roll on my side and look at him. He's already awake, lying on his back staring up at the ceiling, his hands behind his head.

'Morning.' He turns and kisses me.

'Morning.'

He gets out of bed and goes to the window, opening the blinds fully. I shade my eyes from the light. Robert's silhouetted against it, all broad shoulders, firm torso and bed hair.

'Sophie's outside already.'

I scramble out of bed, my head pounding from lack of sleep. 'I need to talk to her.'

Robert's already stepping into shorts. He pulls off the T-shirt he slept in, puts on a clean one and runs a hand through his hair.

'I'll go down and see her,' he says, kissing me.

I'm still in the white maxi skirt and orange linen top I was wearing yesterday. I wind my hair into a messy ponytail as Robert leaves our room. I go to the window and watch him walk across the patio. Sophie's face has worry written all over it, in her frown, the dark circles beneath her eyes and the way her hands clench around her mug. I take a deep breath; I need a shower, I need to clean my teeth, put clean, fresh-smelling clothes on, but first I need to talk to my daughter, ease her worry and let her know that even though Robert and I aren't getting married today, we are still together, still in love and looking forward to a party to celebrate being together.

First Sophie, then Ben, Vicky, and our friends find out the details of the last twelve hours or so. I notice Sophie slip away when I'm telling everyone our decision to not get married but to still be together. By the time she returns to the courtyard our news has been delivered and breakfast is under way with a rather confused Despina filling one of the tables with *tchereki*, croissants, bread and cheese.

I leave Robert's side and go to Sophie. 'Amy's gone?'

She nods. 'Yes. I think she'd gathered from seeing you two together this morning what your decision was. She'd already called a taxi.' She takes hold of my hands. 'I want to stay in touch with her though – I have no interest in attempting any father-daughter relationship with Elliot, but Amy… She's nice, and she's a victim of his lies same as I am.'

'Good, I'm glad. She's your half-sister after all. And the other two.' I glance back to the courtyard, at Robert, Ben and Vicky laughing together. Thea's chasing after Vicky's son Joshua, and Alekos is chatting with Jocelyn and Kim. 'It's funny, isn't it, how we've gone from it being just the two of us for so many years, to a big messy but wonderful extended family.' I hook my arm in hers. 'Come on, I'm starving. Let's eat.'

After breakfast, everyone disperses to spend a few hours relaxing on the beach, by the pool or heading into Omorfia for lunch. Robert and I hang back at Birdsong Villas, and while Sophie and Alekos are busy putting the finishing touches to the party, Thea helps me lay the tables and put out presents before she runs off to help Sophie blow up balloons.

'I'll finish off here.' Alekos takes a pile of napkins from my hands and glances over at Robert who's taking photos of the decorated courtyard. 'You two should take a break, have a walk. Get out of here for a bit.'

'You trying to get rid of us?'

Alekos frowns and I nudge his side. 'I'm teasing you.'

'What's going on?' Robert asks as he joins us.

'Alekos is putting his foot down and making us have a break. Actually to be honest there's been no persuading needed; I fancy a walk.'

'Sounds good to me.'

Alekos places a hand on my arm. 'Before you go though, I want to ask you something.' He looks between me and Robert. 'Ask you both.'

He walks away, out of earshot of Sophie and Thea and we

follow. He turns back to us, his tanned arm resting on the wood of the gate.

'This might be totally inappropriate, and just say if it is, but um, after everything that's happened over the past few days, with me and Sophie and, well you know…'

'Alekos, seriously, whatever it is, just ask.'

'How would you both feel if I asked Sophie to marry me this evening?'

'Are you kidding?' I grab his hands. 'I'd be delighted. Robert?'

'I think it's long overdue.' He grips Alekos' shoulder.

To think I believed that Alekos was little more than a holiday fling and that Sophie was mad to throw away her life for a man she barely knew anything about. I'm glad she proved me wrong, glad she knew her own mind. I mean, he's still hot as hell, but there's more to their relationship than just good looks and a night of passion on a beach.

Thea squeals as she races after a lost balloon that's spiralling into the air.

'Honestly, Aleko,' I say, 'after everything that's happened over the past few days, I couldn't think of anything I'd like more.'

Boy am I glad I didn't choose a traditional white wedding dress. I slip into my saffron-yellow one. It's fitted around the bust and shows just enough cleavage, the skirt floating out and ending a little above my knees. It's the perfect choice for a non-wedding. Robert's dashing too, in smart dark grey fitted trousers and a white shirt with a matching yellow handkerchief tucked into the pocket.

Nothing has gone to waste. Sophie and Alekos have done an incredible job of being my wedding planners, and Birdsong Villas looks even more stunning than it usually does, decked out in fairy lights, bunting and balloons, the backdrop the whitewashed villas and the view of the Ionian Sea. There's a juggler and face painting to keep the children (and us adults) entertained, and Alekos' old band along with Aphrodite are back ready to play once it gets dark. We're all sitting at six tables set up around the olive tree about to start on our desserts. Thea's on my lap, her fingers twisted in my hair, when Robert stands up next to me and and conversation fades away.

'I didn't actually prepare a speech and after the events of last night and this morning, I'm relieved I didn't. For a wedding day without an actual wedding, it's been perfect…' He pauses to catch his breath and I can tell he's fighting back tears. 'After losing Jenny I never dreamed I would ever find someone I would want to spend my life with, let alone love as much ever again. But Leila, you are so very special. I love you.'

I know how much Jenny meant to him, and still means to him after our heartfelt and honest talk in the early hours of the morning. I take his hand and kiss him. I lean close and whisper, 'And I love you, more than anything.'

He smiles and turns back to everyone. 'Now, before the band get their chance to play, Alekos, I believe you had something you wanted to ask?'

It's Alekos' turn to stand.

'I have no idea how I can follow that, except to say…. Sophie Keech.' He gets down on one knee. Candy gasps. Kim grabs Jocelyn's arm. Sophie's face is a picture: shock and delight plastered across it.

'*Po po,*' Despina says.

'*Ti kanis,* Baba?' Thea calls across from my lap. I squeeze her tighter and kiss the top of her head, her curls tickling my nose.

Everyone laughs and Despina puts a finger to her lips and says 'shush'.

'I've done it properly this time, Sophie,' Alekos says in English, 'and asked your mum and Robert this morning if they'd give me their blessing to ask you to marry me.'

'And I said we'd be delighted!' I call out.

Feet drum on the courtyard paving.

247

'So, Sophie Keech, for not the first, but hopefully the last time, will you marry me?'

Sophie holds her hands to her chest, her eyes not wavering from his face. 'Yes.'

There's absolute silence in the courtyard. Even the kids remain quiet, Thea completely still on my lap watching her baba stand up and place the ring on her mum's finger. I squeeze Thea and bury my face in her sweet-smelling hair.

It's such an intimate moment. They're totally wrapped up in each other, almost as if they're not aware of anyone or anything else. Robert's hand slides on to my thigh and I smile. I only catch snippets of what Sophie's saying to Alekos, but it's evident just how much they love each other.

Sophie looks around, her cheeks damp beneath the fairy lights as her gaze goes from Alekos to Candy, to Robert, to Thea, to me. She looks up into the branches of the olive tree above her, closes her eyes and smiles. When she opens her eyes again she looks at Thea snuggled in my arms, and then back to Alekos.

'I promise I will always love you,' he says.

'And I'll love you. I always have done, even the times when we've been apart.'

Alekos takes hold of her hands and whispers something in her ear – I'd put money on it, it's about that night on the beach.

Thea slips off my lap and runs round the table, throwing her arms around her parents' legs and they lean down and encircle her in their embrace. I wipe away fresh tears and Robert takes my hand.

'Maybe now, you give me another grandchild!' Despina calls out.

'Mama!' Alekos pulls away from Sophie and Thea, and shakes his head at her.

I raise my glass. 'Hear, hear!'

Despina tips her glass in my direction, then blows a kiss to Alekos.

The moment of stillness is broken by laughter, and conversation starts up again around the tables. The children play, released from the confines of their chairs after the excitement of the proposal.

I lean close to Robert and kiss him. 'Well, this all turned out pretty well for a wedding that's no longer a wedding.' I release his hand, lift the edge of my dress and stand on my chair. I rattle a fork against my glass until everyone is looking at me. 'Right, now we've got all that lovey dovey stuff over and done with, let's please have some music and get this party started!'

The strum of a guitar and Aphrodite's smooth voice fills the courtyard. I go over to Sophie and put my arm around her waist. 'Congratulations. About bloody time too. I cannot think of a better way for what was to have been my wedding day to end.'

Norfolk, 2012

After tearful goodbyes at Birdsong Villas, we reminisce on the plane about our ten days on Cephalonia, memorable and impactful for so many reasons. I feel like I'm a different person flying home, not a married Mrs Leila Thurston as I thought I'd be, still Leila Keech but with a changed attitude to life, to love, to my past, to my future. To *our* future. I slip my arm in Robert's and rest my head on his shoulder. Kim, Jocelyn and Pamela are laughing together; Fraser and Bella are watching a film on Ben's iPad; and Candy and Ben are sitting behind them whispering together. Old friendships have been brought together and new relationships have been made over the last couple of weeks.

We reach Gatwick and we splinter off; Ben back to London with Fraser and Bella after a long embrace with Candy, while Vicky and Joshua head to Norwich. Candy is crying even before she hugs me, Robert and Pamela goodbye, then she joins Kim and Jocelyn on the drive back to Bristol. Robert's car feels empty with just the three of us now we're missing Ben, Sophie and my friends, and the mood is subdued on the drive back to Marshton. The landscape passes in a blur of grey motorway merging into leafy countryside lanes as we reach Norfolk.

We take a detour via Kingfisher Hall to drop Pamela off and then it's just the two of us zipping along fast country roads, sunlight filtering through the luminous green leaves above. The past couple of weeks has been such a whirlwind of emotions, I feel the need for some time and space to process it all.

'It's been quite a few days,' Robert says as he pulls into the potholed lane and we bump our way down to Salt Cottage.

'It certainly has.' I realise he probably needs time to process the events of the last week as much as I do. I get out of the car and push open the gate. The sun's low in the sky, casting a wonderful glow across the countryside. However much I'm going to miss Sophie, Alekos, Thea and Birdsong Villas, I love coming back here.

The car crunches over the gravel and Robert pulls into the space next to my car. There's bird mess across its roof and front window where its been sitting under trees unused for ten days. Robert keeps the engine running and I go over to his open window.

'You're not coming in?'

'I want to check in at the pub, see everyone, make sure it's all okay. How about meeting me down there in a bit for a bite to eat?'

'I'm not sure I'm hungry.'

'You might be later.'

'I'll wander down.'

We have a lingering kiss before I pull away and wave him out of the gate and down the drive.

It's been a hellishly long day, so much travelling, so many goodbyes. At the best of times after being away I feel sad when I get home but this time it's amplified. It's early evening but it feels later, and I guess it is with us having been up an extra two hours because of the time difference in Greece. I heave my suitcase into the hallway and pick up the post scattered across the floor, nearly two weeks' worth of bills, statements and other rubbish.

I don't feel like unpacking but I want something to take

my mind off the feeling of loss I have from leaving Sophie, Alekos and Thea behind and saying goodbye to my friends. I unzip my suitcase, take out the bag of washing and dump it next to the washing machine in the kitchen. I fill the kettle with water, switch it on and push open the back door. I love the view at Birdsong Villas, but this… There's nothing better than knowing that this view is mine.

Sophie sent me home with a *tchereci* and I'll enjoy a slice or two with coffee over the next few mornings to remind me of breakfast at Birdsong Villas. I put it on the work surface next to foil-wrapped *spanakopita* that Despina insisted I took with me. No arguments from me; I'm going to miss the food and laid-back lifestyle in Greece, not to mention the sunshine, heat and sea views.

I drag my now half-empty suitcase upstairs and take out the rest of my clothes, hanging summer skirts and dresses in my wardrobe and folding blouses and strapless tops away in the chest of drawers, hoping I'll get to wear them again at some point during the British summer.

With the suitcase empty, I sit on the end of my bed unsure what to do next. It's too late in the day to start tackling any work and I don't want to even think about how many emails will be waiting in my inbox. Nope, that can all wait until tomorrow. I feel twitchy, like something's playing on my mind but I'm not exactly sure what. I acknowledge the sadness from having left behind Sophie and family in Greece, but it's more than that, an unsettled feeling making my chest tighten. There doesn't seem to be any reason for it; I'm home, a place I love, the evening sun shining over the garden, birds singing in the trees.

I wander around the house, looking in each room exactly like I did after I returned from Cephalonia when I left Sophie and Thea there for the first time. Little things remind me of Robert: his favourite brand of coffee in the kitchen cupboard, his toothbrush next to mine in the bathroom, but nothing else. No clothes in the wardrobe, no book on the bedside table, no muddy wellies next to mine by the back door. He's a visitor in my house, sleeping here, having a wash, brushing his teeth before returning to his flat above the pub to change his clothes and start his day.

I know what's bugging me.

I lock the back door, leave the teabag stewing in a mug and unhook my shoulder bag off the end of the bannister. I open the middle drawer of the console table in the hallway and search through the random assortment of takeaway menus, odd buttons, and batteries until I find the spare keys. I fold them tightly in my hand and close the drawer.

Outside I breathe in the heady scent of honeysuckle. The weather's almost as good as it had been on Cephalonia, but fresher, my garden and surrounding countryside greener, the Ionian Sea replaced by farmland. I breathe in the sweet scent again and set off along the path and across the gravel drive. It's funny how everything has slotted into place over the past few days. I've spent so many years living in confusion about who I loved and what I wanted from life, and yet everything's been here, right under my nose for a long time. Letting go of the past is the best thing I've ever done.

The large wooden door to The Globe is wedged open, allowing the breeze to filter through making the cosy interior with its beamed-ceiling less claustrophobic on such a sunny day. The large conservatory dining area that leads directly from the bar helps with the airiness, daylight flooding through the windows. Most people are eating there or outside, there's only a couple with their dog at a table in the bar. And there's no sign of Robert.

One of the waitresses is stacking plates and mugs on a tray.

'Is Robert around?' I ask her as I pass.

She turns and smiles. 'Hey Leila, congratulations on your wedding. He popped upstairs.'

'Thanks.'

I follow the corridor that leads to the kitchen and take the stairs two at a time. So Robert's obviously not told anyone yet about what happened on Cephalonia, and our non-wedding, wedding party.

I knock gently on his door but push it open anyway without waiting for him to answer. He's on the far side of the open plan living area, leaning against the edge of the L-shaped kitchen unit, chatting on his mobile.

He smiles and waves me in.

I work out he's talking to Vicky, now safely back home with Joshua. I'm gripping the keys so tightly they dig into my palm.

He says goodbye to Vicky and turns to me. 'I didn't think you'd get down here so soon. Are you ready for dinner?'

'No, not yet.'

He walks over, his frown morphing into a smile as he glides his hands down my tense arms. 'Ah, you were missing me already were you?'

'Actually, yes.'

He was joking but it's true. From being someone so fiercely independent and not being able to imagine ever sharing my life or my home with a man – not really being that great at sharing it with anyone, even Sophie – I now can't imagine life without Robert. I don't want us to be deciding whose place we're going to stay at like we're students embarking on little more than a fling. I don't want to not know if I'm going to see him each day or not. No more uncertainty.

I open my fist to reveal the house keys.

'Move in with me. Or I can move in here; it's just there's more space at Salt Cottage and it might be nice for you to escape from work and the pub…' The words tumble out, muddled because I've not actually thought through what I want to say. 'I want us to be together, you know, like a proper unmarried couple, living together.'

His hands are still on my arms and he's looking at me with that intensity that was off-putting when I first met him, but which I now love.

'Are you sure?' His hands relax as they slide down my arms and he takes my hands in his.

'I've never been more certain about anything in my life.' I place the keys in his hand, folding his fingers around them. I reach up and kiss him. 'I'm going to go back and cook us some dinner. I'll see you at home later.'

I walk out of his flat, back downstairs, through the bar and out into the bright sunshine. I have an overwhelming sense that this was a bigger moment for us than saying 'I do'. I set off up the road, a lightness to my step as I notice the beauty of the day, the blueness of the sky, white wispy clouds, the rumble of a lawnmower coming from someone's back garden, the hedgerow along the side of the road speckled with bright pink and white flowers. I head down the lane that leads to Salt Cottage, avoiding the sharp flint stones that stick out at all angles through the sandy soil. I reach the open gate and close it behind me. I lean against it and look at the cottage. It's how I imagined it would be once I'd stripped away the years of neglect.

Home.

There have been a few places I've called home over the years: my parents' house in Sheffield, Duncan's flat when I first moved to Bristol, our terraced house in Hazel Road, but Salt Cottage is where my heart is. It's the place I dreamt about all those years ago, a country cottage with honeysuckle climbing its wall.

And Robert. I love the thought of waking up next to him here, every morning for the rest of our lives.

ACKNOWLEDGEMENTS

It's thanks to readers who left reviews of *The Butterfly Storm* and *The Birdsong Promise*, asking for Leila's story that *The Honeysuckle Dream* came about. Leila is a wonderful character – fun and feisty with a colourful past, she deserved a story of her own. I loved writing *The Honeysuckle Dream* because Leila is a joy to write. She has plenty of flaws which any 'real' character needs, and a back story that I hope shows why she made some of the choices she did in the first two books. It's honestly been one of my favourite books to write and I hope you enjoyed it as much as I did writing it.

So firstly, a huge thank you to the readers who asked for Leila's story, and to everyone who has read, reviewed and supported *The Butterfly Storm* series from the beginning.

As always my lovely friend and fellow writer, Judith van Dijkhuizen, gave me an enormous amount of feedback on the manuscript; her thoughts and suggestions are invaluable. My thanks also to Kimberly Hays Grow and Kayleigh Louise Brown, my two beta readers who read the book to ensure it worked as a standalone novel as well as part of a series. Their verdict; it did! Thanks, ladies!

Helen Baggott gave the book a final edit and proof read, picking up a couple of plot holes and spotting my errors, making it publication ready. She's always efficient, helpful and great to work with.

I'll never tire of the excitement at getting a cover designed. Yet again, Jessica Bell did not disappoint, coming back with three beautiful prototype designs. Hands down the one I chose was the winner, capuring the essence of the story. It works as part of the series but is a beautifully strong cover to stand on its own too.

The timeline of *The Honeysuckle Dream*, starting in 1978 and finishing in 2012 was an interesting juggling act, piecing Leila's story together, weaving together past and present. My parents and Judith helped me with the details for the 1970s, and I had great fun trawling through family photograph albums from the late 1970s and the 1980s to add authenticity to the periods of time I was writing about. I had a lot of fun reminiscing too – I was born in 1977 so was a child of the 80s.

My biggest thanks as always go to my family, my biggest supporters. My hugely supportive husband Nik, my enthusiastic son Leo, and my wonderful parents who have championed my writing from the beginning. Thank you.

ABOUT THE AUTHOR

Kate Frost writes fiction for children and adults. Her women's fiction, which includes *The Butterfly Storm*, *Beneath the Apple Blossom* and *The Baobab Beach Retreat*, tackle serious subjects such as infertility, broken families and infidelity, often with a romantic element running through them.

Kate Frost's children's books couldn't be more different – *Time Shifters* is a time travel adventure series for 9-12 year-olds. *Time Shifters: Into the Past* was published in autumn 2016 and won Gold in The Wishing Shelf Book Awards 2017. *Time Shifters: A Long Way From Home* and *Time Shifters: Out of Time* complete the series.

Bristol, in the south west of England is home, which Kate shares with her husband, young son, and their Cavalier King Charles Spaniel. Bristol is a vibrant and creative city offering plenty of opportunities for writers. Kate's the Director of Children's and Teen Events at the Hawkesbury Upton Literature Festival, and she's also involved in helping to start Storytale Festival, a week-long series of interactive and creative events for children and young adults in her hometown.

If you'd like to keep up to date with Kate Frost's book news please join her Readers' Club. To sign up simply go to www.kate-frost.co.uk/minetokeep and enter your email address. Subscribers not only receive a free ebook on sign up, but occasional news about Kate's writing, new books and special offers.

If you enjoyed *The Honeysuckle Dream* please consider leaving a review on Amazon and/or Goodreads, or recommending it to friends. It will be much appreciated! Reader reviews are essential for authors to gain visibility and entice new readers.

You can find out more about Kate Frost and her writing at www.kate-frost.co.uk, or follow her on Instagram @katefrostauthor, or search for Kate Frost – Author on Facebook.

Printed in Great Britain
by Amazon